ıss to Ellen Crosby's
y Mystery series

THE BORDEAUX BETRAYAL

"Crosby's plot is taut and her dialogue crisp. A touch of history and a wealth of suspense make this novel a journey not to be missed."

—Mystery News

"Mystery lovers will enjoy the intelligent plot and well-drawn characters, oenophiles will savor the winemaking angle, and Virginians will revel in Crosby's spot-on descriptions of people and places. Give this one the order of merit."

—Richmond Times-Dispatch

"Completely charming . . . luminous . . . a complex mystery with very human emotions."

—Romantic Times

"Filled with an insider's knowledge of wines and the wine industry. . . . Crosby has concocted a rare vintage that offers many subtle flavors of romance, scandal, passion, and violence."

—Alfred Hitchcock Mystery Magazine

THE CHARDONNAY CHARADE

"An engaging mystery with likeable characters. . . . A quick and fun read."

—Associated Press

The Wine Country Mysteries are also available as eBooks

"Complex, likeable Lucie's suspenseful second is another hit."

—*Kirkus Reviews*

"A wine lover who delighted in history class and kicks back with mysteries couldn't ask for much more."

—Washingtonian.com

"Nicely plotted and paced. . . . A particular treat for oenophiles."

—*Booklist*

"Deft use of setting . . . and pleasingly drawn characters."

—*Chicago Sun-Times*

"Plot twists and romantic tension add body, developing into a smooth finish."

—*Publishers Weekly*

THE MERLOT MURDERS

**Best Mystery Debut of 2006
(*Sun-Sentinel*, South Florida)
2007 *Wine Enthusiast* magazine Summer Read**

"A neat whodunit supported by enough wine-making lore to give it some extra body."

—*The New York Times*

"A fast-paced intriguing debut that holds interest from cover to cover."

—*Kirkus Reviews* (starred review)

THE
BORDEAUX
BETRAYAL

A Wine Country Mystery

ELLEN CROSBY

POCKET BOOKS

New York   London   Toronto   Sydney

Pocket Books
A Division of Simon & Schuster, Inc.
1230 Avenue of the Americas
New York, NY 10020

The author gratefully acknowledges permission to reprint excerpts from *Thomas Jefferson's European Travel Diaries: Jefferson's Own Account of His Journeys Through the Countryside and Wine Regions of the Continent, 1787–1788*, edited by James McGrath Morris & Persephone Weene, © 1987 Isidore Stephanus Sons, Publishing, Ithaca, New York.

First Pocket Books paperback edition August 2009

POCKET and colophon are registered trademarks of Simon & Schuster, Inc.

For information about special discounts for bulk purchases, please contact Simon & Schuster Special Sales at 1-800-506-1949 or business@simonandschuster.com.

The Simon & Schuster Speakers Bureau can bring authors to your live event. For more information or to book an event contact the Simon & Schuster Speakers Bureau at 866-248-3049 or visit our website at www.simonspeakers.com.

Cover illustration by Wendell Minor

Manufactured in the United States of America

1   3   5   7   9   10   8   6   4   2

ISBN: 978-1-5011-0195-3

For Tony and Belinda Collins

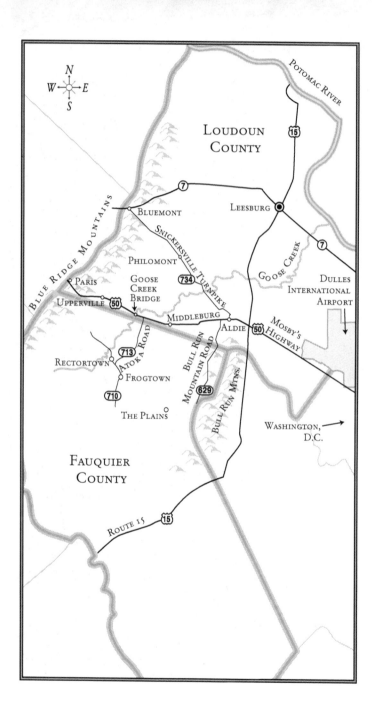

MONTGOMERY ESTATE VINEYARD

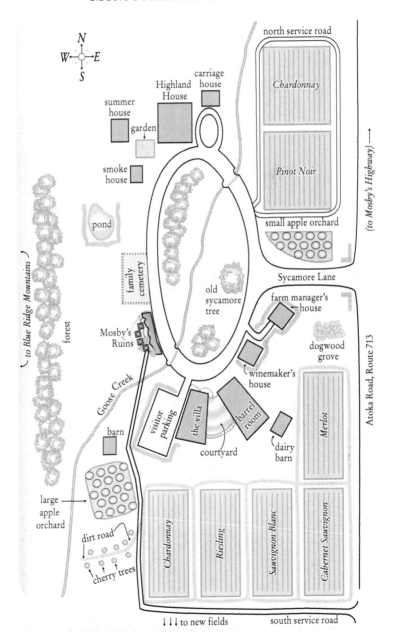

Wherefore by their fruits shall ye know them.
—Matthew 7:20

Always do sober what you said you'd do drunk.
That will teach you to keep your mouth shut.
—Ernest Hemingway

Chapter 1

St. Thomas Aquinas once said sorrow could be alleviated by good sleep, a bath, and a glass of wine. Lucky him, if that's all it took.

Hector died shortly before Labor Day, the last event in a tumultuous summer weighed down by heat straight out of hell's waiting room. He'd been like a father to me, managing the crew at my family's vineyard in the foothills of Virginia's Blue Ridge Mountains for the last twenty years. His death came hard on the heels of my second auto accident in the past three years, when the front end of my old Volvo collided with the back end of a large buck. And that event had been preceded by Hurricane Iola, whose wicked ways wreaked havoc just as we were about to harvest our white wines. If the month of August had been a fish, I would have thrown it back.

Fortunately autumn arrived in a kinder mood. The withering temperatures receded and the low-slanted sunlight washed everything in softer colors, blurring the sharp edges of the shadows. The air no longer smelled as though it had been boiled and the relentless metallic sound of the cicadas began to wane. Tonight, on an October Indian summer evening, the bullfrogs' serenade sounded plaintive.

I'd invited Mick Dunne, my neighbor and a man with whom I'd had a white-hot affair last spring, to dinner and a lecture on wine at Mount Vernon. Though we'd only just arrived, he'd glanced at his watch three times in the last fifteen minutes. Each time, I pretended not to notice.

When Joe Dawson, my cousin's fiancé, had given me the tickets, I figured asking Mick would be a good way to let him know I'd moved on since last spring and that we could still do things together as friends. Besides, he'd just planted thirty acres of vines on land adjacent to mine. We needed to get along.

Right now, though, unless George Washington himself turned up to offer Mick a tour of the place or told him they could nip down to the whiskey distillery, I already regretted the evening. Though Mick tried to mask his restlessness with well-bred feigned interest as only the British can, I knew he was bored.

We walked along a shady path that bordered an expanse of lawn known as the bowling green. Washington had planted some of the larger trees—tulip poplars, white ash, and elms—himself. I reached for Mick's arm to keep from stumbling on the uneven terrain. Ever since a near-fatal car accident three years ago left me with a deformed left foot, I needed a cane to keep my balance. Mick glanced down as I slid my arm through his. Another opportunity to peek at his watch.

I gave it one more try. "There's a fabulous view of the Potomac River from the other side of the mansion. Wait until you see it."

"Really? How marvelous." It sounded like I'd just offered him a cigarette before he got the blindfold.

"There's also a sundial in the middle of the courtyard. Too bad it's nearly sunset or you could check the time there, too," I said.

There was a moment of stunned silence before his laugh erupted like champagne fizz. "Sorry, love. I'm distracted tonight." His arm slid around my waist. "I didn't mean to be rude."

Love. Had the word slipped out, or was it intentional?

"Why did you come tonight, if you're not interested in this lecture?" I asked.

His arm tightened. "I am interested. But not in some woman giving a dull talk."

My face felt warm. "Joe said she's supposed to be riveting."

She was also Joe's friend. I moved out of the circle of Mick's arm.

"Not many people here," he said. "She can't be too riveting."

"That's because it's a select audience. I'm sure she'll be fascinating."

He stuck his hands in his pockets and grinned like I'd said something amusing. "Have you read her book?"

"I haven't even read the newspaper since August we've been so busy with harvest."

"Then let's have dinner and slope off. Come on, Lucie. Who cares if we stick around?"

"Joe cares. I promised him we'd stay for the whole evening. Anyway, I think her book sounds interesting. She followed Thomas Jefferson's voyage through the European vineyards when he was ambassador to France."

I got another gun-to-the-head look from him. "Why isn't she at Monticello if she wrote about Jefferson? What's she doing here?"

"Because Jefferson bought a lot of George Washington's wines for him. And she is going to Monticello. I think Joe said she's going to wrap up her book tour in Charlottesville. She just finished traveling around California. Now she's doing the East Coast."

We had come to the ivy-covered colonnade connecting Washington's servants' quarters to the main house. In the distance the river gleamed like dull pewter. I led Mick to the embankment where the ground fell away, leaving a view of the Potomac that stretched to the horizon. In the dusky light, the river—friendlier to pleasure boaters and fishermen where it snaked ribbonlike past Washington— looked vast and depthless here at Mount Vernon.

We stood in silence until finally he said, "You were right. It's an incredible view."

I had not expected him to sound wistful. "I thought you'd like it."

"Those cliffs remind me of Wales." His voice was soft with nostalgia. "We used to go up from London on summer holiday when I was a boy. My Lord, how I loved it there. On the north coast, the castles are perched on the bluffs just like this, except it's all rocks to the Irish Sea."

I believe that it is possible to miss a place you love so much that the ache is physical. I'd read that Washington pined terribly for his home when he was away from it—which was often—fulfilling his duties as commander in chief of the Continental Army or in Philadelphia as the first president. Staring at his cherished view, which had changed little since he and Martha looked out on it centuries ago, I knew I, too, would be homesick for this breathtaking place, just as Mick sounded homesick now for the north coast of Wales.

A bell rang behind us and I turned around. The western

sky was the color of liquid gold and the mansion appeared to be sitting inside a rim of fire. Silhouetted figures began to converge on the columned piazza.

"The tour must be starting," I said. "I wonder where Joe is."

"He'll turn up." Mick's arm slid around my waist again and this time I let it linger. As we reached the house, I saw a man and woman framed like a cameo in one of the colonnaded archways. Lantern light from the east courtyard illuminated his face as he leaned close to her, placing a hand on her shoulder. The woman tucked a strand of shoulder-length blonde hair behind one ear. Then she reached up and pulled his head down for a long, slow kiss. I couldn't stop watching them. The man was my cousin's fiancé, Joe Dawson. I did not know the woman, but she sure as hell wasn't Dominique.

"Come on," Mick said. "The crowd's moving. We'll miss what the guide is saying."

Either he hadn't seen what I just witnessed or else he didn't recognize Joe.

"Coming."

I had taken this tour so often over the years I could practically give it, but Mick, who had moved to Virginia six months ago, had never been to Mount Vernon. We began in the dining room, the largest room in the house, which had been restored to its original colors—two eye-popping shades of Washington's favorite green. I was glad to see Mick interested in the docent's talk, but I couldn't stop thinking about Joe and that blonde.

It didn't take long before I found out who she was. Someone jostled an elderly woman as the group moved out of the dining room. The book she'd been holding hit the floor and landed at my feet. I picked it up. *European Travels with Thomas Jefferson's Ghost* by Valerie Beauvais.

Joe had been making out with the guest of honor.

"Thank you so much, dear." The woman smiled, pearl-white teeth in a face as wrinkled as old fruit. "So clumsy of me."

"So clumsy of whoever bumped into you." I'd picked up the book facedown so I was staring at the author photo. No wonder they'd splashed it on the back cover. She had the racy good looks of a fashion model, a slightly lopsided smile, and a sly, almost naughty expression like she'd been talking dirty with the photographer. Stunning but tough-looking. By the time our tour finished winding in and out of the house and up two flights of stairs, I decided I didn't like Valerie Beau-vais.

Turned out I had company. After we'd seen the house, everyone spilled out on to the lawn where buffet tables had now been set up for dinner. I saw Ryan Worth, wine critic for the *Washington Tribune,* sitting in one of the Windsor chairs lining the piazza. He got up and waved, heading to-ward Mick and me. On the way he flagged down a waiter holding a tray of champagne flutes. Ryan handed a glass to me, then helped himself to two more for Mick and himself.

"Don't be a stranger," he said to the waiter. He clinked his glass against ours. "Tell me why you two have to be here. I came because I'm getting paid to introduce the guest of honor." He looked like he'd been asked to gargle with Drāno.

Ryan wrote "Worthwhile Wines," a weekly column that was syndicated in more than two hundred newspapers, a statistic he frequently enjoyed quoting. Short, wide, in his late thirties, with thinning black hair, his Van Dyke and pursed-lip smile made him appear slightly sinister, or else like he knew something I should but didn't. He had an encyclopedic knowledge of wines and wine history, though sometimes he took himself too seriously, acting as though he were sharing information he'd brought down from the mountain on stone tablets. Still, I respected him. He knew his stuff.

"I'm here because Lucie dragged me," Mick said.

"Oh, come on," I said. "We've been over this. Dinner and a talk. How bad can it be?"

"Obviously you've never heard Valerie." Ryan covered his mouth and faked a yawn. "She may look like a babe but she can clear a room faster than someone yelling 'fire.' As for her book—"

"Talking about me behind my back?" Valerie Beauvais had a husky Bacall-like voice with a hint of a drawl. "Hello, Ryan. I hear you've got the pleasure of introducing me tonight." Her smile seemed to mock him.

Close up, her eyes were even more arresting as she took us all in, dismissing me and settling suggestively on Mick, as though there were already some private joke between them. I wondered where Joe was.

"Don't let it go to your head, Val," Ryan said. "I'm not doing it for free. Besides, your publicist groveled and I took pity on him."

For a moment she seemed startled, then her eyes grew hard. "Funny. He said the same thing about you." She focused a slow-burn smile on Mick, ignoring Ryan. "I don't think we've met. Valerie Beauvais."

She held out her hand and Mick shook it. "Mick Dunne. And Lucie Montgomery."

Valerie didn't shake my hand. "I've heard of you," she said. "You own a vineyard and you're holding that auction."

Who had told her that? We'd barely publicized the

auction, a fund-raiser for a program for homeless and disabled kids in the D.C. metro area. One of my former college roommates, now the program's executive director, came to me for help after I'd raised a bundle of money for the local free clinic last spring.

"That's right," I said to Valerie.

"How'd you manage to get that bottle of Margaux?" she asked. "You must be very persuasive."

It didn't sound like a compliment. "You'd be surprised," I said. "And it's for charity."

In 1790, Thomas Jefferson ordered a shipment of wine for himself and his good friend George Washington from four of the greatest French wine estates in Bordeaux—Châteaus Lafite, Margaux, Mouton, and d'Yquem. Apparently some—or perhaps all—of the shipment never made it to either Mount Vernon or Monticello. One bottle, with the initials "G.W.," the year, and "Margaux" etched in the glass, turned up more than two centuries later in the private collection of Jack Greenfield, owner of Jeroboam's Fine Wines in Middleburg, Virginia. A week ago Jack called me and offered the wine for our auction. That was the good news. The bad news was that it was in poor condition. More than likely, he'd said, it had turned—now probably a bottle of very old, very expensive red wine vinegar.

Still, it represented liquid history. And it would be the jewel in the crown for our little charity auction. When Ryan heard the news, he'd offered to write about it in "Worthwhile Wines."

"You'll get national attention thanks to me," he said. "Syndicated in—"

"I know. More than two hundred newspapers," I said. "Thanks. That would be fabulous publicity."

But his column didn't run until tomorrow. Someone had already told Valerie about the wine. Her smile was gloating. She knew I had no intention of asking how she'd found out.

Ryan polished off his champagne and grabbed another flute from a passing waiter. "Anyone else? No?" He gulped more champagne and stared hard at Valerie. "God, Val, you're priceless. Just because you have to sleep around to get what you want doesn't mean everyone else does. Who told you about the Margaux? I wrote about it in my column, but it isn't out yet."

She laughed like he'd just told an off-color joke that she'd enjoyed. "I had lunch with Clay Avery at a place called the Goose Creek Inn. He let me read it," she said. "You know he wants me to write for the *Trib,* don't you? Sorry, but he's bored rigid with your columns and all that trivial crap you write about. Plus, he says you're a pompous ass." She winked. "Guess you ought to start calling it 'Worth-less Wines,' huh? You might want to dust off your résumé. Don't tell Clay I told you."

Clayton Avery owned the *Washington Tribune,* but he'd retired from actively managing it. He still had an eye for the ladies—the younger, the better—so I could easily imagine him taking Valerie out to lunch and letting her flirt with him. What I couldn't imagine was Clay, a true Southern gentleman, telling Valerie what he thought of his wine critic in such crass terms.

Ryan's face turned a mottled shade.of red. "Maybe Clay had a little too much to drink at lunch, but I doubt he'd hire you," he said. "If an original thought ever ran through your head, Valerie, it would be lonely. And that includes your Jefferson book. Has your editor discussed the plagiarism with you yet?"

For a second I thought she might throw her champagne at him, but then she must have remembered that he was introducing her after dinner.

"You'll pay for that." Her lips barely moved. "You don't know what you're talking about. Excuse me. I'm at the head table. Don't screw up my introduction, Ryan. Try to stay sober. I've heard stories about you, too."

Ryan stared at his nearly empty glass after she left, waggling it back and forth. "'Scuse me, folks. I need a moment. Save me a place at your table, will you?"

"Sure," I said.

"Let's make sure we don't sit too near the head table in case they start throwing the cutlery at each other," Mick said after Ryan left.

"I think they already both drew blood. Wonder how much they're paying him to introduce her," I said.

"No idea, but he must be desperate for the money. God, he hates her."

As we walked over to the buffet table I saw Joe Dawson holding Valerie's chair for her. She sat, flashing her lopsided grin as he took the seat next to her. They kissed briefly and she stroked his cheek. This time Mick noticed.

"Is that Joe with Valerie?" he asked.

"Sure is."

"Anything wrong between him and Dominique?"

"There might be, after tonight," I said. "Joe said he knew Valerie when they were doctoral students at UVA. He never mentioned they were such good friends."

"They're more than good friends," Mick said. "They've slept with each other."

I didn't need to ask how he knew. An electrical charge ran through me from the barely-below-the-surface voltage lines we'd laid down on the nights he and I slept together.

"Dominique was still living in France when Joe started working on his Ph.D.," I said. "It must have happened before they met."

Mick stared at me in the restless, hungry way that both scared and aroused me. He picked up my hand and kissed my fingers. I shivered. "They're still lovers," he said.

Ryan finally joined us, holding a plate heaped with food and another full glass of champagne.

"You all right?" I asked.

"Have a seat," Mick said.

"Thanks. I'm fine. Sorry about that scene earlier."

"Forget it," Mick said.

"She's a fraud," Ryan said. "And she knows how to goad me. I shouldn't have let her get to me."

"You accused her of plagiarism," I said. "Are you sure about that?"

He blew out a breath that sounded like air leaving a tire. "Hell, yeah, I'm sure. You think she wrote that book herself? Or her other one, on the first harvest at Jamestown?"

"If she didn't, who did?"

"The Jamestown book." He ticked items off on his fingers. "One, she was sleeping with one of the archaeologists when they discovered that James Fort wasn't washed into the river like everybody had thought it was for the past two hundred years. Two, the glass they found, the artifacts dating from the first harvest in America in 1609—she got lucky because he was the one who unearthed them. Three, her boyfriend spoon-fed her everything. It doesn't get much easier than that."

"What about the Jefferson book?" Mick asked.

Ryan looked pained. "That book was my idea. I planned that tour of the vineyards Jefferson visited. When I went down to the UVA library and Monticello for some preliminary research, I ran into her and stupidly told her about it over a drink. Next thing I know, she pitched it to her publisher and they bought it. I was dead in the water when I finally got around to putting my proposal together."

"So who wrote the Jefferson book?" I said.

He was incredulous. "Have you read it?"

I said, "No," and Mick shook his head.

"A kid in grade school could have done a better job. She plagiarized the good parts. What she wrote is pathetic. The reason she's traveling all over the country on a book tour is because her publisher is trying to recoup the whopping advance she got based on the Jamestown book." He sat back in his chair and downed more champagne. His Van Dyke quivered and the pursed-lip smile looked pinched.

Someone came over and tapped Ryan on the shoulder. "You're on," he said. "Time to introduce her."

I wondered if he was the groveler from Valerie's publisher.

Ryan stood up and put a hand on the table to steady himself. "Sometimes I hate myself for being such a whore," he said. "I wish I hadn't said yes to this."

Despite his acrimonious feelings, he gave a perfectly correct, if unenthusiastic, introduction to Valerie and her book. He also apparently decided to cut his losses since Valerie knew about the Margaux, and brought up the wine, its connection to George Washington, and our auction. He ended by plugging his column. Valerie glared at him as she got up to take her place at the podium but he walked past her and kept on walking. He never did return to our table.

Her talk was a sleeper, literally. Mick leaned back in his chair and closed his eyes. A moment later, I heard his breathing, regular as clockwork. Even Joe's head bobbed once or twice like he might be nodding off. We'd clearly been invited to pad the attendance numbers. When Valerie finished, I nudged Mick.

"It's over," I said. "Safe to wake up now."

"What happened?"

"Jefferson made it back to Paris at the end of his trip."

"I like happy endings. Guess I don't need to read the book."

"Me, neither. Let's go. I'd like to avoid both Valerie and Joe."

Mick took my hand and we started to walk across the lawn toward the colonnade. Someone touched my arm.

"I want to talk to you," Valerie said. "I don't have much time."

"About what?" But I knew about what. The Washington wine.

"I'll meet you out front in the courtyard," Mick said, "after you're done here."

I nodded, wishing he'd stayed.

"I'm giving a talk to some kids at Middleburg Academy tomorrow," Valerie said. "I thought I'd drop by your vineyard on my way and see the wines you've got for your auction. Check them out for myself. Let's say nine o'clock. That will give me time to get to the academy by ten."

Middleburg Academy was the private girls' high school where Joe Dawson taught history. So he and Valerie were seeing each other tomorrow, too.

I hate being bullied or told what I will or won't do. "The public will get a chance two days before the event to preview all the wines we'll be auctioning. You're more than welcome to have a look then."

Her eyes widened and she drew her head back. She looked like a snake about to strike. "Honey, you haven't got a clue what you've got sitting in your wine cellar. If you're smart you'll let me come by tomorrow."

I leaned on my cane and moved my face close to hers. "I'm plenty smart and I know the Margaux isn't in the best condition. Don't worry. We'll be up-front about it."

"The Margaux." She gave me an imperious look. "I knew you didn't know what you had. I'm talking about provenance."

"Valerie!" Her publicist showed up at her elbow. "Where the hell have you been? People are leaving. You've got to get over to the signing table now. Come on."

She said over her shoulder as he hustled her back to the piazza, "I'll see you tomorrow, Lucie. Nine o'clock."

I told Mick about the conversation on the way back to the gravel parking lot just outside the mansion grounds.

"Do you think she knows what she's talking about?" I asked.

"There's one way to find out, isn't there?" We'd reached his car, a black Mercedes. He opened the door for me. "Let her look at the wine and hear her out."

"I don't like the way she tried to push me around."

"So don't let her look at it."

"This affects you, too, you know. You agreed to have the auction at your home."

"I'm missing some connection in your logic."

"You don't seem that bothered by what she said."

"I'm not." He glanced over at me. "Darling, stop it, will you? Make a decision and forget it." His words were clipped.

I stared out the window as the D.C. skyline came into view across the Potomac. The Capitol and the Washington Monument stood out like cardboard pop-ups on the otherwise flat landscape before disappearing as we turned west for the forty-five-mile drive home to Atoka. Mick found a jazz station on his satellite radio and we listened in silence to wailing saxes, piano riffs, and smoky voices for the rest of the trip.

"Are you all right?" he asked. We had stopped at the lone traffic light in Middleburg. The next town was Atoka. "You've gone awfully quiet."

"Just thinking."

We didn't speak again until he turned off Atoka Road onto Sycamore Lane, the private road that led to the vineyard and Highland House, my home.

"If you don't let her come by tomorrow you're not going to be able to get it off your mind. So do it and that'll be the end of it," he said.

I smiled in the darkness, wondering how he knew what I was thinking. "All right, although I think she just wants to stir up trouble. What would she know about that bottle that Jack Greenfield wouldn't know? Ryan implied she's not that bright."

"You know the difference between men and women? Women make up their minds more than once. You agonize over every detail. Blokes just decide and we're done with it."

"Is that a criticism?"

He pulled into the circular drive in front of my house and stopped the car. "Take it anyway you like."

I knew what was coming next. After four months of abstinence his kiss was like drinking from a well after a journey through the Sahara. I'd forgotten how much I missed him, or maybe I hadn't let myself think about it. His breathing was hard and shallow as he laid me back against the seat. I wondered why he wanted to make love here first when we could just go inside and do it in my bed.

I felt dizzy as his hands moved to unzip my dress. I arched my back to make it easier for him.

"Bloody hell!" He sat up suddenly. "I knocked my knee on the gearshift."

I started to laugh and pull him down on top of me, but it was over for him as quickly as it started. He untangled himself from my arms and sat back up. "Maybe we shouldn't. Not tonight. Sorry, love."

My face was flushed and my clothes were disordered. He'd unhooked my bra and I was having trouble rehooking it. I tried to dress without looking at him.

"You all right?" he said. "Sorry. I just—"

"Please don't apologize. We haven't come to that, have we?"

"No, of course not. Look, Lucie—"

"It's okay. Good night. Thanks for coming with me and being a good sport about this evening."

I escaped from his car before he could say anything else. I'd taken two steps when I realized I'd left my cane in the Mercedes. My face burned as he handed it to me.

"Let me know how it goes with Valerie," he said.

I kept my voice deadpan. "Sure."

As soon as I got inside I undressed and went straight to bed. All night long he'd been sending an unmistakable message that he wanted to rekindle our relationship, hadn't he? So what had just happened? Did he want to jerk my chain to see if I'd still respond?

He found out, all right, but I had no intention of letting it happen again.

At least I hoped not.

Valerie never showed the next day. Nine came and went and so did ten. I went to my office to finish the monthly tax return we needed to file with the Alcohol and Tobacco Tax and Trade Bureau. It was overdue but harvest had been a bear and we'd worked almost around the clock. I punched figures into a calculator and wondered why the government couldn't find someone to draw up these forms who spoke the same English I did.

The phone rang and "Middleburg Academy" showed up on the display. After last night I didn't feel like talking to Joe. I let the call go to the answering machine.

He sounded agitated. "Sorry to bother you, Lucie, but I was wondering if Valerie Beauvais was still there. I've got a second period American History class in the middle of meltdown. She promised to come by and talk to them this morning and she hasn't shown. Could you call me when you get—"

I picked up the phone. "Hey, Joe. You're looking for Valerie? She never came by here, either."

"You serious? I just called her cell and got her voice mail," he said. "The academy put her up at the Fox and Hound last night. She hasn't checked out but she doesn't answer the phone in her cottage, either. The staff swears she's not on the property and says her car's gone. I can't figure out where she went."

"Sorry I can't help." I didn't like sounding brusque but Valerie could take care of herself and if she was lost then she wanted to get lost.

"I hate to impose but do you think you could possibly—"

The Fox and Hound was just up the road from the vineyard. He wanted me to check on his girlfriend. I cut him off. "I'm pretty tied up here."

"I'd go myself but I can't leave the kids and I'm worried about her. Please, Lucie? If you could just swing by and see what's up, I'll owe you. It'll take you less than fifteen minutes."

I propped my bad leg up on the credenza and stared at the photos lined up on it. Framed pictures of my parents, Chantal and Leland Montgomery—now both dead—as well as my brother, Eli, with his wife and daughter; my sister, Mia; Hector and his family; and photos taken with Quinn, our current winemaker, and Jacques, our former winemaker, with our crews at harvest. I picked up a silver-framed photo of Dominique and Joe at the Goose Creek Inn's fortieth anniversary party when she officially took over as owner. Both of them laughing and clowning as they fed each other cake. Except for the clothes they were wearing it could have been their wedding day.

He had been trying to get her to set a date for the past few years but my workaholic cousin always found a reason to postpone. Joe was a patient man, a good man—like an older brother to me.

"All right," I said. "How do I get in touch with you after I check the Fox and Hound?"

I heard his sigh of relief. "Call the school and they'll put you through to the phone in my classroom. And thank you."

"Don't mention it," I said.

I'd left my new car, a red Mini Cooper convertible with white racing stripes, in the winery parking lot. I put the top down and grabbed a baseball cap from the backseat to keep my hair from blowing in my eyes.

Many of the roads around Atoka and Middleburg were ancient Indian trails now lined by Civil War–era stacked stone walls. Some were paved but many were still dirt or gravel because this was also horse-and-hunt country and it was better for the horses. Almost all of these pretty country lanes were hilly, filled with twists and turns that followed the contours of the land or Goose Creek as it meandered its way to the Potomac River just past Leesburg. I could drive them with my eyes closed because I knew them so well, but the corners were treacherous for anyone new to the area or not paying attention.

The bright yellow SUV lay on its roof in Goose Creek at a sharp elbow bend in Atoka Road. The moment I saw it I knew it was Valerie's. I pulled off the road and reached for my phone, murmuring a prayer. As near as I could tell she had made no effort to get out of the SUV.

The woman who answered my 911 call asked calm, quiet questions. I gave her what little information I could. She promised help was on the way and I hung up.

I waded into the chilly water until I got close enough to see inside the car. When I did, I felt sick. Valerie hung suspended upside down, trapped by her seat belt. Her face was bloody and she wasn't moving.

I wondered if I was too late and she was already dead.

Chapter 2

—⊗⊗⊗—

I didn't expect the water to be so cold, nor the current so strong. Fortunately the creek was only knee-deep where her car had gone in and I could use my cane to keep steady against the swiftly flowing water.

I called her name as I looked through the passenger window, but she didn't stir. The car was full of water as high as the creek level. The noise as it rushed through the open windows roared in my ears. Near Valerie's body it was a pale shade of pink and my stomach churned some more.

I guessed that her car must have rolled like a barrel down the embankment headfirst because the roof was crushed in at the windshield and her air bag had been deployed, meaning the front end had struck something solid. A faint gunpowder odor still permeated the air inside the car. So far Valerie's face was above water but the caved-in roof—which looked like it was responsible for her injuries—had diminished the interior headroom, leaving little clearance between Valerie and the water level. The ends of her blonde hair, which she'd worn loose, skimmed the surface of the eddying water as did both hands since her arms were now thrown above her head like a supplicant.

I sloshed around to the front of the car, hanging on so I wouldn't slip. At one point the chassis rocked crazily and I let go in a panic. Had it landed on a tree limb or something else that made it so unsteady? Whatever it was, I had to get Valerie out of here—release her from her seat belt and get her to the bank of the creek.

I hung my cane on the side mirror and fought the urge to throw up as I looked through the driver's side window. Valerie's face and hair were blood-soaked and it looked like she'd sustained some injuries on the left side of her chest. Her eyes were closed and she didn't appear to be breathing. I tried to find her carotid artery and my hand came away bloody.

She was dead.

"Oh, God, Valerie," I said to her. "I'm so sorry. I'm getting you out of here, honey. They shouldn't find you looking like a trussed fish."

The collapsed roof had crushed both front doors making them impossible to open. The back doors were locked. I found the unlock button and heard the click releasing all four doors.

Once I undid her seat belt Valerie would drop like a stone straight into the water. I'd have to grab her before she did, then try to pull her out of the car. She was taller than I, and probably weighed about ten pounds more—maybe a hundred and thirty, give or take. Hopefully I'd be able to carry her, but I wouldn't be able to use my cane. If worse came to worse, I'd have to drag her.

It no longer mattered if her injuries worsened.

The only way to get into the car was through one of the back doors. The frame between the doors on the driver's side was also bent, but not so badly that I couldn't open the back door. I tugged hard on the handle and the car rocked back and forth again.

"Oh, God," I said under my breath. "Please stay where you are." I jerked the door and the motion caused my cane to jump and slip off the side mirror. It dropped in the creek with a graceful plop and immediately caught the current, floating downstream. I started to go after it, then let it go. I'd never catch it.

By now the water in the car was a darker shade of pink, almost cherry-colored. I squeezed between the front seats. If I could get Valerie's seat to recline fully, I could pull her straight back once I released her seat belt, though it meant I needed to do both actions nearly simultaneously and some-how keep my balance in the cramped space.

I snaked my hand between her seat and the door and found the lever. The seat groaned with her weight but I pulled on it so the back was nearly horizontal. Valerie's face was suddenly right next to mine, bloodied and battered. I sucked in my breath.

"Okay," I said to her. "Let's do this on three." I counted and pushed the release for her seat belt. It caught a button on her blazer and I tried to loosen the belt as she fell on me knocking me backward against the rear seat. My bad foot collapsed and I lost my balance, though at least I didn't swallow any water.

I backed out of the car and stepped into the creek, trip-ping over something. Valerie came along with me and we went down together. My head snapped like it was on a spring and my back felt like someone had sliced it open with a razor. This time I did swallow water and it tasted like sour metal. I coughed and spat. God Almighty, what did people dump in Goose Creek?

By the time I got us both to the riverbank, her blood had seeped into my clothes and I was shivering from cold and pain. My back felt like it was on fire. I'd seen what I'd fallen on. Tree limbs.

I dug into my pocket for my cell phone. Waterlogged and ruined. No way to call 911 again, or anyone else.

When the first fire and rescue trucks showed up, I was lying on my side next to Valerie. I heard someone shout that there were two victims as a man in firefighter's gear knelt by me.

"What happened?" he said.

"Her car went off the road into the creek. I got her out but I think I was too late."

"We'll get you to a hospital, miss," he said.

I tried to sit up. It felt like there was a vise around my head and my back throbbed.

"I wasn't in the car," I said. "I tripped over a tree branch in the creek when I pulled her out. I've got some cuts on my back and probably some bruises, but that's all."

A paramedic joined us. "You're going to the hospital."

He meant Catoctin General over in Leesburg. I'd spent months there three years ago learning to walk again after my accident. I didn't want to go back, especially for something as minor as a few scratches. Even visiting someone there dragged up memories I'd rather forget.

"Thank you, but no thanks," I said. "I don't need to go to any hospital."

He was young with short wiry hair, a wholesome, square face, and friendly eyes. The eyes widened in surprise and I expected him to contradict me. Instead he said, "Let me look at your back."

He had to cut my shirt open. "Looks like a tic-tac-toe board here. How did you manage to do this?"

"I lined up the tree limbs before I fell on them."

"Nice," he said. "Look, I'm going to clean and dress these cuts and put some antibacterial ointment on them. Might sting a bit."

"It stings now."

He taped gauze bandages over the deepest cuts. I gritted my teeth and only groaned once while he did it.

"Easy," he said. "Almost done."

"Thank you."

"I hope you can sleep on your stomach for a few days," he said. "Change those dressings regularly—actually, have someone do it for you. Once the cuts scab over it will be better to let them heal uncovered."

"Will I have scars?" I didn't add that I had no "someone" to do it for me.

"You might. Sure you don't want to go to the hospital?" He wrapped a Mylar blanket around my shoulders since my shirt was in shreds. I glanced over and saw that Valerie's body had been covered by some kind of drape.

"Positive."

"I've got to fill out some paperwork that says you're refusing further medical treatment. And someone needs to come get you once they release you here," he said. "You're in no shape to drive."

A female deputy from the sheriff's department squatted next to both of us. "I'd like to talk to you, Miss Montgomery, if you don't mind," she said. Her badge said "G. Hernandez."

"Sure." More emergency vehicles had arrived, blocking the road. Valerie's car still lay in the creek but now half a dozen deputies and firefighters in rubber boots surrounded it.

"What happened?" She flipped open a spiral notebook.

"When I got here, the SUV was in the creek. I guess she missed the turn."

Hernandez tapped her pen against the edge of the notebook. I followed her gaze from the road to the trajectory Valerie's car might have taken into Goose Creek. "We'll know more after we hook her car and the CRU goes over it."

"CRU?"

"Crash Reconstruction Unit. Did another car pass you before you got here?"

I shook my head. "No one."

"You just happened to be driving down the road and saw her?"

"Actually, I was looking for her."

Hernandez straightened up. "How come you were looking for her?"

"She was supposed to come by my vineyard this morning for a meeting. Then she was going to speak to a group of kids at Middleburg Academy. The teacher called when she didn't show and told me she was staying at the Fox and Hound up the road. He asked me to go by and see if I could find out what delayed her."

"What's her name?" Hernandez kept writing and didn't look up.

"Valerie Beauvais."

"Spell that, please? The last name."

I told her.

"You a friend of hers?"

"Not really. I met her last night at a dinner at Mount Vernon. She gave a lecture about a book she just wrote."

"She mention car trouble at Mount Vernon? A flat tire, maybe?"

"Not to me. Why?"

She pointed to the SUV. "You didn't notice one wheel is missing?"

For the first time I noticed that the back driver's side tire on Valerie's car was gone. "Oh my God. I didn't realize." Hernandez watched me. "All I wanted to do was get her out of the car."

"Right." Hernandez indicated the Mini. "Is that your car over there?"

"Yes." Two officers stood next to it. I watched one of them lean over the windshield and write something down. Probably the VIN number.

"Excuse me. You don't think I—?" I stared at Deputy Hernandez. She gazed back clear-eyed, but I could tell she was still taking stock of my stunned reaction.

"I'm sure you realize we need to check out every possibility," she said. "One, you were on the scene. Two, you know the deceased."

"Do I need a lawyer?" I asked.

"You're not being charged with anything at this time. I understand you're refusing to go to the hospital?"

My paramedic nodded. "I dressed her injuries. She needs to take it easy for the rest of the day but she should be okay. And she shouldn't be driving."

"An officer will take you home." Hernandez stood up. "But it might be a while. Unless there's someone you could call—a family member, maybe?"

My waterlogged phone lay on the ground next to me. "Can I borrow your phone, please?"

She handed it to me and I flipped it open, suddenly unsure whom to call. Hector was gone. If I asked my brother, Eli, he would moan, once he finally got here, that he really ought to be finishing a set of drawings for some building or the client would hit the roof and would I please not drip water or blood on the custom-leather seats of his precious Jaguar. My sister, Mia, was away at college in Harrisonburg.

I started to dial Mick's number and punched "end." Hernandez watched me.

"We can take you—"

"Thanks. That won't be necessary." I called Quinn Santori, my winemaker. When he answered I said, "I'm in kind of a jam. Any chance of a lift home? A deputy from the sheriff's department and a paramedic have told me I can't drive."

He took a moment to reflect on that. "And I thought my day was bad with the pump acting up. Where are you?"

He showed up in his metallic green El Camino ten minutes later, pulling in behind a crane and a flatbed truck with the Loudoun County Sheriff's Department logo on it. As usual he was dressed in combat fatigues, an old Hawaiian shirt, and more jewelry than most women.

Deputy Hernandez looked Quinn over. "That your ride?"

"That's my ride."

Shortly before my father passed away last year, he hired Quinn when our first winemaker, whom I adored, returned to France after suffering a small stroke. Quinn wouldn't have been my first choice, probably not even my last. I knew he would have said the same about me. But in the past few months he'd finally stopped acting like everything I knew about wine-making could be summed up in ten minutes as long as I spoke slowly. And I finally got used to working with someone with the attitude of Dirty Harry and the sartorial taste of a thrift shop habitué.

"What happened?" His face, to my surprise, looked pale under his fading summer suntan. "Are you all right?"

I told him everything.

"You went in the creek after that woman?" he said.

"She was still in her car. I couldn't just leave her there."

"You've got blood all over you. What happened?"

"I slipped in the creek and a tree limb got in my way. I've got a few scratches on my back. Can we go now, please?"

"Sit tight. I'll have to carry you."

"I don't need to be carried. I can walk just fine, if you can help me up. And maybe let me lean on your arm."

"Where's your cane?"

"Somewhere between here and Leesburg, depending on the creek."

He helped me up. My bad foot buckled and his arm went around my waist. "Stop being a martyr and let me carry you."

"I'll be fine."

"Sure, jelly-legs. I've got half a mind to throw you over my shoulder."

"That would be a very bad decision on your part." The faint scent of his favorite Swisher Sweet cigars clung to his shirt. I breathed it in like calming incense, glad I'd called him after all. "Maybe Manolo or one of the other guys from the crew can come back for the Mini."

"I'll take care of it. Let's get you home first."

"There's one other thing."

"Yeah?"

"The wheel came off Valerie's car. It's probably the reason she went into the creek. They're not charging me with anything, but since I knew her and they found me at the scene—"

"That deputy believes you ran an SUV off the road with that windup toy?" He glanced over at the Mini. At least he sounded like he didn't believe I'd done it.

"I don't know." My cuts burned and my head ached. "They're checking it out."

Quinn held the door of the El and I slid carefully into the passenger seat. "Jesus," he said. "That's a hell of a way to start the day."

I washed my hair in the sink and took a sponge bath to keep my bandages dry. By the time I finished and swallowed a double dose of ibuprofen, Manolo, who'd taken over Hector's old job, had brought the Mini back to the house.

Short of wearing a body bag, there was no way to hide my injuries, especially since I now had some spectacular-looking bruises, which appeared in large red blotches, on my arms and legs. I went through my closet and finally settled on a long black-and-white cotton halter dress with a low-cut back for comfort and a black pashmina shawl for camouflage.

Joe had left messages at the winery, at my house, and no doubt on my now-defunct cell phone. I decided to tell him about Valerie face-to-face. It wasn't right to deliver news like this in a phone call. And to tell the truth, I wondered about the relationship my cousin's fiancé had with the deceased. Had they been lovers? Joe sure hadn't taken any pains last night to conceal that they were more than casual friends.

I had to ease myself slowly into the Mini, but at least I felt clearheaded enough to drive. And I had the ibuprofen bottle for backup.

Middleburg Academy sat on fifty secluded acres of manicured lawns and well-kept gardens. I had attended Blue Ridge High, the local public high school, which had all the architectural charm and style of a maximum-security prison. The academy's pretty campus of ivy-covered gray stone buildings with crenellated walls and turreted towers was stamped with the imprimatur of old money and tradition. Its students were the daughters of senators, sheikhs, CEOs, and famous Hollywood names. In addition to the academic program, the staff encouraged the girls to bring their horses and board them on the grounds during the school year—most of them did.

I drove up the oak-lined private road past a fountain surrounded by a garden of fall mums arranged in burgundy and gold stripes for the school colors. In the spring the gardeners made floral designs based around the initials "MA." If anything died or wilted to spoil the perfection, it was replaced instantly. I left the Mini in the lot near the main building, parking a few cars away from Joe's red Toyota Camry, recognizable for the "Virginia: First in Wine" bumper sticker I'd given him.

The school's reception area, with its dark paneled walls, velvet sofas, worn oriental rugs, stone fireplace, and oil paintings of headmistresses and significant donors, looked like the lobby of an elegant English hotel. The woman behind the front desk wore a smart black suit and a single strand of pearls.

"May I help you?" She removed her horn-rimmed glasses and looked me over.

My shawl had slipped off one shoulder. Her eyes flickered from my face to my shoulder and I followed her gaze. She was staring at a raw, red bruise the size of a fist.

I hiked the shawl back into place and said, "I'm here to see Joe Dawson."

"Dr. Dawson is teaching at the moment." Judging by her voice, I hadn't made a good first impression.

"It's an emergency or I wouldn't be here."

She raised one eyebrow. "If this is a domestic matter—"

Great. She thought my boyfriend beat me up.

"There's been an accident involving someone he knows," I said. "Someone else. Not me. Please, it's important."

"Oh." She put her glasses back on and now she really looked me over. "I assumed it was about you. Please have a seat. I'll find him right away. Whom shall I say is calling?"

I told her and she picked up the phone.

Five minutes later I heard footsteps on the marble staircase around the corner from the front desk and Joe bounded into view. As I stood up from the sofa, my shawl slipped again. Joe's eyes, like the receptionist's, went straight to my shoulder.

"My God, Lucie! What happened? I've been trying to call you all day." He moved quickly across the lobby and reached for my hands. At a school this posh, the staff was expected to look smart and dress appropriately. Joe had missed a spot shaving this morning, his tie had a stain on it, and there was eraser dust on the sleeve of his navy blazer. His eyes had dark circles under them. Hopefully the board of visitors wasn't in town for a meeting.

"Can we talk someplace private?" I asked.

"Sure, sure." He turned to the receptionist. "Janice, anybody using the conference room?"

Janice looked like she wished we could stay right where we were as she was dying to know herself. "Uh, no. It's free. Go right ahead."

There were more paintings of dead headmistresses in the cool, airless room. All wore slight smiles of amused superiority and had eyes that seemed to follow wherever I moved. Joe flipped on the lights and pulled a mahogany chair with a burgundy leather seat away from the conference table.

"Sit down, cupcake."

He was smiling but his eyes were grave. At least he'd used his favorite nickname for me. I sat gingerly and leaned the metal cane the hospital had given me after my car accident against the table.

Joe took the chair next to me and crossed his legs. His socks were mismatched, too—blue and brown.

"What happened to you? Can I get you something? Water?" he asked. "Where's Valerie?"

"Nothing, thanks." I shook my head and took one of his hands in both of mine. "I'm so sorry to have to tell you this, but Valerie was in a car accident this morning. That's why you didn't hear from her."

Joe's baby-faced good looks and dimpled smile still got him carded when he tried to buy liquor even though he was in his mid-thirties. His face sagged and suddenly he looked a lot older. "She's in the hospital?"

"No," I said. "Her car went off the road at that hairpin turn between the Fox and Hound and my vineyard. One of the wheels came off somehow and she went into Goose Creek. She didn't survive the accident. I thought I should tell you in person."

He'd been nodding as I talked and he kept on nodding when I finished like he was still processing what I was saying and hadn't gotten to the part about Valerie being dead.

"I'm sorry," I said again.

He quit nodding and the light went out of his eyes. "Is that how you got these bruises?"

"I pulled her out of her car. It was filling up with water. She was dead when I got there. No one could have saved her."

"I see." He removed his hand from mine and touched the edge of my shawl, rubbing his fingers over and over the fringed edge until I thought the dye would come off on his hand. "You're pretty banged up. And you're sitting funny. What did you do to yourself?"

"I fell when I was getting her out of the car. It's nothing serious."

He leaned over and his arms went around me. "How could a wheel come off her car?" His voice was thick with grief. "How could she be dead?"

"The sheriff's trying to find out." I didn't tell him they also were looking into whether I had anything to do with her accident. "They're going to reconstruct the crash."

He buried his face in my hair. "I should have driven her here this morning. It never would have happened. She'd be fine."

"Don't."

He dropped his arms and stood, staring at a portrait of a dark-haired headmistress dressed for foxhunting in breeches, boots, a white shirt and stock, and the red riding jacket worn by someone accorded the honor of Master of Foxhounds. I wondered if he was trying not to cry.

"She wasn't just an old friend from school like you told me, was she?" I said. "I saw you together last night. You were in love with her. At least, that's what it looked like."

He shifted his eyes from the painting to me. His face hardened and I knew I'd crossed a line into territory where he felt I didn't belong. "I cared about her. What of it?"

"What about Dominique?" I said. "Your fiancée?"

He looked as though I'd just slapped him. "Jesus, Lucie. What do you take me for? I guess she didn't tell you. Probably too busy to mention it. We're not engaged anymore. Or at least, it's on hold. We both needed a little space."

"I didn't know that." Though he certainly hadn't wasted any time filling his share of that little space.

He jammed his hands in his pockets. "I'd better get back to the kids. And I appreciate you coming here to tell me about Valerie."

He walked me to the main entrance and we both stepped out into the warmth of the balmy afternoon.

"Beautiful day, huh?" His voice was ironic. "Guess we ought to savor them when we can. Because you never know—"

"No," I said. "You don't."

"I'll call you some time, cupcake."

The carved wooden door with its fancy iron scrollwork closed with a loud clunk behind him. There was no spring in his step this time as there had been when he had come down the stairs to meet me.

I wanted to feel sorry for him but I couldn't. There was something odd about the rushed intensity of his relationship with Valerie. Something odd about her accident, too.

I drove home and wondered what she wanted to tell me about the Washington wine Jack Greenfield donated and why she'd been so sure I didn't know about its provenance. Before the auction took place at the end of the month I needed to find out—even if it was nothing more than a wild goose chase.

Chapter 3

Quinn was in the lab just off the barrel room when I showed up at quarter past three. I'd changed into a baggy sweatshirt and loose pair of pants. He looked me over like yard sale merchandise the sellers ought to be paying you to take. "Shouldn't you be in bed?"

"If I was, I'd just lie there and think about how much it hurts. Anyway, I'm too restless, especially since we still have to bring in the Cab. Did you do the field tests yet?"

"I'm about to. Want to come along?"

"Sure."

The only grapes left to harvest this year were Cabernet Sauvignon, the most celebrated red wine grape in the world. The best-known and most sought-after Cabs come from Bordeaux, a place God created on His best day, granting it a perfect climate, sun-drenched days, and the kind of rocky soil vines thrive on.

Unlike the French, Americans name wines by grape varietal rather than region, but a French Bordeaux, an American Cabernet Sauvignon, and what the English call "claret" are all the same wine. Most of these are blends of more than one grape—usually Merlot or Cabernet Franc, though sometimes a little Petit Verdot or Malbec is added as well. The trick, for a winemaker, is figuring out how much of which grape to add to get the perfect wine—though by law, the "other" grapes can't be more than 25 percent of the blend, or it can't be labeled Cabernet Sauvignon.

Quinn was a born fiddler and I knew he was already pondering our blend even though we hadn't yet picked the grapes. We'd brought the Merlot in a few weeks ago, putting most of it in barrels, but keeping what we planned to blend with the Cab in stainless-steel tanks.

"Let's buy some PV this year," Quinn had said at the time. "A few tons. It'll give the wine a nice garnet color."

"We're not buying someone else's Petit Verdot. I don't want a different *terroir* in our wine. You know we always use only our own grapes," I'd said.

Terroir was the indefinable "X" factor in a wine—literally it meant "the taste of the land" and made each wine distinctive from the next. Changing the soil or the region meant changing the wine. Last spring we planted fifteen acres of new varietals, including a few acres of Petit Verdot—but it would be three years before we got a harvest from those grapes.

"Stop being such a purist," he'd said. "I'm talking about five percent. It'll make all the difference in the wine, but it will still be our *terroir*. You know I'm right. You're just digging in your heels because that's how your mother did it."

It still hurt that he'd once called my plan to run the vineyard as my mother had done "professional suicide." I was proud of what she and Jacques had accomplished—with little help from Leland—to build our reputation. Giving Quinn carte blanche to do as he liked meant he'd change everything—use shortcuts and take advantage of the tricks he could play with modern technology.

"The wines she and Jacques made were some of our best vintages," I'd said, angry that he'd invoked my mother to make his point. "It's thanks to them we've got such a good reputation today."

"*Were* some of the best vintages," he'd said. "We'll do better."

I gave in, but I was adamant the grapes had to come from Virginia. I knew a few vineyards that bought grapes from California and, as a result, had to call their wine "American wine." We made *Virginia* wine—I wasn't ever giving ground on that.

"I've got the refractometer. If you get everything else, I'll bring the Gator around to the crush pad," he said to me now. "Pick you up in five."

He pulled up in the Gator, an all-terrain vehicle that looked like a cross between a golf cart and a tractor, and I climbed into the passenger seat. The breeze felt like a warm caress against my sore body, the sky was a limitless blue, and the sunshine sharp and clear. In the distance the soft-shouldered Blue Ridge Mountains seemed to have fused with the sky so it was hard to tell where one stopped and the other began.

Quinn turned down the south service road. "Bonita called while you were out," he said. "From Mexico."

He'd been living with Hector's daughter for the past few months until her father died. Hector and his wife, Sera, liked Quinn well enough, but they were traditional parents who didn't approve of their twenty-one-year-old daughter living with a man nearly two decades older than she was. Especially one who didn't plan to make an honest woman of her.

"Did they finally have Hector's funeral?" I asked.

Though I'd offered Sera a plot in my family's private cemetery with its view of the mountains he loved so much, she wanted to take him home to Mexico. Bonita made all the arrangements. They left two weeks ago.

I drove them to the airport and watched Sera, frail as a bird, strong-willed as a bull, and Bonita, all girly sensuousness and seduction, pass through the security checkpoint at Dulles Airport. When Bonita's eyes met mine just before they disappeared into the passengers-only labyrinth, I knew I'd probably just said good-bye to both of them for good. I'd never told Quinn.

"Yeah, they had some big Catholic shindig with all the family." He took a corner too sharply and I grabbed the edge of my seat. "I don't think they're coming back."

We had reached the large apple orchard. The trees were full and heavy and the Virginia creeper, which twined around the split-rail fence, had already turned ruby-colored.

He could have been talking about the weather or he could have been talking about someone who just broke his heart. With Quinn it was hard to tell.

"Did she say they weren't?" I asked.

"Nope. Didn't say much of anything."

"I don't think they're coming back, either," I said. "You okay with that?"

"You mean, because of Bonita?"

"I don't mean because of Sera. She was ready to skin you, boil you, and hang you out on the fence for the coyotes to dine on."

"She was, wasn't she?" He grinned. "I dunno. First Angie moves out on me, now Bonita. It wasn't really working. You were right about it not being a good idea to get involved with someone you work with."

I'd nearly forgotten about Angie, a former high school classmate of mine who worked as an exotic dancer at a local club. That relationship hadn't lasted long, either.

He pulled up at the first marker for the Cabernet block and cut the ignition.

"Was I?"

Though the sunlight was behind him, he squinted at me like he was having a hard time focusing. But his eyes lingered on mine and I saw in them—as I know he saw in mine—the unspoken acknowledgment about the occasionally precarious state of our own relationship.

"Yes," he said. "You were." He climbed out of the Gator and said, "Let's do this."

He took the refractometer, the telescopelike instrument we used to measure Brix, out of his shirt pocket. I got the other things we needed—resealable plastic bag, small bucket, graduated cylinder. As we walked down the row of vines, he pulled out a switchblade and cut random grapes from clusters and dropped them in the bag I held open.

"Dammit." He knelt by the bottom trellis wire. "The groundhogs are eating the lower clusters. I thought the guys knew they were supposed to cut them off."

"Talk to Manolo," I said. "Get him to remind the crew. They forget."

He brushed away a soporific yellow jacket already drunk on fermenting juice.

"We've got enough for a sample," he said, taking the bag and mashing the grapes. When it was full of juice, he emptied it into the cylinder. "Manolo's head isn't in his job the way it used to be."

"He's worked for us since he was a kid. Started practically the day he arrived here from Mexico. I'll talk to him."

I poured a few drops of juice onto the measuring prism of the refractometer.

Quinn held the eyepiece up to the sunlight. "Twenty-one point two. It should be twenty-two by Monday since this Indian summer weather is supposed to hold. Here, see what you get."

Brix was the most important field test we did because it measured the amount of sugar in the grapes, which, in turn, determined when they were ready to be picked. It also allowed us to calculate what the percentage level of alcohol would be once we made the grapes into wine. Because the federal government set strict standards for how much alcohol was allowed in each varietal, it wasn't something we wanted to screw up.

I watched the refractometer level float up and down before settling on twenty-one point two. "I get the same thing you do."

"Let's sample some more clusters near the Merlot block," he said. There Brix was higher though still below twenty-two so he decided we'd pick there on Monday and finish the rest on Tuesday.

On the way back to the winery he said, "You've been kind of quiet. I know you had a rough day. I could swing by your house and drop you there, if you want."

"I'm all right. It's just that I can't stop thinking about Valerie Beauvais. I wish I knew what she wanted to tell me."

"Tell you about what?"

"She said something last night at Mount Vernon about the wine Jack Greenfield donated for the auction. Asked me how I managed to get him to give us the Margaux. Then after dinner she told me I didn't know what I'd got and that it had something to do with the provenance."

"What about it?"

"I don't know. She wasn't going to tell me until she came by."

"And now she can't." He swung the Gator around by the equipment barn and parked. "The phone's been ringing off the hook ever since Ryan's column ran in the *Trib*. Everyone and his grandmother wants to know about the auction and the Washington wine now."

I chewed my lower lip. "How would Valerie know something about Jack's wine that he wouldn't know?"

He climbed down from the Gator and handed my cane to me. "Ask him."

"If I did he'd be insulted. Ryan said she was a phony."

"Then I'd believe Jack and forget about it."

"I guess so."

He gave me the look that said he knew I didn't plan to and headed for the barrel room. I got the Mini and drove over to the Fox and Hound.

I stopped at the turn on Atoka Road where Valerie's car had gone into the creek. The tall grass was matted and the bushes were broken and beaten down at the place the sheriff's cruisers and the emergency vehicles had parked earlier. The asphalt was torn up in a long strip where it looked like the axel of her car and the undercarriage had dug into the road after her wheel came off. The marks—ugly as a scar—ended where her SUV had left the road, probably beginning to roll over until it landed in the middle of the creek.

I put my hand over my mouth and wondered if it had seemed like a slow-motion nightmare to Valerie, or if it had been so fast she never realized what was coming. It looked like the wheel had fallen off in the worst possible place—in the middle of an elbow-bend turn—and she'd lost control.

No doubt the sheriff's department or CRU had already found the wheel, which would help them piece together the rest of the scenario.

On any other day, the woods and the creek were pretty and peaceful—the kind of scene that would have made an appealing photo for a travel brochure. I said a prayer for Valerie and got back in my car. Three minutes later, I was in the parking lot of the Fox and Hound.

Even without knowing that the owners, Grace and Jordy Jordan, were Anglophiles, the red telephone box with "EIIR" and the London cab parked by the entrance were dead giveaways. The Jordans visited Britain every year for one of Jordy's historical sightseeing jaunts, but they also brought home antiques, English china, and fine art to furnish the rooms and cottages of their elegant bed and breakfast.

I found Jordy in his office off the foyer. Grace had recently redecorated the entrance in shades of sage, cream, and butternut after falling in love with some William Morris textile prints on her last visit to the Victoria and Albert Museum in London. Oil paintings of English hunting scenes lined the walls. A large Portmeirion vase on the console table held dried flowers that smelled of cinnamon and cloves.

Jordy was in his early sixties, gray-haired, avuncular, and comfortable as a favorite reading chair. He set down a copy of *Majesty* magazine when he saw me. He looked tired.

"Hello, my dear. Have a seat. Move those newspapers off that chair, will you, and hand them to me?"

I picked up a pile of *The Guardian* and *The Times* from a chintz-covered Queen Anne chair and gave them to him before I perched on the edge. The ibuprofen was starting to wear off and the cuts on my back throbbed once again.

"The place has been in a state all day," he said. "A couple of guests checked out early, what with the sheriff's department here for most of the afternoon, carting off that poor woman's belongings from Cornwall Cottage. Our guests expect privacy and discreet service."

"She was on her way to see me when her car went off the road," I said. "Any chance I can take a look at that cottage?"

Jordy shook his head. "The sheriff strung up crime scene tape around the place like Christmas garland. I can't even take a look at it." He folded his arms across his belly. "We had a couple who booked it beginning tomorrow. I called them this afternoon and explained that we needed to move them down the path to Devon. Just as nice and bigger. They asked why, so of course I told them the truth. You know what? They canceled their reservation."

"Crime scene tape? The sheriff doesn't think it was an accident?" I asked. What else had they found at the creek? Or in Valerie's car?

"Apparently not," he said. "Of course I'm sorry she's dead, but that tape will upset our guests until it comes down. So disturbing. Though we did get a lot of calls all day on account of that auction you're having at the end of the month. Place is full up for that weekend thanks to you. We've even got a waiting list in case of cancellations. I read the column in the *Trib* about that bottle of wine Thomas Jefferson bought for George Washington. An amazing story. Very generous donation from Jack Greenfield."

"I know," I said. "Jordy, Valerie Beauvais was on her way to the vineyard to look at that bottle of wine before she gave a talk at Middleburg Academy."

He made a clicking sound with his tongue. "Such a shame. I heard you found her and pulled her out." His eyes strayed to my hospital-issue cane. "You all right, Lucie?"

"I got banged up when I slipped in the creek, but I'll be okay. You mind if I take a look around here, anyway? I'll stay away from the crime scene tape."

He steepled his fingers. "What are you looking for?"

"I don't know. Probably nothing."

"Something to do with that bottle of wine?" He leaned back in his desk chair and regarded me.

"Valerie wanted to talk to me about something. Whatever it was, she never got a chance to do it. I guess I'm just scratching an itch, that's all."

Jordy and Jack Greenfield played poker with a local group of men known as the Romeos. It stood for Retired Old Men Eating Out and they could spread gossip faster than a strong wind could spread a fire in a dry spell. I'd just aroused his curiosity and he knew I'd been deliberately vague. The topic would come up for sure at the next poker game.

"Help yourself." His smile was bland. "Don't imagine you'll find anything, but you're welcome to look."

"Thanks." I stood. "I see you've got a copy of her book."

His chair squeaked as he swung around to retrieve it from a gate-leg maple table. "Here. Take it, if you'd like. Put it in the wine library in your tasting room."

"Don't you want it?"

Jordy looked embarrassed. "My dear, I'm sorry to speak ill of the dead, but it's unreadable."

I took the book and thanked him. He walked me to the front door.

"Did you see her leave this morning?" I asked.

He shook his head. "She didn't even show up for breakfast. Surprising since Gracie put out one of her award-winning English spreads." He patted his stomach. "One of those will keep you until dinner. Tomorrow's dinner."

I kissed him good-bye and he closed the door. But as I walked toward Cornwall Cottage I saw the lace curtain in his office flutter and drop back into place. Jack Greenfield would definitely hear about my visit.

In the waning afternoon light the crime scene tape around the cottage gleamed. I walked up and clamped my hands around my eyes like goggles and peered through the windows. Luckily the curtains hadn't been drawn.

The living room was immaculate as though ready for new guests. The bedroom was a different story. Covers thrown back on the king-sized bed with the sheets tangled and twisted. An antique quilt lay in a heap on the floor. I moved around to the kitchenette window. A can of nuts and a couple of empty bottles of wine sat on the counter. There was half a pot of coffee in the coffeemaker.

That was it. Jordy had been right—there was nothing to find, especially after the sheriff's department had cleaned the place out. I started back down the flagstone path toward the parking lot.

The rubber tip of my cane came down on something hard wedged in a crevice between two stones. I looked down. It was a piece of metal—something round and dull-looking. I bent down and almost picked it up.

Fortunately I didn't, because on closer inspection it looked a lot like a lug nut from the wheel of a car.

Chapter 4

If I was right and it came from Valerie's car, then someone had tampered with her wheel while she was in the cottage. I reached for my cell phone to call the sheriff before remembering the phone was waterlogged and I'd left it at home. Jordy wouldn't be happy about the sheriff showing up at the Fox and Hound twice in one day, especially if what I'd found was something that had fallen off a lawnmower. Whatever it was, I left it where I'd found it and headed back to the house.

A young redheaded woman with a scowl on her face came out onto the back porch, slamming the door hard behind her. She muttered something before she saw me and realized I'd been watching. Her face turned scarlet.

"Afternoon, miss." She spoke with an Irish lilt. "May I help you?"

"No, thank you. I'm just on my way to talk to Mr. Jordan."

"I believe he's in his office," she said. "Sorry about the door. Long day." She pulled a pack of cigarettes out of her purse and fished around until she found a book of matches.

"I'm sure. You work here?"

"I do."

"I guess you were here when the sheriff showed up?"

"Oh my, yes. Such goings on." She moved closer and extracted a cigarette from the pack. "Everyone was in a state. Especially Miss Grace and Mr. Jordy."

I didn't have to prod much. She was full of the importance of what she knew.

"It must have been difficult." I kept my voice friendly and noncommittal. "Did you talk to one of the deputies?"

She lit up and dropped the match on the ground, blowing out a stream of smoke. "No, they only spoke to the girls who take care of Cornwall Cottage." Her smug smile lit up her pale green eyes. "No one asked me, so I didn't say nothin'. Didn't want to get him in trouble, he's such a fine man and all. Tips me nice when I look after one of their guests."

"Get who in trouble? One of what guests?"

She examined her cigarette and I knew I'd pushed too hard. "Oh. Well, nobody. I shouldn't be talkin' this way."

I slid my purse off my shoulder and took a twenty out of my wallet. "I'd really like to know. Do you think you could tell me?"

She barely contemplated the money. No wrestling with her conscience before she took it and tucked it in her bra. I'd half-expected her to hold out for more.

"Dr. Dawson," she said. "His school puts guests up here all the time and he comes round a lot."

"He was here last night?"

She nodded. "With Miss Boo-vase. I'd finished up the dinner dishes and stepped out for a quick fag. Saw his car as he drove past me on the way to Cornwall Cottage."

"What time?"

"About eleven. Just after she showed up."

"He saw you?"

She colored again. "I didn't have the porch light on, so I suspect he didn't."

"Did you see him leave?"

"No, but he stayed a while." I waited and she added, "I overheard a couple of deputies who came into the dining room for coffee. They found . . . well, he'd been takin' precautions, you see."

Mick had been right. Still lovers. "A condom?"

She puffed on her cigarette. "Several."

"Oh." It was my turn to blush. "What's your name?"

"Bridget. Why?"

"You need to tell the sheriff about seeing Dr. Dawson, Bridget."

"Lord have mercy, no! I cannot!" She dropped the cigarette and stubbed it out under a heavy-soled shoe. "I'll get in trouble. I'm not supposed to be smokin' on the job. And Mr. Jordy will think I've been spyin' on the guests."

No point stating that Mr. Jordy would have been right.

"I'm sorry, but you have to. You won't get in trouble. I'll make it okay with Mr. Jordy. Come on."

"No. Really, I can't."

I held out another twenty. "Please?"

She shrugged and took the money, then bent and picked up the cigarette butt and her match. I almost missed the sleight of hand as she tossed them behind a rhododendron next to the house. Probably not the first time.

I rang the doorbell as Bridget squirmed next to me, popping a breath mint in her mouth. Somehow she didn't seem destined for a long period of employment at the Fox and Hound.

After I'd explained everything, Jordy handed me the phone and eyed Bridget. I called Bobby Noland, whom I'd known since we were kids. Now a detective with the Loudoun County Sheriff's Department, he'd done a one-eighty since high school when he'd been a regular in the principal's office. His decision to go into law enforcement surprised everyone except his mother, who claimed it was irrefutable proof that God answered prayers.

Bobby arrived in an unmarked cruiser a short while later, wearing jeans and a black polo shirt with the sheriff's department logo embroidered on the pocket. He shook hands with Jordy and Bridget and nodded at me. We'd adjourned to the parlor where Grace had brought tea and scones, frowning at Bridget as she left the room.

Bobby took a scone but passed on tea. Then he got right down to it. "There's crime scene tape all around that cottage, Lucie. What were you doing there? I could haul you in for messing around where you're not supposed to be."

If it had been anybody else but Bobby, I probably would have been intimidated. We had too much history together growing up. I knew his weaknesses and he knew mine.

"I didn't go inside," I said.

"You still shouldn't have been there," he said. "And you didn't answer my question."

"Valerie Beauvais was on her way to see me when her car went into the creek," I said. "She wanted to talk to me about some of the wine that's been donated for our auction."

"What about it?"

"I don't know. That's why I dropped by—in case she left anything behind. When I found her car this morning in the creek, I thought her accident was an accident. How was I supposed to know you put crime scene tape up?"

"Well, we did. So maybe that should have been your first clue the place was off-limits."

"I found a lug nut."

"You found what?"

"A lug nut. At least, I think that's what it is. By Cornwall Cottage." For his benefit I added, "I didn't touch it."

"Let's go take a look." He didn't sound happy.

"Before we go, there's something else you should know." I glanced at Bridget. "Go on, tell him. He won't bite."

Her cocky confidence had disappeared and her voice was barely louder than a whisper. "Miss Boo-vase had a guest last night. I saw Dr. Dawson's car drive by on his way to the cottage."

If they'd found condoms, Bobby already knew Valerie had been with a man. Hard to tell if the identification of her visitor was news or not. His eyes met mine, giving away nothing, then slid to Bridget. "What time?"

She told him. He asked a few more questions and said to me, "Show me that lug nut now. Jordy, Bridget, thanks for your help."

I set my dishes on the silver tray and nodded at Bridget. Jordy walked Bobby and me out.

"I promised Bridget she wouldn't get in trouble if she told the truth," I said. "I gave my word."

Jordy sighed. "All right."

"Thank you."

When Bobby and I got to Cornwall Cottage, I showed him what I'd found. Turned out it was a lug nut, though Bobby said it didn't mean it came from Valerie's car. Still, he took photos with a digital camera and bagged it.

"I'll bet you anything it's from her wheel," I said. "What about the other lug nuts? Did you find them?"

"You know I can't say."

"You didn't, did you? That means this one's really important."

"No comment."

We walked back to the parking lot. "Joe didn't tamper with Valerie's car, Bobby."

"What was he doing here last night if he's engaged to your cousin?"

"The engagement's off."

He rubbed a hand across his forehead and closed his eyes like he was trying to excise a headache. "Is that so? You know anything about Joe's relationship with Valerie Beauvais? Whether or not it was sexual?"

I decided not to mention that Bridget had told me about the condoms. "I saw them together last night at her lecture at Mount Vernon. They kissed a couple of times, but that's all I saw."

He still held the bag with the lug nut between his thumb and forefinger. "I wonder if he was the only visitor she had," he said. "Guess I'll be talking to your cousin's ex-fiancé."

I nodded. More than one lover—I hadn't thought of that. Either way, it didn't look too good for Joe.

My answering machine beeped as I walked in the front door of my house just after six o'clock. Three messages. All from Katherine Eastman sounding increasingly irate.

Kit, like Bobby, went back to my sandbox days. Best friends all twelve years of school, we'd finally split up in college—she studied journalism in North Carolina and I went to Williamsburg for history and French. We got back together after graduating, both landing jobs in D.C. She worked in the newsroom of the *Washington Tribune,* a place she used to refer to as "the shark tank." I got a job with an environmental group that tried to convince policy makers that scientists hadn't invented global warming to scare the public or obtain more funding.

Three summers ago Kit's mother suffered a stroke and a few weeks later a car I was in, driven by a now-ex-boyfriend, slammed into the wall at the entrance to our farm as he brought me home one night in the middle of a rainstorm. Kit returned to Atoka to be near her mom, asking for a transfer to the *Trib*'s Loudoun bureau. I spent a few months in Catoctin General learning to walk again before moving to a house my French mother's family still owned on the Côte d'Azur, where I spent two years adjusting to life with a cane.

The time stamps on the answering machine indicated Kit had been calling for the past three hours. I listened to her last message. "Dammit, how come you don't answer your cell anymore? I finally tried here. Four times. Where the hell are you? Call me or else."

I took more ibuprofen and called. "It was only three times. Or else what?"

"I don't know. Or else I'll call again and make it four. Where have you *been*?"

"Here and there. My cell is dead after a swim in Goose Creek." I picked it up from the console table in the foyer. Definitely destroyed. "Looks like I need to replace it. What's so urgent?"

"What do you mean, 'what's so urgent'? You pulled that woman out of the creek. I'm writing the story. How about a little cooperation?"

"How about dinner? You buy, if you want me to talk."

"The *Trib* isn't made of money. Take my salary, for example."

"Is that a yes or a no?"

"Meet me at the Goose Creek Inn at seven. And you better have a lot to say. I already get grief about my expenses."

The Goose Creek Inn, which had won every major award for dining and "most romantic setting" in the Washington area over the last forty years, was a whitewashed auberge on a pretty country lane just outside Middleburg. As usual, the parking lot was full, but I found a semilegitimate space small enough for the Mini and tucked it in there. Fairy lights twinkled in the trees and the air smelled of wood smoke.

The large foyer, with its walls of bright primitive oil paintings and vintage posters advertising French alcohol, cigarettes, and travel, was filled with groups waiting for their tables on a busy Friday night. Here people still dressed for dinner and men were required to wear jackets in the evening. Jeans were prohibited.

Provençal china and antique copper pots sat on a sideboard next to a copy of *The Goose Creek Cookbook*. As usual, the cookbook was opened to the recipe for the famous chocolate cheesecake created by my late godfather, who founded the place. I would have preferred not to know about the obscene amounts of butter, dark chocolate, and cream cheese that went into Fitz's cheesecake, but that recipe sold a lot of cookbooks.

Kit had arrived before I did and was talking to Dominique near the maître d's stand. My cousin caught sight of me through the crowd and gestured for me to join them. One of the perks of being related to the owner. We would be seated right away, probably at her table.

Usually Dominique radiated the pulsing energy of a

supernova, running the inn and Goose Creek Catering with a skimpy velvet glove over her small iron fist, but tonight she looked like she'd been dragged through a knot-hole. We both had inherited our ambition from our mothers, who'd been sisters. But unlike me, Dominique didn't have an off-switch. She also had a way of acting like she'd just been invited to expand the Blessed Trinity to a quartet. When that happened, her staff usually tried to stay out of her way. This afternoon Joe had implied that her worka-holic habits had finally gotten to him.

My cousin looked elegant in a black cashmere sweater, black trousers, and a thick gold necklace, but I smelled heavy cigarette smoke on her breath when she kissed me on both cheeks in the French way. She'd begun chain-smoking again.

Kit gave me an air kiss that wouldn't ruin her Marilyn Monroe red lipstick. She wore a tight green mini-skirt with buttons down the front and a khaki-colored top that looked like it had spent too long in the dryer. All her clothes fit like that. She'd picked up forty pounds since high school and still managed to convince herself it was only twenty.

"We were just talking about the accident," Kit said. "You don't look so good. I heard you got kind of banged-up."

"Some scratches on my back and a few bruises. I'll be fine in a day or two."

"A couple of the Romeos came in for cocktails this evening," Dominique said. "That's how I found out. *Mon Dieu,* it must have been awful." She picked up two menus. "Someone said Joe was at Mount Vernon last night with the woman who was killed. Is that true?"

She'd probably learn soon enough that their evening hadn't ended at Mount Vernon, but I didn't have the heart to tell her right now. "Yes."

"You're at my table. I'll take you there." She turned so abruptly she almost collided with a waiter. I noticed two bright pink spots on her cheeks as she excused herself.

When we were seated, Kit pulled out a reporter's notebook and a pen, setting them on the table. "What was that all about?"

I turned the small vase with its single red rose so the open flower faced us. "She and Joe broke off their engagement."

Kit's eyes narrowed. She'd overdone it with the eye makeup as usual so it looked like she had on football eyeblack. "She tell you or he tell you?"

"He did."

She opened her notebook and clicked her pen. "They've been engaged longer than some marriages last. What happened?"

"I don't know. He didn't elaborate and she hasn't brought it up."

"That's too bad." She clicked her pen a few more times. "So tell me about finding the Beauvais woman's car."

Kit was Bobby Noland's girlfriend, but she'd told me once that he'd made it clear pillow talk would get his ass kicked by the sheriff and that she should expect to go through the same channels every other member of the press did for her information. I gave her the expurgated version of what happened and waited to see what other questions she asked.

A waitress brought two glasses of a Chilean Cabernet Sauvignon, a bread basket filled with warm *petit pains,* and took our orders. Kit clinked her glass against mine. "I heard that the car might have been tampered with," she said.

"The rear wheel on the driver's side was gone."

"So I understand." She watched me. "You know something."

"You can't use it."

"Aw, come on—"

"Sorry." I folded my lips and shook my head.

"Okay, okay. What is it?"

"I found a lug nut by her cottage at the Fox and Hound. Bobby came by and bagged it."

Kit set her wineglass on the table. Her red lipstick had left a perfect kiss mark on the rim. "What were you doing at the Fox and Hound?"

"This doesn't go in your story, either. It's probably not even relevant to what happened."

"Talk to me."

"It has to do with Ryan's column today. I assume you read it."

"I don't have to. He reads them to me himself since he's got the office next to mine. Some days I could strangle him with the power cord from his laptop." She eyed me. "So go on."

"Clay Avery brought Valerie here for lunch the other day and showed her the column. Last night Valerie said—in front of Ryan—that Clay wanted to hire her to write for the *Trib*. She suggested he dust off his résumé."

Kit pulled back the napkin that covered the bread basket and took a roll. "News to me."

"Really?" I said. "Then just as we were leaving Mount Vernon, Valerie found me and said she knew something about the provenance of the wine Jack donated. But she had to come by and see it before she'd tell me what it was."

"You mean that bottle Jefferson bought for Washington?"

"She asked how I'd managed to get hold of it—like I had to sleep with Jack or something."

"Jeez, did she really?" Kit made a face. "That's disgusting. Provenance, huh? Do you think she meant the bottle might have been stolen?"

"I don't know," I said. "I'm worried she was going to tell me it was counterfeit."

"Fake wine?"

"Sure. People do it all the time. Blend a couple of okay wines to taste like something world-class or put phony labels on mediocre wine—stuff like that. Collectors buy those bottles to lay down—if they ever drink it at all. So it's years before they figure out they've been duped."

Our dinners arrived—cassoulet for Kit, ragout of autumn vegetables with orzo for me. We'd ordered a bottle of Swedenburg Estate Cabernet to go with our meal. The waiter opened it and poured some for me to try. I nodded and he filled our glasses.

"How are you going to find out if it's fake or not?" Kit asked.

"I don't know. You know what else? I'm not even sure I ought to believe her. Ryan said she plagiarized parts of her book. So she wasn't exactly honest."

Kit set down her fork. "You mean she might have made the whole thing up?"

I sighed and stared into my wineglass. "I have no idea. Maybe she was just trying to stir up trouble."

"She sure sounds like someone who knew how to do it. Could be that's what got her killed."

"Ryan couldn't stand her."

"Ryan has a temper and an ego," she said, "but I don't think he'd do anything that drastic. You're talking about manslaughter."

"An act of passion or extreme provocation," I said. "You know what Bobby says. Under the right circumstances— or the wrong ones—anyone is capable of anything. Even something that seems out of character."

"There's your answer. Maybe he did it, maybe he didn't."

"Somebody did it." I didn't want to bring in Joe and the fact that he and Valerie were probably in flagrante delicto at the moment someone was outside her cottage tampering with her car. "Sorry I wasn't much help with your story."

"Forget it."

It wasn't like Kit to let me off the hook so easily. I looked at her plate. She'd hardly touched her food. "You feeling all right?"

"Yeah, fine." She kept her eyes downcast.

"What's going on?"

"Nothing."

"Are you . . . wait a minute. Are you pregnant?"

Her cheeks turned scarlet. "Jee-sus, Lucie! Don't be ridiculous. How could you even think such a thing?"

I waited.

"Okay," she said. "It's something, but not that. I've been offered a job in Moscow. Number-two correspondent in the bureau."

"Moscow, *Russia*?"

"We don't have a bureau in Moscow, Idaho."

"Oh my God, you're serious. You're thinking about taking it?"

"Will you stop looking at me like I said they want to shoot me into outer space with a cannon? I was on the foreign desk before I got transferred to Loudoun, in case you forgot."

"I remember. But it's just so . . . far away. I thought you needed to stay here because of your mom."

"My mom says I need a life and it shouldn't be chained to hers." She picked up a piece of roll and sopped up some of the sauce from her cassoulet. "I've never owned a passport in my life. First time I'd really get to see the world. All those places named Something-Stan." She sounded wistful.

"You sure you're ready for something that drastic?"

"It's a honking big pay raise."

"Because it's a senior job?"

"Because it's a hardship post and they don't have people falling all over themselves to volunteer for it."

"What does Bobby say?"

"I haven't told him."

"You sound like you're ready to say yes."

She shrugged. "I have to make up my mind by the end of the month. Language training starts after Christmas. I wouldn't leave until June."

"Just after the snow melts in Russia?"

"Ha, ha. You want dessert?"

I shook my head. "That chocolate mousse looks out of this world," she said. "Maybe I'll ask them to box up my cassoulet and take it and some dessert to go. I've got to get back to the office."

She asked for the check and we drank the last of our wine.

"I'll miss you if you take that job," I said.

"I'll miss you, too." She signed the bill as the waiter set down a Styrofoam box. "I don't know what to do. One minute I want to go, the next I don't."

When we got back to the lobby Dominique was still at the maître d's stand, talking to some of her guests. Kit waved good night but I stayed and waited until she was free.

"How was your dinner?"

"Excellent. It's always excellent. You know that," I said.

She smiled but her eyes were grave. I didn't want to keep up this façade any longer. "Joe told me, Dominique. I'm so sorry. Are you going to be okay?"

She put out her hand as if to physically ward off my words. "Of course I am. Anyway, I expected it. It's not rocket surgery to understand why we decided to break up."

When Dominique got upset, her English—especially the idioms—usually took a nosedive.

"Want to talk about it?"

"There's nothing to say. And you don't have to walk on kid gloves around me, either."

I hugged her. Her bones felt brittle and hollow as a bird's. She was already so thin she looked anorexic. "Call me if you change your mind."

"I'll be fine."

I said good-bye and went outside. She was wrong. Once word got around about Joe spending the night with Valerie before she died, putting him at the cottage where the lug nut to her wheel had been found, there'd be plenty to say.

And none of it would be good.

Chapter 5

——— ∞∞∞ ———

On weekends, especially when the weather is gorgeous, people flee Washington in droves to soak up the pleasures of country life. On a typical day we can have between two and four hundred visitors passing through the vineyard to taste and buy wine. Some rent limos or pick a designated driver so everyone in the party doesn't have to watch their limit. If we're the last stop on their wine tour and they'd had a few, it could get lively.

Quinn and I finally hired full-time help to work in the tasting room—Francesca Merchant and Gina Leon—who took over organizing events, booking groups, and supervising the tastings. We also compiled a list of waiters and waitresses from the Goose Creek Inn who would moonlight for us on their days off, especially weekends.

The buildings making up the winery had been planned by my mother, a talented artist with an eye for design. She'd wanted something that harmonized the neoclassical architecture she'd grown up with in France with the simpler colonial style of Highland House, built by my father's pragmatic Scottish ancestors. The ivy-covered building that now housed a tasting room, small kitchen, wine library, and our offices looked more like a villa than a commercial structure and the name stuck. A European-style courtyard and porticoed loggia connected it with the barrel room and laboratory where we made and stored wine.

We held picnics, dinners, and concerts in the courtyard with its breathtaking view of the vines and mountains, and served wine and small meals on the villa's cantilevered two-story deck. But most of our events took place at Mosby's Ruins, the remains of an old tenant house near the winery. During the Civil War, it had been a hideout for the Gray Ghost, Colonel John Singleton Mosby, until Union soldiers burned it down trying to flush him out.

On Saturday, McNally's Army, an Irish rock band from D.C., came to play for the afternoon. Guests brought picnic lunches and sat on blankets and deck chairs on the hill in front of the area we'd converted to a stage. We sold wine by the glass or bottle and light snacks. The Army always pulled in a big crowd. Their music, which I loved, blended Celtic and country and their female vocalist had a voice that could haunt like a lost lover.

Joe Dawson showed up as the concert wrapped up and guests were leaving. He came over to the Ruins and stood there, looking like a train wreck, as he watched me pay the band.

"Want a glass of wine?" I asked. "Or a bottle and straw?"

He gave me a hangdog smile. "Got a minute?"

"Sure."

I found an open bottle of Pinot and two glasses with our logo etched on them. He took them and helped me climb up on the raised stage, which once had been the first floor of the old house. We sat on the edge with our legs dangling over the side and watched the sun turn into a fireball as it began its descent behind the Blue Ridge.

Joe poured the wine and handed me a glass. "Looks like I need a lawyer. I called Sammy Constantine."

One of the Romeos, Sam Constantine helped Mia out of a jam last spring. A good man, no bullshit, a straight talker. Hiring him cost a bundle.

"Have you been charged with anything?"

"Not yet. But they linked me to Valerie's cottage at the Fox and Hound that last night," he said. "She, uh, invited me back after her talk at Mount Vernon. The cops, uh, found things. Someone must have seen my car."

I looked into my wineglass. "One of the maids saw you."

He chewed his lip, nodding. "I should have figured."

"Couldn't you have waited, Joe? Why did you have to go right from Dominique's bed to Valerie's? You and Dominique have been together for *years*."

He held his hands up. "Whoa! Hold it right there, okay? What do you want me to say? It's done. I'm paying for it, too, aren't I?"

The sun had moved lower in the sky. It was starting to cool off. He was right. It was over and done with.

I quieted down. "Why do you need a lawyer? You don't have a motive for killing her—do you?"

He didn't look happy that I'd asked. "This is where it gets complicated."

A bad start to a story that already involved sex and lawyers. "What do you mean?"

He drank more wine. "When Valerie was writing her book she needed additional information about Jefferson's efforts to establish a wine industry in the United States.

She asked if I could send her a copy of my dissertation, so I did. You can find it in the UVA library, of course, but I never got around to getting it published anywhere else."

I knew where this was going. "She lifted parts of your dissertation for her book?"

He shook his head, like he couldn't believe it himself. "Not just parts. Whole sections, which she didn't footnote or even acknowledge in the bibliography. You know who else read my dissertation? Ryan Worth. That guy must have a photographic memory because he recognized it. I guess he wanted to share the love because he contacted her editor. And the editor, who got contacted by Bobby Noland, told Bobby."

"That's your motive? Professional revenge for plagiarism?"

"That's what they want to know."

"Did you ever confront her about it?"

Joe stared at the horizon. "I only skimmed the first chapter. Never got beyond page fourteen. Of course they think I'm lying. But honestly I had no idea about the plagiarism and probably nobody else on the planet would have either, except for frigging Ryan Worth."

He refilled our glasses.

"Valerie sought me out at Mount Vernon after her talk," I said. "Told me she knew something about the provenance of one of the wines Jack Greenfield donated for our auction. Kind of taunted me that I didn't know what I had. Then the guy from her publishing house dragged her off." I swirled wine in my glass. "Any ideas?"

"Nope. She mentioned it to me, too, but didn't want to give up any details. Said it would be a bombshell when word got out."

"You weren't curious?"

"I didn't really think about it, you know?"

I looked at him, remembering how Valerie had kissed him in the colonnade at Mount Vernon and the tangled sheets in the bedroom at Cornwall Cottage. "I guess you must have been preoccupied with other things."

His cheeks turned red. "Okay. She did say she never would have known about whatever it was if she hadn't retraced Jefferson's vineyard journey through Bordeaux."

"Bordeaux? The only vineyard both Valerie and Jefferson visited in Bordeaux was Château Margaux. That's the Washington wine." I set my empty wineglass down. "The other place, Château Dorgon, doesn't exist anymore. The third wine Jack donated is a Domaine de Romanée-Conti—a Burgundy."

Joe hoisted himself off the stage with both hands and landed on the hard-packed ground. "Come here." He held out his arms. "I'll help you down."

"Thanks, I'll take the stairs." I knew Joe didn't kill Valerie, but he was getting dragged into whatever brought her down. Part of me thought he didn't deserve it, but another part of me thought that we reap what we sow.

Joe seemed to acknowledge the rebuff as he picked up the empty bottle and our glasses. We walked down the path toward the villa at some distance apart.

"I know you're mad at me because of Dominique," he said. "Wish I could change things. Or turn back time."

I shrugged. "You know, Valerie didn't have much professional credibility with Ryan."

"I heard his story. She stole his idea. That's a load of crap. She wrote that book on Jamestown. She got rave reviews." His voice was hard.

"Ryan said someone handed it to her on a platter."

"Ryan can go to hell. She told me she ran out of time to

get the Jefferson book done so she panicked. Plus she was in a bind financially and that put even more pressure on her. I've known her for a long time. Valerie was a good scholar, Lucie."

"So you think this bombshell, whatever it is, is legitimate?"

"Yeah, I do."

I banged my cane against the ground in frustration. "Dammit, what am I going to do?"

"I don't know," he said. "I'm sure you'll figure out something. Wish I could help but I got my own fish to fry right now."

He left me at the entrance to the villa. I watched him walk down to the parking lot and get into his car.

Whatever Valerie knew, now I really had to find out.

They say when you want to dig up some dirt, go find yourself a worm. As it happened, I knew just the worm.

I called Ryan Worth on his cell and caught him on his way out the office door to an evening wine event in D.C.

"What are you doing at work on a Saturday?" I asked.

"Since it's Columbus Day weekend, the place is quiet. I thought I'd get a jump on the next column so I could take a few days off next week. If I don't get some down time I'm going to go nuts. What's up?"

He sounded friendly but guarded.

"Could I ask a favor?"

"What is it?"

"You were right about the national attention your column would bring our auction," I said. "The winery is getting calls from all over the place. Jordy Jordan told me the day it ran he booked every room at the Fox and Hound for that weekend."

"Glad to hear it. So what's this favor?"

So much for trying to butter him up.

"It's not a local fund-raiser anymore. Now it's a big deal," I said. "Before that column ran we accepted any donation we got, meaning wines that came straight out of people's wine cellars. Bottles they'd gotten as gifts or wine they'd been storing for a while. I haven't begun to catalog any of it, nor do I have any idea what prices to set for the opening bids. Now I think we're going to have a savvy, street-smart crowd bidding on them. Nothing like we anticipated."

"You want me to help catalog your wines?" He blew out a short, sharp breath. "Do you know how much work that is?"

"Please, Ryan. I'm begging. It's for charity. And, uh, one other favor? I'd like you to be the auctioneer. We need a pro now. You'd be terrific."

I could hear him drumming something on the top of his desk, a pen or a pencil, while he thought about it. The rat-a-tat stopped. "You paying for my expertise?"

"Of course." I should have seen that coming. "What's your fee?"

"I'll cut you a break," he said, "since it's for charity. Pay me a thousand and I'll handle the catalog and raise a bundle for your charity. Deal?"

I wondered what his noncharity price tag was. Everyone else was doing this for free.

"Deal," I said.

"Okay, get me a list of everything you've got and shoot it to me in an e-mail. I'll start figuring out your floor prices."

"I'll get you the list, but do you think maybe you could come over here instead?" I asked.

"Why do I have to come over there?" He sounded ominous. I was on my third favor and thin ice.

"I just want to make sure the donations we've got are the
real thing. So I'd like you to actually *look* at the bottles."

"If you want me to do that, I need to ask twelve-fifty."

I hadn't even bargained on paying him the thousand,
but I couldn't afford to lose him. "Okay, okay. Twelve-fifty.
We'll pay you after the auction. From the proceeds."

"Yeah, fine. I know you're good for it."

"How about coming by tomorrow evening?"

"Hang on." I waited, probably while he scrolled through
his electronic calendar. "Looks like I could do five."

"Five's good. See you then."

"How come you didn't corral Jack Greenfield into doing
this? Or Shane Cunningham?" he said. "You know Shane's
running Internet wine auctions now. He and Jack do this
stuff all the time."

Shane was Jack's business partner. I knew about the
wine auctions but I'd been too busy with harvest to check
out what he was selling. Might as well come clean and tell
Ryan the truth before Valerie got here tomorrow.

"Because one of the bottles I'm worried about is the
Washington wine and I can't ask Jack or Shane."

He barked a laugh. "Well, you can relax about that one.
I *did* look that bottle over when Jack had it. I guarantee you,
it's the real deal."

"You're sure?"

"Why wouldn't I be? What's up?"

"Valerie Beauvais said there was something I didn't know
about its provenance. She was on her way here to look at it
the morning she died. I never found out what she knew."

Ryan snorted. "Valerie—God rest her soul—wouldn't

have known provenance if it walked up and slapped her upside her head."

When I was silent he said, "Okay, sorry. That was rude. When I'm over there tomorrow, I'll show you why I'm so sure you don't have anything to worry about. Satisfied?"

I said "yes" but he'd already hung up.

He seemed to know a lot about Valerie Beauvais. And he'd been astute enough to recognize the source of the plagiarism in her book as Joe's dissertation—something he'd had to go looking for at the UVA library.

But if it were true that Clay Avery had been thinking of hiring Valerie to write for the *Washington Tribune,* then Ryan couldn't be too sorry that she was dead and no longer a thorn in his side. And if she were right about the Washington bottle, he'd look like a fool for having staked his reputation on its authenticity.

Which gave him—even more than Joe—more than one motive for murder.

Chapter 6

Another big crowd came through the winery on Sunday as the glorious weather continued to hold. It had only been two weeks since the sun moved from the northern to the southern hemisphere on the autumnal equinox, but the longer, lower rays of sunlight already bathed the vines and fields with a gilded light that came only at this time of year.

We had moved the tasting outside to the courtyard to take advantage of the view and the weather. Francesca Merchant had hired a string quartet to play chamber music for the afternoon.

"I know you like this classical stuff, but it just doesn't do it for me. Frankie says they're good musicians, but everything sounds like the same guy wrote it. Vivaldi, Beethoven—whoever," Quinn said to me as we stood in the shade of the loggia and watched Gina hand out tasting sheets and explain our wines to three older men who'd arrived in a limo with three good-looking young women.

The quartet was playing a baroque piece by Telemann.

"There's a big difference between Beethoven and Vivaldi.

You just don't pay attention." I fingered the collar of yet another of his Hawaiian shirts, this one with skimpily clad girls in grass skirts and postage stamp bras, swaying, presumably, to a hula. "Couldn't you have worn a different shirt?"

"Why, is there a stain on this one?"

"Never mind."

My brother, Eli, showed up midafternoon without my sister-in-law, Brandi, and my one-year-old niece, Hope. As always he looked a little too dapper and even a bit feminine. I knew why. Brandi now picked out all his clothes, like Barbie dressing Ken. She favored pastels so I was getting used to seeing Eli in sherbet colors like the pale yellow shirt and matching linen trousers he wore now.

"Hey, babe," he said. "Thought I could sponge off you this afternoon. What's to eat? The girls went to my in-laws' for the weekend."

"Tapas. I'll make you a deal. Help us out for the next few hours and I'll send you home with leftovers."

Eli pushed his Ray-Bans up so they sat on top of his perfectly gelled hair. "I guess I could stick around for a while." He placed his hands on the complacent paunch that had once been his washboard stomach. "I could use a bite now, though. Woke up too late for breakfast and spent all morning at Jack and Sunny Greenfields'."

"What were you doing there?"

"Jack's renovating his wine cellar."

"Moonlighting?"

Eli suddenly looked weary. "Helps pay the bills."

I knew he was just scraping by. He adored Brandi and couldn't—or wouldn't—tell her the money tree had been picked clean. Last I'd heard he'd borrowed the equivalent of the GNP of a small country to cover what they already owed.

He walked over to one of the tables, returning with a plate filled with enough food for three people. "Good stuff." He stabbed a sausage with a toothpick. "Where'd you get these?"

"The organic butcher in Middleburg. What's Jack doing to his wine cellar?"

"Everything." Eli spoke through his chorizo. "Installing a security system, upgrading the cooling system—really shelling out the bucks for glass murals, limestone flooring, redwood wine racks, map drawers showing where the wine comes from. The whole caboodle. And a computerized inventory—finally. Shane's handling it. Jack's been paying insurance out the wazoo for years without knowing the actual value of his collection."

"Why does he need a security system all of a sudden?"

Eli licked his fingers. "Got a napkin? I don't want to get grease on these clothes. First time I've worn them."

I handed one to him.

"Jack's got, oh, easily thirty thousand bottles. He wants to protect his investment." He picked up a fork and dug into a small mountain of marinated piquillo peppers. "Plus he heard about those wine cellar thefts in California. Decided he needed something more than a padlock on the door. The security guy came by this morning and did his spiel, explaining all the things they can do. I felt like James Bond when M demonstrates the toys."

"It's Q. M is his boss. Q does toys."

"Whatever."

"If you're done with your snack, James," I said, "how about helping me pour wine in the villa?"

"Shaken not stirred," he said. "Just let me grab some more chorizo."

Frankie stood behind the bar in the tasting room when

Eli and I walked into the villa. A pretty strawberry blonde in her early fifties, I liked her low-key, capable ways and gentle, dry sense of humor. So, apparently, did our customers. Since she joined us, she'd acquired a small but faithful group of regulars who dropped by on weekends, claiming they came for the wine. I knew they came to talk to Frankie. You could find an ocean of compassion in those clear blue nonjudgmental eyes.

"Go get something to eat and enjoy your string quartet," I said to her. "Eli and I will take over for a while. I think he left you a sausage. Maybe two."

She smiled. "Thanks. Amanda Heyward called about half an hour ago. Said she planned to drop by to give you the fixture cards for the next few months. Also something about a guest list."

A fixture card was a one-month calendar listing dates and locations of meets for a foxhunt. For more than a century, my farm had been part of the territory of the Goose Creek Hunt. During hunting season their meets commenced at Highland Farm once every five or six weeks. Amanda, the GCH's secretary and an old family friend, was responsible for distributing the cards.

As thanks for letting the hunt ride through our farm so often, she'd also offered to take charge of the guest list for our auction and mail the invitations. Amanda had worked in corporate fund-raising for heavyweight multinationals and big-name museums for years until too many eighty-hour workweeks burned her candle to a charred wick. Her offer was a godsend.

She showed up in the tasting room dressed in mud-spattered jodhpurs, riding boots, and a high-necked white blouse, her long gray-brown hair pulled up in a windblown knot, ruddy face sunburned after an afternoon of galloping across the countryside. She kissed Eli and me and accepted the glass of Cabernet Sauvignon he poured for her.

"I just went riding with Sunny." She climbed up on one of the bar stools and dropped a leather satchel on the floor. "Heard you were there this morning discussing Jack's wine cellar, Eli. All that security stuff he wants to install is driving Sunny crazy. Costs a fortune. What does he keep in there worth that kind of money? The goblet they used at the Last Supper?"

"You'd be surprised," Eli said. "He's got some wines you'll never find anywhere anymore."

"Yeah, but around here everyone's got fantastic or expensive vintages on their sideboard or in the basement. I know I do—and half the time we don't even bother to lock our front door it's so safe." She set her glass on the bar and tucked a stray piece of hair back into her French knot.

"Among other things, Jack has verticals of some of the legendary Bordeaux," Eli said.

"What's a vertical?" Amanda asked.

"A bottle of wine for every single year it was made. Sorry," he said. "I thought you knew wine jargon."

Amanda babysat for us when we were kids and she'd changed Eli's diapers. Mine, too. Eli, acting pompous, didn't impress her.

"I know enough about wine to know some of those years had to be duds," she said. "So he's got swill among the gems."

"Not exactly." I joined her on another bar stool. Some days my bad leg ached worse than others. Today was one of those days. "Most wine is drunk in the year it's produced. It's only the good stuff that gets laid down to drink later. If the year was a dud, as you said, those bottles generally were consumed right away. Later it's harder to find that vintage, which drives up the price. The value of owning verticals comes from the fact that it's a complete collection."

"Fair enough," she said. "But I still think the last time anyone had to worry about locking something up around here was when the Yankees were in town during the War of Northern Aggression. Jack's going really over the top with that bionic password stuff or whatever it is he's thinking about."

I saw Eli suck in his breath. He wasn't going to let this go. I glared at my brother and said to Amanda, "Didn't you want to talk about the guest list for the auction?"

"Oh, sure." She bent to retrieve her satchel from the floor and missed seeing Eli make a face at me and roll his eyes. When she sat up, she put on a pair of reading glasses and opened a paisley folder, pulling out a spreadsheet.

"We have just over one hundred sixty people coming so far. That's not counting the RSVPs we've received since Ryan's column on the Washington wine ran in the *Trib*. We're probably going to be at our max capacity by the end of next week. Then we start turning people away." She looked up over the top of her glasses.

"What a shame," I said. "Why don't we talk to Mick about setting up a tent in his garden? Then we don't have to turn away anybody."

"His house is magnificent," Amanda said, "now that Sunny almost finished redecorating. I'd hate not to use it. We could put a tent any old place."

"Let's think about it. We'll figure out something," I said. "By the way, Ryan agreed to be our auctioneer and said he'll write up the wine notes for the catalog. It looks like we're going to have plenty of donations thanks to the Romeos. They're like the Mafia volunteer squad putting the squeeze on people. Everyone's contributing at least one bottle. Sometimes more."

"I'll bet your new neighbors aren't." Amanda's eyes went cold. "The Orlandos."

"I don't know. They only just moved in," I said. "I haven't met them."

"His law firm represents animal rights groups." She slapped the folder with the spreadsheet shut and jammed her glasses into a small Burberry case with a sharp shove. "She's the kind who throws paint on people who wear fur. They came by the kennels asking about the condition of the hounds. Very confrontational. Shane happened to be there and was more polite to them than I would have been. He said the hounds were well treated and not to worry. Then they insisted on coming inside to see for themselves. So he told them it was private property and asked them to leave. The next day they sent a letter saying we should consider their farm closed to the Goose Creek Hunt. Until hell froze over."

She picked up her wineglass and downed the contents.

"I didn't know that," I said. "I'm sorry."

"They have the right to keep you from foxhunting there if they want to," Eli said. "It's their land now."

"Which has been part of our territory for more than a century." Amanda banged the base of her wineglass on the bar emphasizing each word. "Oh, God, sorry. I'm just livid every time I think about it. I *know* it's their land, but they have no idea what they've just done. What that means."

"No visit from the Welcome Wagon?" Eli said and smirked.

I slashed an index finger across my throat and shook my head. He smirked some more.

"You grew up here," Amanda said. "On this farm. Or

have you forgotten about it, now that you're living in subdivision land?"

"Come on, Amanda, that's not—"

Amanda cut him off. "George Washington had foxhounds. He wrote about hunting all the time in his diaries. So did Jefferson. The earliest surviving record of organized foxhunting in America comes from right here in northern Virginia—a pack organized by Lord Fairfax in 1747." She recited the names and figures, glaring at Eli. "Foxhunting is part of our history, our culture. You know perfectly well how hard we fight for the open spaces, to keep land pristine and undeveloped. The Orlandos came from Manhattan. Acres of concrete between two rivers. The only place more disconnected from reality and the world of nature is Disneyland."

"Have you tried talking to them?" I eyed my brother, who grinned at me and picked up my cane, hooking it around his neck to fake a swift stage exit.

Amanda looked at Eli like he was dryer lint, then glanced at her watch. "Not yet. There's a meeting at the kennel in half an hour to discuss what we're going to do. In the worst case, how to work around losing all that land. I'd better get going. I'll call you about the guest list in a day or two, Lucie." She nodded stiffly at my brother. "Eli."

After she left I looked at my October fixture card. They'd scheduled a meet at Highland Farm for the sixteenth, in nine days. Mick now rode with the Goose Creek Hunt. Maybe I could ask him what the hunt decided to do about losing the Orlandos' land as part of their country. With the auction coming up, I didn't want to get Amanda worked up on that subject again.

Eli picked up her glass and set it in a dish drainer behind the bar.

"Man," he said, "is she pissed off."

"You didn't help."

"I just played devil's advocate. You know it's their right to close their farm. If she takes their head off the way she just did with me, your neighbors are in for it, babe."

"Sure sounds like it," I said.

Ryan Worth showed up at five o'clock, just as we closed for the day. I'd warned Quinn he was coming by.

"I'll be sure to get lost," he said. "And leave you two lovebirds alone together."

Ryan had panned one of our wines—our Pinot Noir—in a recent review. Quinn was furious. Without telling me, he called Ryan and gave him a piece of his mind.

Apparently that was the high-water mark of their conversation because after that Ryan brought up Le Coq Rouge, the California vineyard where Quinn worked before joining us. Quinn hadn't known Ryan's good friend was Tavis Hennessey, the owner. Nor had he known that Ryan was completely au courant of the scandal involving the winemaker—Quinn's former boss—who'd gone to jail for selling adulterated wine on the black market in Eastern Europe. Business at the winery tanked and Hennessey finally closed Le Coq Rouge. Though Quinn had never been charged with anything, Ryan had made a when-you-lie-down-with-dogs-you-get-up-with-fleas crack to Quinn. As far as I knew they still weren't speaking.

"Why did you have to call and yell at him like that?" I'd asked. "I didn't think the review was fair, either. But you get more with honey than you do with a club."

"Maybe," he'd said, "except you don't feel as good afterward."

I met Ryan by myself at the ivy-covered archway to

the courtyard. A gust of wind blew an unused cocktail napkin that had eluded our cleanup crew in front of us as we walked to the barrel room. I picked up the napkin and stuffed it in my pocket, glad I'd worn a jacket. The temperature had dropped at least twenty degrees since this afternoon.

"Your winemaker joining us?" Ryan asked.

"Unfortunately he's got another appointment this evening he couldn't get out of." With his washing machine.

"Too bad."

Ryan held the door to the barrel room for me and I hit the lights as we walked in.

"How many lots have we got so far?" he asked.

"Fifty-five and still counting."

The barrel room smelled of the tangy, slightly acrid odor of fermenting wine. About the size of an Olympic swimming pool, the semiunderground cave had thirty-foot ceilings, fieldstone walls, and four interconnected bays, where most of our oak barrels lay undisturbed in cool darkness. The stainless-steel fermenting tanks stood along the far wall. The gentle gurgling of the glycol-and-water solution circulating inside the refrigeration jackets was soothing as we walked the length of the room.

Ryan pulled out a chair from a long table we used for winemaker's dinners and private parties. He sat down, flung his briefcase on the table, and took out a reporter's notebook.

"We'll take the top forty and put them in the live auction." He began making notes. "Everything else we'll do as a silent auction. It'll take me about ninety minutes to dispense with forty lots. After that, the natives get restless and you don't get as much bang for the buck."

Above his head, my mother's cross-stitched sampler

hung over one of the archways leading to the recessed bays. She'd stitched one of her favorite quotes from Plato—"No thing more excellent nor more valuable than wine was ever granted mankind by God."

I stared at the sampler and nodded. Ryan had brought up things that never would have occurred to me. Thank God he'd agreed to help, fee or no fee.

"How much longer should we keep accepting contributions?" I asked.

"Cut them off soon. I still have to do the write-ups and figure out which ones to do live. Then we've got to get the catalog to the printer."

"Sunny Greenfield will handle the printer," I said. "We're using one of my mother's paintings of the vineyard on the cover."

"Nice. I always liked her art." He looked around. "Hey, bartender, any chance of a drink? This is going to take a while."

I decided against the Pinot and got a bottle of Cab. For the next two hours he checked bottles against the list I'd made, writing about each one in his notebook.

At last he threw down his pen and sat back in the chair, rubbing his eyes with the palms of his hands. "Can we call it quits here? We'll get those last few on the next round. Plus whatever else comes in."

"You're in charge."

He reached for the bottle of wine. I covered my glass with my hand, so he filled his own.

"You've got some nice wines. A few clunkers but I didn't spot any outright fakes."

"Can we talk about the Washington bottle?"

"Sure. Where is it?"

It was in a different bay, on its own. I retrieved it and

set it on the table in front of him so it wasn't in the direct beam of an overhead spotlight. The bottle, its contents dark and viscous as blood, gleamed mysteriously.

He picked it up like he was holding the Holy Grail. "Amazing."

"You're sure it's real?"

"Let me give you a little history lesson." He set the bottle down carefully. "Until the late 1600s, there was no such thing in France as a wine produced by a single château. They mingled the grapes harvested from different places, so what they produced didn't have much connection with the land."

"Terroir," I said, and he nodded.

"Château Margaux—which you've got here—was one of the first châteaus to make wine from vines grown solely in their own vineyard. That put them at the head of the curve in wine-making methodology and they stayed there." He ticked off his fingers. "Two things. Glass and cork. By the time this wine was bottled, heavier glass suitable for aging wine and shipping it had come into use. Plus the French had switched from capping their bottles with a layer of olive oil and wax to using cork."

He paused to fill his own glass with the last of the Cab. "What was I just saying?"

"Using cork instead of olive oil and wax."

"Right. So now they could ship wine. By the eighteenth century the Portuguese—the primary suppliers of cork—had invented an elongated bottle with a short neck and a shoulder. Of course since every bottle was blown by mouth the shapes were slightly irregular." He caressed the Washington wine from the neck down to the flared shoulder with the back of his index finger. "Anyway, the new shape meant the bottles could be stacked on their sides—instead of keeping them upright—so the corks would no longer dry out and the wine wouldn't spoil. Good for long voyages, like crossing the Atlantic."

He indicated the Margaux. "This bottle is perfectly consistent with what was historically available in 1790. Also, Thomas Jefferson always asked for his wines—especially his Bordeaux—to be shipped in bottles rather than casks."

"Wouldn't it have been cheaper to ship in casks?" I asked.

"Sure, but the odds of the wine he ordered and the wine he got being one and the same were slim to none." Ryan drank more Cab, then pushed back his chair and hunched down so he was eye level with the broad-shouldered bottle. "If the French—especially in the south of France—hadn't doctored the wine to fake Jefferson out and give him what he thought he'd ordered, then the men on the boats who brought the wine across the Atlantic or up the river drank their fill of his casks and topped them off with river water afterward so they were still full."

I made a face. "That is disgusting."

"Jefferson thought so, too." He sat up again. "Eighteenth-century wine fraud. We've got no monopoly on it. Happened all the time. Which is why TJ insisted on bottles, especially for Bordeaux. And, as we know, not all of those bottles made it to Monticello or Mount Vernon. Like this one."

"The wine in this bottle," I said, "is not in very good condition."

"Would you be in good condition if you were almost two hundred and fifty years old?" He brushed his finger lightly over the rough-etched lettering in the glass—1790, Margaux, and the initials, G.W. "Look at that color, though. Spectacular."

"A lot of the wine is gone," I said.

"Down to mid-shoulder." Ryan said. "I don't have a problem with that. You know you're going to get seepage in a wine this old. The cork is slightly dry, but in excellent condition, considering."

What he didn't mention, though, was that the ullage—the space between the wine and the cork—was filled with oxygen. Just as too much oxygen can rust metal or turn apples brown, too much air kills wine.

"It's a shame the châteaus didn't keep records that long ago," I said. "I guess we're lucky Jefferson did."

"Exactly." Ryan drained his wineglass. "Here's what you've got. The bottle is the right age. Mid-shoulder level is consistent with a wine that old. And here's the clincher. When Jefferson came back to the United States after serving as ambassador to France, he wrote a letter in 1790 ordering a large quantity of Bordeaux for himself and George Washington. In that letter he specified that the shipments should be marked with their respective initials so they'd get to their proper destinations. You're looking at one of the bottles he never got."

I chewed my lip and stared at the initials.

"Why are you shaking your head?" he said.

I leaned closer to the bottle of wine. "I wonder what Valerie knew that we don't."

"Oh, for God's sake. Are you still on about her?" He threw up his hands and accidentally brushed against the bottle. It teetered and we both grabbed for it. I caught it.

"Jesus." He looked stunned. "Wouldn't that have been something, knocking it over right here?"

"I'll just put this big boy back where he belongs for safe-keeping. You sit tight."

When I returned he was rolling the balloon of his

wineglass between both hands, staring into it like he was looking into a crystal ball.

"You're absolutely sure that it's authentic?" I said. "Stake your reputation on it?"

He smiled wickedly. "Not a hundred percent sure. But there is a way of finding out."

"What's that?"

"We could drink it."

"Nice try." I swiped his wineglass and put both of our glasses on a counter for washing in the morning. "Thanks for your time."

"You'll get my bill."

I walked him to his car. "How well did you know Valerie Beauvais?" I asked.

"Well enough to know what a snake in the grass she was."

I didn't say anything.

"Yeah, I know," he said. "Gives me a motive for killing her, doesn't it?"

"You need more than a motive," I said. "What about opportunity?"

"Apparently I had that, too," he said. "Two deputies already talked to me and they don't like my alibi."

"Which is?"

"Home alone in bed. I've got a witness but the dog doesn't like officers of the law so he's not talking."

I smiled. "Did you do it?"

He looked startled. "Hell, no." He pulled his keys out of his pocket and tossed them in the air. As he caught them he said, "Guess I got lucky. Someone else beat me to it."

Chapter 7

A beam of red light shone outside my kitchen window as I finished my dinner dishes. I watched it bob up and down as it moved past the rosebushes toward the summerhouse. When Quinn wanted to preserve his night vision he used a red flashlight. It was just after eight o'clock. Early for him.

Of all the surprising discoveries I'd made about my eccentric winemaker, the most unexpected was his passion for astronomy. Before he died, my father gave Quinn permission to bring a telescope to the summerhouse with its panoramic and mostly un-light-polluted view of the night sky from the valley all the way to the Blue Ridge. But Quinn and I had a falling out a while back when I thought he was turning the place into a love nest. In a fit of anger, he'd removed the telescope and his copies of *Stardate,* a magazine I once thought pertained to online dating.

Maybe he'd brought the telescope back and forgotten our tiff. I pulled on a hooded sweatshirt that had been hanging on the back of a chair and got my cane. My night vision hadn't adjusted as well as his and I yelped when I got caught on the thorns of one of the rosebushes.

He came out of the summerhouse. "What are you doing here?"

"Impaling myself in the dark. What do think I'm doing here? I came to see what you're looking at." I tugged the sleeves of my sweatshirt so they covered my hands. It was cooler than I expected. "Did you bring your telescope?"

In the near darkness his face was darker shadows and planes, his eyes black pools of negative space. "I thought you didn't want me stargazing out here."

He hadn't forgotten the argument.

"That was a misunderstanding and you know it," I said.

"It's still at my place," he said. "Packed up."

"You could bring it back, if you wanted."

"Is that so?" he said. "Thanks. I'll think about it."

I didn't like the way he kept staring at me. "If you don't have your telescope, what made you come here tonight?"

"Wanted a view of the harvest moon. There's only one each year. Tonight's the night. Too many trees at my place for a good view." He walked back to the summerhouse and opened the door. I heard something scraping inside. "Grab that door, will you?"

He hauled one of my mother's weather-beaten Adirondack chairs outside and positioned it so it looked out over the valley.

"You staying?" he asked. "Or were you just checking up on me?"

"I'll stay."

"You don't need to."

"I'd like to. Unless you'd rather be alone."

"Don't complicate things. I asked, didn't I?" He went back inside and got another chair.

"There are lots of harvest moons," I said.

"Nope. There's only one that's closest to the autumnal equinox. That's the real harvest moon." He set the second chair close to the first. "Have a seat. Moon's behind that cloud bank. When it moves away, you'll see it."

I set my cane down and sat next to him, leaning against the weather-coarsened wood. He pulled a cigar out of his jacket pocket, unwrapped it, and rustled in another pocket for matches. I watched the familiar ritual as his match flared and he bent his head, puffing until the cigar was lit. The tip glowed like a mini-moon and I breathed in the familiar scent of his tobacco.

He sat back as the clouds slowly moved off and the enormous moon, the color of a ripe wheel of Leicester cheese, hung in the sky above our heads.

"It's gorgeous," I said.

"Yup." He stretched his legs out in front of him and crossed them.

"You know in France, they used to care for the grapes according to the phases of the moon," I said. "Planting, picking, pruning. Maybe we should try it some time."

"The French also believe it's bad luck to have women around at harvest." He looked at me and puffed on the cigar. "I don't suppose you'd like to try that sometime?"

I tucked my feet under me and wrapped my arms around my knees. "You are such a Neanderthal, you know that?"

He laughed. "I just don't buy into that crap, that's all. Give me science any day. Speaking of which, I've been thinking about the Cab blend."

"You think about it nonstop." But to tell the truth, so did I. Until we got the grapes picked and into the barrels, I'd be as restless and preoccupied as he was.

"Damn lucky for you that I do," he said. "I want this year to be out of this world. We could screw up everything else, but you know how much rides on this one."

I didn't expect him to sound so somber. Most of the time he acted like he had a grace and favor relationship with St. Vincent, the patron saint of winegrowers, who whispered in his ear. But I understood what he meant. Of all the wines we produced, Cabernet Sauvignon was our most valuable—the one whose sales really paid the bills at the vineyard.

"It'll be great," I said. "As long as we aren't picking too late. If we get an overnight freeze while that wine is still sitting in the vats, there goes fermentation until next spring when it warms up again."

"If we pick early there'll be too much acid," he said. "You want people getting heartburn when they drink our wine? It's a nightmare to fix wine with too much acid."

"You're still talking like a Californian," I said. "Out there you never had to worry about high acidity. If you pick too late your only problem is that the alcohol content goes through the roof."

His cigar glowed serenely in the dark. "High alcohol content's easier to take care of than too much acid."

"Sure," I said. "You just add water to rehydrate the yeast."

The minute I said that, I regretted it. I glanced over at him but he was still staring straight ahead, watching the sky. His profile looked like it had been cast in steel.

"I was talking about stuck fermentation," I said.

"I know you were." But he sounded brusque and I knew it was because I'd indirectly brought up Le Coq Rouge. "Adding water is not the only way to deal with it, either. You can use a glycol heater."

"I know."

Too bad I hadn't mentioned that instead, though my comment could have hit a nerve for any winemaker. We all wrestled with the dilemma of how much to fiddle with a wine to fix it or improve it, and still consider it the "original" wine. California had problems when their grape sugar stopped converting to alcohol, known as stuck fermentation. In Virginia we had the opposite problem. Our alcohol content was often too low so we added sugar to boost it, a practice known as chapitalising. Both processes meant we were tinkering with the wine—but no winemaker considered them fraudulent.

So if that was okay, was it also acceptable to top off bottles from an outstanding year with a bottle of the same wine from a less stellar year? It was only a small amount of wine and the practice was known as recorking. Had the winemaker diluted the fantastic vintage, or was it still worth the same price? And where did you draw the line at how much was too much?

"I'm sorry," I said to Quinn.

"Forget it." He stirred in his chair. "How'd it go with the asshole?"

"You shouldn't call Ryan that and it went fine. We need him. He knows his stuff."

"He's still an asshole." He puffed again on the cigar. "By the way, Mick left a message at the vineyard earlier. Asked if you'd call him. Something about Amanda and a tent."

"For the auction. We've got so many people coming we might need to move it outside, on account of the Washington wine."

I wondered why Mick had called the vineyard instead of calling me directly. Maybe he'd tried my dead cell and the mailbox was full. Maybe he just wanted to leave a message and avoid talking to me after the other night.

Quinn read my thoughts. "What's going on with you two? You back together again?"

"The thing at Mount Vernon was a business-related dinner. That's all." I didn't want to discuss it. "Look, I'd better get inside. We have an early start tomorrow."

"Yeah, I'm ready to go, too."

He stood up and held out his hand. I took it and he pulled me up. His skin felt rough and callused. Nothing like Mick's, who, I'd heard, had a manicurist come to his home on a regular basis.

"Lucie!"

"What?"

"I asked what time you're getting there in the morning."

"When are you getting there?"

He rolled his eyes. "I just told you. Six-thirty."

"Okay, I'll be there at six-thirty, too."

He was still holding my hand as we walked through the rose garden. "Watch your step near those thorns." He let go of my hand once we passed by the roses and fished in his pocket for his car keys. "See you in the morning."

"Good night." I didn't look back, but I was sure he stayed and watched me cross the lawn to the veranda. A moment later I heard his car engine start and the sound of tires on the gravel driveway.

I lay in bed and wondered what, if anything, had just happened between us. Only the other day he'd said what a mistake it had been to start an affair with Bonita. And that it was a bad idea to mix business and personal relationships.

When I finally fell asleep I dreamed I found Valerie's car

on its roof in Goose Creek again and I needed to rescue her. But when I finally managed to fling open the car door, another woman hung suspended in mid-air.

Not Valerie. Me.

Harvest is morning work. We pick when it's cool and generally stop by noon or shortly afterward, depending on the heat. On this October day, Columbus Day, sunrise came at six forty-five. I woke in darkness just before my alarm went off at six and switched on the light on my bedside table. The local Leesburg radio station promised another Indian summer day once the sun came up. Temperatures in the low eighties. Perfect weather. I dressed and drove over to the vineyard.

Jacques Gilbert, our first winemaker and, unlike Quinn, a classical music aficionado, used to compare the process of growing grapes and making wine to the movements of a symphony. Allegro during spring and summer when the vines flourished and *veraison,* or ripening, began. Andante in winter when the vineyard was blanketed with snow and the vines were dormant. Harvest was presto, and vivace meant the release of a new wine. I loved his analogy except for harvest, which for me demanded a music of its own. Something Latino that pulsed and throbbed—songs like the ones the men played on their boom boxes as they worked and sang in the fields. Earthy, sensual . . . with sizzle, flashing skirts, and stiletto heels. Something sexy.

Quinn was working on the pump, which he'd moved to the crush pad by the time I arrived. He was dressed in jeans and a UC-Davis T-shirt that looked new. Probably a gift from Bonita, who'd studied viticulture and enology at Davis. I wondered why he'd worn it today—or if it were just the first clean thing he'd found in his drawer.

Manolo showed up at seven driving Hector's old Superman blue pickup with our regular crew and half a dozen day laborers from a camp in Winchester sitting in the open back. It still tugged at my heart that Hector wasn't behind the wheel as he'd been last year. I waved at Manolo, who stopped at the crush pad to let off a few of the men. He waved back and drove on, taking the rest of them out to the fields. By now it was light but the sky was still colorless. I watched the small, dark figures drop gracefully off the back of the truck and pick up yellow lugs at the end of the row before disappearing into the tangle of vines, grapes, and leaves.

No wine can be better than the grapes from which it came. But it can be a lot worse if the winemaker screws anything up—picking at the wrong time or making a bad call during the fermentation process. Quinn looked stressed as he often did at harvest, chewing on an unlit cigar and giving orders in a brusque, businesslike voice. Any tenderness he'd shown last night at the summerhouse had evaporated like morning mist off the vines. I got busy weighing the lugs when they came in filled with grapes. Later Quinn asked me to run the tests in the lab.

By one o'clock we'd picked everything we were going to for the day. I was finishing the last Brix tests when he showed up in the doorway. We'd turned the fans on because fermentation had already started, giving off enough carbon dioxide to kill us both unless we kept the air moving.

"The crew's cleaning up and Manolo's hosing off the crush pad." He had to speak up over the drone of the fans and the noise of the circulation system cooling the whites in the tanks. "I think we're done here until we have to punch down the cap this evening. I'm going over to Leesburg. I busted the channel lock wrench when I was working on the pump. We need a new one since the pump's still acting up."

"Cheaper than a new pump." I rinsed a beaker and hung it upside down on a rack to drain. "I need a new cell phone. Store's in Leesburg. Want to go together?"

His eyes narrowed and I blushed. He was staring at me like I'd just invited him on a date. I folded a dishtowel into a neat rectangle and set it on the counter.

"On second thought, you go on ahead," I said. "I need to go home and take a shower and change first."

Quinn looked down at his clothes, which were spattered with dull purple blotches, just like mine. We both looked like we'd been shot repeatedly. He stared at me some more and I could tell he was thinking about something other than my clothes.

"You don't need to change," he said. "We'll take the El. Meet me in the parking lot when you're done here."

We didn't talk much on the drive to Leesburg. He dropped me off at the phone store and said he'd pick me up when he'd done his errand. A teenager who looked like he spent most of his time and money at the tattoo parlor was busy transferring my phone number from the old phone to the new one when Quinn showed up carrying a bag from T. W. Perry Hardware.

On the way back to the car I said, "You think we could stop by Jeroboam's on the way home?"

"Why?"

"I thought maybe I'd ask Jack about the provenance of that Washington bottle."

The El was so old he had to unlock the doors manually. He unlocked mine and said, "What do you want to do that for? You already said he'd be insulted."

"I'm curious and I can be diplomatic. I'll tell him it's for the catalog."

"Follow your own advice and forget it." He looked over at me. "Damn, Lucie. I can hear the gears whirring inside that little brain of yours. You gotta know, don't you? You're not going to let it go. Just like a dog with a bone."

"A girl could get a swelled head from all the nice things you say, you know that?"

"Part of my charm."

He took Route 15 to Gilberts Corner, then Mosby's Highway west to Middleburg, instead of the small country roads as I did. As usual he drove too fast, eyes riveted on the road, working a tiny muscle in his jaw that meant he was pondering something. I knew so little about him. An Italian father who abandoned him and his Argentine mother when he was a kid. She'd raised him on her own somewhere in California. He never talked about his parents, or any siblings, either. If he had any.

We parked in an unmetered space on South Liberty near the old magnolia tree in the churchyard. Jeroboam's was on the corner on East Washington. Washington Street—East and West—had gotten its name from George, who'd visited when he was surveying the region for Lord Fairfax. And here I was more than two centuries later wondering about a bottle of wine that Washington might have drunk if it had ever been delivered to Mount Vernon.

Jack Greenfield bought Jeroboam's sight unseen a year ago to appease his beautiful wife, the sensational Sunny, because she hated the commute from their home in Georgetown when she rode with the Goose Creek Hunt or visited her many Loudoun County clients for her interior design business. He hired someone to run Salmanazar's, the D.C. wine store his family owned for sixty years, and called the new, smaller store in Middle-burg "Jeroboam's." It was an inside wine joke since the biblical names were also the terms for large-sized bottles used for champagne—a Salmanazar being the equivalent of twelve champagne bottles and a Jeroboam holding four champagnes or six bottles of Bordeaux.

In Middleburg, we still said that people who moved here came from "away," which distinguished them from the locals who'd been born and bred in Loudoun and Fauquier Counties. Technically Jack and Sunny were from away, but they had generously invested time and talent, becoming well known as part of the community in the short time they'd lived here.

Sunny had decorated Jeroboam's with her customary flair so it resembled a fine English hunting lodge, whose walls happened to be filled with wine bottles. The few empty spaces, including the little stairway that led to a lower-level tasting room, had been turned into an informal art gallery with all of the paintings for sale. Jack was clearing up glasses and bottles in the dark-paneled tasting room when we arrived. He dressed to sell wine like he worked for a Fortune 500 company—bespoke blazer, starched shirt, silk tie, fine wool slacks, and well-polished tasseled loafers. He came around from behind the bar when he saw us.

Usually I got a friendly kiss on the cheek, but Jack took one look at our wine-stained clothes and held back. "You two look like you could use a drink," he said.

"Don't mind if we do," Quinn said. "What's cookin', Jack?"

"Plenty of things are cooking." He walked back to the bar.

Jack was no nonsense, with a strong face and silver hair,

stylishly combed back from a high forehead. Jet-black eyebrows that slanted downward toward the bridge of his nose gave him the look of an erudite devil.

"My esteemed business partner has gone to the airport to pick up his latest girlfriend." The eyebrows arched with the resigned look of a parent lamenting a child's behavior. "Sunny and I've decided that Shane needs a wife. Too much time being the playboy. Left me here to handle a tasting for a temperamental caterer handling a wedding reception in Upperville next spring. Couldn't make up her mind about anything."

"That's women for you," Quinn said. I elbowed him.

Jack set out two glasses. "Try this Cab from a vineyard near Charlottesville. Give it a moment to open."

I drank my wine. "Lovely. Good nose, nice long finish. I like the pepper."

"A bit young for me," Quinn said.

"He's such a critic when he's thinking about our blend," I said. "Ignore him."

Jack smiled. "So what's cooking with you?"

Quinn concentrated on his nice, young wine. He wasn't going to help me ask about the Margaux.

"I was hoping you could tell us more about the provenance of the Washington bottle," I said. "Ryan's writing the notes for the auction catalog and that bottle is now the star of the show."

"I know it is," Jack said. "I've been getting calls from all over the world. People want to know if I've got another bottle, or even if they can buy a case." He tapped his forehead with his index finger. "You wonder, sometimes."

"Not me," Quinn said. "We get people who want to know if we put real apples in the Riesling when we say it tastes like apple. Or how much pepper we put in the Pinot when we talk about the peppery taste. Do we grind it or put in whole peppercorns?"

Jack laughed. "Good thing you don't tell them it tastes like leather."

"So how did it come into your possession?" I asked. We'd veered away from the Margaux.

With some difficulty, he recorked the wine we'd just tasted. Quinn and I both noticed.

Jack looked rueful. "Arthritis acting up again. Don't get old. To answer your question, Lucie, my family was in the wine trade in Germany from the mid-1700s until just after the Second World War. Then my father moved here and started again in America. In Germany we used to have close ties to every major producer in Europe, especially the French. I found the bottle in the cave at my family's old warehouse in Freiburg after my father passed away. Someone could have given it to us, or it could have been there for a century."

"Your father never mentioned that Bordeaux to you?" I asked. "Ever?"

"He did not. When I found it, it was not in good condition which makes me suspect that we acquired it after a previous owner kept it poorly cellared. Or else it was badly transported. Possibly both. I told you it's probably vinegar by now. But I know you will get a lot of money for it. Some people will pay a small fortune for the thrill of owning a wine once destined for George Washington."

The last line sounded like a mild rebuke. It was Quinn's turn to do the elbowing. "We know that, Jack," he said. "And we're grateful for your donation. It was extremely generous of you, right, Lucie?"

"It was," I said. "But if you think of anything between now and the auction—"

"My dear, I've already told you everything." He folded his arms across his chest. "Everything."

"We should be going," Quinn said. "Thanks for the wine."

When we got outside Quinn said, "You can thank me now for saving your bacon. He was getting pretty pissed at you playing Spanish Inquisitor with him. If you'd pushed any harder I bet he would have asked you to return the bottle."

"I just asked where it came from. That's all."

"He didn't like it."

"I know," I said. "I wonder why."

"Don't go there, Lucie. I mean it."

A gunmetal-colored Porsche pulled up and parked behind Quinn's El Camino. "That's Shane," I said, "and his new friend."

We watched him help a stunning brunette from the car. "She's lovely," I said.

"Goddamn." Quinn sucked in his breath. "What the hell is *she* doing here?"

"You know her?" I asked.

The raw pain in his voice gave away he not only knew her, but she'd broken his heart when he did.

"Yes," he said, "she's my wife."

Chapter 8

He was married.

How had he managed to keep that a secret? To keep *her* a secret?

"What's she doing with Shane," I asked, "if she's married to you?"

"Ex-wife, I meant." He was curt. "We're divorced."

I watched Shane and the brunette cross the street and saw recognition dawn in her eyes. Her step faltered and Shane, unaware of the lightning arcing between his girlfriend and my winemaker, slid his arm around her slim waist.

Quinn's eyes never left her face.

When they joined us, he said, "Hello, Nicole. Long time no see."

It was clear they hadn't parted amicably. And that she still got to him. Hard to tell what was going through her mind other than the shock of seeing him again.

She wore a russet suit that set off her dark hair, brown-black eyes, and honey-colored skin. Short, fitted skirt and flared jacket. Silk blouse unbuttoned just low enough to tantalize. Lace bra showing through the sheer fabric. The suit was either Armani or Versace. Quite the contrast to the classic outfit I had on. Levi's and the Gap. Torn, dirty, and stained.

"Quinn—" She spoke his name like a caress. "What a surprise. What are you doing here?"

"I live here. What about you, Nic?" His voice was like cold steel.

"You two know each other?" Shane's eyes roved between Nicole and Quinn. Though Shane was always pleasant to me, I thought there was something a little too beautiful and preening about him that came across as what the French call *m'as-tu vu?*—"have you seen me?" I'd heard stories that he was a high school dropout who grew up in a rough part of Baltimore, but he'd shed his past—including the Bawlmer, Murlin, accent—so thoroughly that anyone who didn't know better figured Daddy left him a nice trust fund after he'd graduated from an East Coast university. He certainly lived like he had a rich relative with the expensive cars, knockout women, and gambling trips to Vegas.

"We know each other," Quinn said, "don't we, Nicole?"

She blushed. I watched as she put her arm through Shane's and twined her fingers with his. "Quinn is my . . . that is, we used to be married. A long time ago."

Shane pulled Nicole closer and kissed her hair, his eyes on Quinn. "Then you're divorced. Nikki and I met in Vegas a few months ago. We've been together ever since." He still looked taken aback by the news.

"Good for you." I recognized Quinn's go-to-hell voice. It seemed like Nicole did too, judging by the way her expression turned cold. "See you 'round some time."

Quinn laid his hand on my shoulder and started to propel me across the street.

"You're not going to introduce me to your friend?" Nicole called after us. It sounded like a taunt.

Quinn stopped and we both turned around. "Lucie Montgomery meet Nicole . . . what name are you going by these days, sweetheart? It was hard to keep track for a while."

"My maiden name." Her eyes flashed. "Martin." Then she looked at me, taking in the cane and my limp. "Where have I heard of you?"

"I have no idea." The sooner we got out of here, the better. She kept staring, like she was trying to recall some forgotten piece of information. "I'm sure we've never met," I said for emphasis.

"Let's go." Quinn walked me over to the El and opened my door, holding it while I got in. Across the street, I saw Shane whisper something in Nicole Martin's perfect ear. She watched us, nodding. Guess he'd explained what was what. Or who.

Quinn revved his engine. "Do not hit that Porsche," I said. "I don't care how much you hate him for being with your ex-wife."

"I don't hate him," he said. "He's welcome to her."

We drove back to the vineyard in silence that echoed. He looked at me just once—his face like granite, his eyes dark as obsidian. I knew then that seeing her again had opened a wound that had never healed. Now she was walking around in his mind.

He was grieving, hurt, angry. And still very much in love with his ex-wife.

When we got back to the vineyard he dropped me at my house and said, "I'm going out in the field for a while. And don't worry about punching down the cap tonight. I got it covered."

I nodded. "Okay. If you're sure."

"I'm sure."

I knew better than to offer sympathy, let alone pity. He would have thrown it right back in my face. So I let him go, saying nothing, and tried not to think about the look in his eyes when he talked about going out into the field alone.

Around nine o'clock the phone rang. I was in the parlor, trying to plow through *European Travels with Thomas Jefferson's Ghost*. The nearest telephone was in the foyer. I reached for my cane and half-ran to catch it, hoping it might be Quinn. By the time I picked up the receiver, the answering machine had kicked in.

"Lucie, *ma chère*." The well-loved voice on the other end sounded slightly muffled—filtered, no doubt, through the smoke of a bad-smelling Boyard and a snifter of Armagnac, before being piped through my machine. It was 3 A.M. in Paris. My eighty-two-year-old grandfather would be an hour or so away from calling it a day and going to bed. *"Désolé que tu n'es pas là—"*

"I'm here, Pépé," I said in French. "How are you? It's so good to hear your voice."

My end of the conversation reverberated like a bad echo through the two-story foyer and I regretted not getting to the phone sooner since now I'd have to hear the entire conversation in stereo.

"I'm well," he said. "Very well. I just returned from China."

I often hoped I'd lucked out and inherited most of my DNA from my mother's family rather than any of the self-indulgent, weak-willed genes my father might have passed along. Pépé had sent a postcard from the Great Wall, writing that he and a few friends hiked part of it. They'd also traveled the Silk Road as far as Kyrgyzstan.

"I hope you're going to take it easy after that trip. It sounded quite strenuous," I said.

I heard the flare of a match. Probably relighting his cigarette. Boyards, banned years ago by the European Union because of their toxicity, were made of black tobacco and maize paper. The only cigarette I knew that constantly extinguished itself. Pépé allowed himself one or two a day from his dwindling hoard.

"I shall definitely be taking it easy. My next trip is to Washington."

"Here? It is? When?"

He paused. "I am sorry to spring this on you at the last moment, *mon ange,* but I'm flying in tomorrow." Another pause. "I have a hotel reservation at the Marriott near Dulles Airport but I hope we can see each other and you'll let me take you to dinner at least once while I'm in town."

Pépé had been a career diplomat. He was unfailingly polite. I knew better than to be hurt that he hadn't asked if he could stay with me, because he'd worry he was imposing. He probably hadn't even unpacked from China, much less gotten over jet lag. I thought about the refrain from a song Leland used to teasingly sing to my mother, lamenting how hard it was to keep 'em down on the farm after they'd seen Paree. You couldn't even keep my grandfather in Paree.

"First of all, you can cancel your reservation at the Marriott," I said. "You're staying here with me. And second, what time does your flight get in? I'll come get you."

"Absolument pas," he said. "I'm renting a car. Not to worry, I'll drive myself to your place."

I didn't realize he was still driving. I adored Pépé but

he drove like a Formula One racer hell-bent on breaking the record. Most of the rest of the family—in particular, Dominique—flat-out refused to get in a car with him any-more.

"I don't think that's such a good idea," I said. "They've raised the penalties for traffic violations here in Virginia. A thousand dollars for reckless lane-changing. Some fines are even higher. I'll drive you wherever you need to go."

I didn't mention the fines applied only to drivers with Virginia licenses. Or that our legislature had imposed the excessive penalties hoping they'd motivate the good citizens of the Commonwealth—some of whom also drove like bats out of hell—to behave better behind the wheel.

"I don't want to be a burden," he said. "Harvest is such a busy time of year for you. I've got meetings with *les vieux amis*—my old friends—and several dinners planned. It would be better if I have my own transportation."

"Sure. You'll get on the Beltway and think you're on the Autoroute du Soleil," I said. "It would be better to let Do-minique or me drive than bail you out of jail."

"I drive like every other Frenchman." He sounded miffed.

"Exactly. So don't rent the car. What time's your flight?"

He told me and I wrote it down.

"Have you told Dominique you're coming?" I asked.

He sighed. "Not yet. You know how she fusses over me and treats me like an old man. I am not as old as she would like me to be, you know."

"You still need to call her. She should hear the news from you that you're coming. You don't want to hurt her feelings, do you?"

"Mais non," he said. "Of course not."

"Then call her. And don't worry. Everything will be fine once you get here. We'll have a good time."

"Mon trésor," he said. "I forget how much I miss you until we speak. I cannot wait to see you." Another sigh and the sound of a match being struck once again. "And your cousin."

I hung up and a moment later, the answering machine beeped. Tomorrow was harvest and another early start, but I was too restless to go to bed. I hit the delete button and erased our conversation.

Maybe Quinn had gone back to the summerhouse. I put on a jacket and went outside. The Adirondack chairs were exactly where we'd left them last night.

Where was he? Maybe I should call him. We often spoke late at night, especially during harvest when there was work to do in the barrel room. But this wasn't work and we'd never crossed the line this far into intimate territory. Tonight would be a bad night to start.

I went back inside, threw my jacket on the chair by the phone and walked into the library. It had been Leland's book-lined office until a fire destroyed most of the room, along with much of the downstairs. As part of the renovation I'd had the cherry bookcases rebuilt as they'd been before. But the shelves, once jammed with double rows of Leland's extensive collection of books by and about Thomas Jefferson, were nearly bare. It still startled me each time I saw the empty spaces.

A copy of Jefferson's diary of his voyage through the European vineyards, reprinted on the bicentennial anniversary of his trip, was one of the few books to survive the fire. I'd been trying to read Valerie's tome before Pépé called. The bad reviews were justified.

The odds weren't good that Jefferson's actual diary,

written more than two centuries ago, would provide a clue to what Valerie had hinted at about the provenance of the Washington wine, but I pulled it off the shelf anyway. A slim volume, just over one hundred pages. I wiped dust off the cover. *Thomas Jefferson's European Travel Diaries. Jefferson's Own Account of His Journeys Through the Countryside and Wine Regions of the Continent, 1787–1788.*

I took it upstairs and began reading in bed.

Words to the Wise from the Author for Americans Traveling Abroad.

When you are doubting whether a thing is worth the trouble of going to see, recollect that you will never again be so near it and that you may have to repent the not having seen it.

What had Valerie seen in Bordeaux? Whatever it was, now I was the one who repented "the not having seen it." And what about Jack Greenfield? A matter of "the not having *said* it." Claiming no knowledge of how such a fabled bottle had come into his family's possession. It seemed implausible. I closed the book and turned out the light. In a few hours it would be daylight and the second day of harvesting the Cab.

In the morning, I'd see Quinn.

He showed up before the crew arrived, unsteady on his feet and dressed in the clothes he'd worn yesterday. Bloodshot eyes, wild hair, and unshaven, he looked like something somebody forgot to shoot. When he came closer I thought I detected a faint scent of perfume clinging to his shirt, more Rite-Aid than Lord & Taylor. Hard to tell since it blended in with his own body odor and the essences of booze and stale tobacco. God, what had he done last night? Where had he been and who had he been with?

I nearly asked if he'd cruised some bar and picked up somebody—anybody—to console himself after seeing Nicole with Shane, but it was none of my business. What was my business was that in twenty minutes the crew would be here and they'd see their boss looking like he'd single-handedly drunk Loudoun County dry in one night.

We worked around dangerous equipment. I couldn't let him stay here in his state.

"Go home." My voice was hoarse with anger and disappointment. "You're drunk, you stink, and you look like hell. I don't want anyone else seeing you right now. You have a goddamn nerve showing up like this. Especially today with what's at stake for us."

"Well, good morning to you, Susie Sunshine. Wake up on the wrong side of the bed of nails, did we, darlin'?" He still slurred his words. I wanted to strangle him.

"Get out of here! Go home and sleep it off. I don't want to see you until you're sober."

He straightened up. "I'm fine." His eyes looked crossed as he tried to focus on me and he swayed slightly.

"You are still drunk. You will *not* be here when the crew shows up." My voice shook and so did my hands. "That's in fifteen minutes. Just—go, will you? Please!"

"Who are you tellin' to go?" He lurched closer.

For a moment I thought he might fall down at my feet. I wanted to move away from him and the messiness of this tawdry scene, but I gritted my teeth and said, "My employee."

He looked like I'd just slapped him. I turned and half-walked, half-ran into the barrel room, leaning on my cane like an old woman. My legs felt like jelly as I slammed the door without looking to see if he'd followed. It took me so long to turn on the fans to dissipate the overnight buildup of CO_2 I began to feel light-headed from the gas.

I hoped he hadn't noticed how badly I was trembling. Though in his state he probably wouldn't have noticed if Manolo ran him over in the pickup. God help him if he was still there when the crew showed up. But when I went back outside ten minutes later, he was gone.

When Manolo arrived I told him Quinn was sick and, ignoring the surprise in his eyes, said the two of us were running the show. Manolo was young and good-looking and he knew the bars, too. If he'd run into Quinn, he wasn't talking.

"Lucie," Manolo said. "You all right? I just said something twice and you didn't answer. You don't look too good. Maybe what Queen has, you got, too?"

"I'm pretty certain what Quinn has isn't contagious," I said. "Sorry. I was distracted. Let's get to work."

The fact that we had one less person helping out—and it happened to be the one who usually ran the show—kept me focused, too busy to think about the kick-your-stupid-ass speech I planned to deliver once he'd sobered up enough to hear it. We had less to pick today, but we also had a delivery of Petit Verdot to deal with. Quinn had ordered it from a Culpeper vineyard that grew grapes but didn't make wine. I'd nearly forgotten about it until the truck drove up to the crush pad.

The phone rang when I was in the lab running the final tests. Frankie, calling from the villa. "Sorry to bother you, Lucie. Someone's here to see you."

"Who is it?"

The deliberate silence on her end was the code we'd

set up to identify someone who'd sampled a few too many wines and was getting out of hand.

"I'll get Manolo to come with me," I said.

"These guests have asked specifically for you."

I wondered why she wanted me to come alone. "I'll be right there. By myself."

"Great." She sounded grim.

I did not recognize the well-dressed man and woman sitting on one of the sofas around the stone fireplace in the center of the tasting room. Frankie was the only other person there, reading behind the bar.

She walked over to the couple when I entered. "Lucie, these are your new neighbors, Claudia and Stuart Orlando. Mr. and Mrs. Orlando, meet Lucie Montgomery."

For Frankie not to like someone they had to break at least three of the Ten Commandments. She clearly didn't like the Orlandos. She pivoted on her heel and went back to the bar to retrieve a gardening catalog.

"I'll be outside on the deck. Call me if you need me," she said to me.

Claudia Orlando was a pretty redhead with porcelain skin who looked like she could have stepped out of a painting by Titian. Stuart was big and beefy with a ruddy spider-veined face that said unhealthy lifestyle. Older than his wife by at least a decade, if not more. He colored his hair. It was too black.

I'd bet money they'd come to talk about the Goose Creek Hunt, but I figured I'd wait for them to bring it up. "What can I do for you, Mr. and Mrs. Orlando?" I sat down on an adjacent sofa and propped my cane next to me.

"It's Claudia and Stuart, hon." Her delicate beauty and the nasal Brooklyn accent were a total disconnect. She pronounced her name "Claw-dee-er."

Stuart indicated my cane with a finger that looked like an overstuffed sausage. "Hunting accident?" he asked pleasantly, but I knew he was probing.

I smiled. "No."

He waited for the rest of my explanation. When I remained silent, his eyes narrowed and he leaned forward. "We'll get right to the point, Lucie. Claudia and I, here, have decided that our land will be off-limits to those foxhunters who claim that it's part of their so-called territory. We believe strongly that what they do is inhumane. Not just what they do to the fox, but also to those poor dogs."

"It's cruel," Claudia said. "They're just so helpless."

"Hounds," I said.

"Pardon?" Stuart asked.

"They're not called dogs. They're called hounds."

"Hounds, shmounds." He waved a hand like he could care less. "We're here to ask you to join us. We can shut them down, or at least curtail what they do, if both of us prohibit them from hunting on our land." He smiled. "It's a start. And then we can take it to the next level."

"The next level?"

"Why, outlawing foxhunting." Claudia tapped a finger on the glass coffee table and a wristful of wire-thin gold bracelets jingled like wind chimes. "Stuart is a lawyer. A smart lawyer. Orlando and Thomason. You must have heard of the firm. They represent most of the animal rights groups."

I nodded. No point telling them I'd heard from the secretary of the Goose Creek Hunt. "I have."

Stuart looked satisfied. "Are you with us, Lucie? I certainly hope so."

"I'm afraid not," I said. "The Goose Creek Hunt has been hunting on my family's land for more than a century.

They will always be welcome here, as long as I have something to say about it."

"Why?" Claudia looked puzzled and distressed. "What they do is *savage*."

"This isn't England," I said. "They rarely kill the fox and when they do it's usually because the animal is old and diseased, or has rabies. It's more like fox chasing. It's not a blood sport in this country."

"I do not understand how you can condone it." Stuart had switched to what I assumed was the courtroom voice he used to eviscerate an unfriendly witness.

I flinched and he saw it. He pressed on.

"I don't like making threats." He smiled in a way that said he relished it. "But this could escalate into an unfortunate situation and I'm sure neither of us wants that to happen."

Meaning I didn't want it to happen. He looked smug, but Claudia still looked shocked. Maybe I had a chance if I tried explaining things to her.

"George Washington went foxhunting in this valley." I looked her in the eyes and ignored Stuart. "So did Lord Fairfax. Foxhunting began right here in the earliest days of our country. We are, at heart, a farm community. Nature takes its course and hunting is part of it. I'm sure coming from Manhattan it must seem totally alien to you, but hunting and racing are an integral part of life and the culture of our region. You've only just moved in. Why don't you spend some time learning about your neighbors before you judge and criticize us?"

Stuart reached for his wife's hand and leaned over to whisper in her ear. I heard him anyway. "She's hopeless, sugar pie. Forget it."

I reached for my cane and stood up. Claudia looked

upset but I'd just baited Stuart and the ugly expression on his face said he planned to come out swinging next round. They stood as well.

"For the record," I said, "I don't hunt."

"You're going to regret this, Mrs. Montgomery," he said. "I promise you."

We'd moved back to formal names. "I doubt that very much," I said. "And it's 'Miss.'"

Claudia looked at me with pity. "That explains a lot," she said. "We'll see ourselves out."

Frankie walked inside as the door to the villa slammed behind the Orlandos. My face burned. The spinster remark stung.

I swung around to Frankie. "You were eavesdropping."

"You bet I was," she said. "He's despicable. Unfortunately, she'll do whatever he tells her."

"He threatened me," I said. "I don't like that."

"I don't think he threatened you," Frankie said. "I think he just declared war."

Chapter 9

I told Frankie to close up early and take the rest of the afternoon off.

"Where's Quinn?" she said. "He hasn't been around here all day."

"He came down with a bug so he stayed home."

She frowned. "And missed harvest? What'd he have? Bubonic plague?"

"I don't know. Look, I'd better get going. My grandfather's plane arrives at Dulles at half-past four and you know what a bear traffic is."

She nodded. "Your nose is growing, Pinocchio. See you tomorrow."

My face was still red. She'd probably drop by Quinn's on her way home to find out if he'd recovered from his mysterious ailment and then she'd know. I wasn't sure why I made up that lie and didn't tell her outright—or maybe I was.

It was just after three o'clock. Was Quinn still sleeping it off or did he get lost for the day like he'd done in the past? I detoured by his cottage on my way to the airport.

He'd parked the El Camino at an odd angle in front of his porch. The blinds on the front windows were closed. He was probably still sleeping. Manolo had promised me earlier that he and a couple of the men would punch down the cap this evening, so it didn't matter whether or not Quinn showed up in the barrel room today.

Punching down the cap was a chore that lasted as long as the wine continued to ferment, and not anybody's favorite task. The "cap" was a ten- to twelve-inch-thick layer of wineskins and pulp that floated to the top of the fermenting vats and congealed into wet purple concrete. It was a product of the chemical process that occurred as the yeast that was added to the grape juice converted the fruit sugar to alcohol—so everything bubbled like the witches' brew in *Macbeth*.

Twice a day we needed to break up the sludgy mass and submerge it in order to give the wine its tannins, taste, and color. The larger vineyards handled this mechanically but we still did it the old-fashioned way, using paddles, Eli's old baseball bat—and our hands. Each vat contained a ton of wine so it was a physically demanding task that involved being submerged in wine up to our armpits and pushing against a solid purple block that didn't want to give way. My shoulders always felt like they were coming out of their sockets and my fingernails remained stained for weeks. I got out of performing the chore today because I needed to go to the airport, but my turn would come soon enough.

Pépé's flight from Paris arrived on time. I waited in the cordoned-off area of the international arrivals terminal and watched the lighted board blink with information on which flight had landed and when the passengers moved on to customs. My grandfather finally came through the automatic double doors, pushing a luggage cart, staring straight ahead, a slightly puzzled and bemused look on his face as though something about the eccentricities of my country had already tickled his fancy even though he'd barely set foot on American soil.

I called to him and waved from behind the low metal barricade. His well-lined face lit up and he waved back. When we met, he kissed me three times and murmured my name. I hugged him and took in the smell of Boyards and a whisper of his familiar old-fashioned cologne. But what I mostly smelled were the memory scents of the things I loved—and missed—about Paris. Years ago my mother told me I was my grandfather's namesake—his first name was Luc—and it was an open secret in the family that I was his favorite.

He refused to let me push his luggage cart and I didn't bother to argue. My grandfather came from the generation where chivalry and gallantry were as instinctive as breathing. Luckily I'd managed to park near the terminal so we didn't have far to walk. He insisted on stowing his suitcase in the Mini, also without help, though when he sat next to me in the car, he seemed winded by the exertion.

"*Tu vas bien?*" I asked.

"*Oui, oui.*" He flicked his hand, brushing away my concerns. "*Un peu fatigué, c'est tout.*"

"You can rest when we get home," I said.

"*Mais non.* We're having dinner this evening at the Goose Creek Inn with Dominique." His eyes crinkled with amusement. "So you see, I did call your cousin."

"You sly old dog. I knew you'd come round."

"*Ma belle,*" he said, looking pleased with himself. "Certainly not 'old.'"

I laughed. "Certainly not. You still haven't told me the reason for this visit. Not that you need one."

He folded his hands in his lap. "*Eh, bien,* a reunion. *Les vieux amis.* My colleagues from the war."

He meant World War II.

"The colleagues you worked with on the Marshall Plan?" I said.

The plan had been the brainchild of Secretary of State George C. Marshall back in 1947, a massive humanitarian aid project conceived to help a shattered Europe rebuild after the devastation of the war. The stipulation for receiving aid, however, was that the European countries needed to draw up a unified plan for how they would use the money—acting as a single economic entity rather than a fractured group of nations. Pépé had been the lead member of the French delegation and one of the major European architects in forging the union the Americans sought. He'd spent more than a decade from the mid-1940s to the mid-1950s as a counselor at the French embassy in Washington.

"We still meet once a year," he said, "usually in Paris at a dinner and lecture at the American embassy. But every so often we come back here to Washington where it all began."

"I think it's incredible you still get together after all these years," I said.

"Ah, but it was an incredible time when friends helped friends. America built much goodwill in the world with its generous wallet and kind heart. A respected nation the whole world once emulated." He paused. "So much has changed since then."

I thought he'd emphasized "once" ever so slightly. We were driving along Route 28, farmland until high-tech businesses moved in and transformed it into a busy industrial corridor near the airport. A large American flag snapped from a pole in front of a mirrored glass and stone building belonging to a company that designed computer programs used in the defense industry. I watched Pépé's eyes follow the flag as we passed.

"I guess the world is a lot more complicated now," I said.

His eyes were no longer smiling. "Indeed it is."

I thought I could persuade my grandfather to rest before dinner once we arrived at Highland House, but he wouldn't hear of it. Instead he wanted a tour of the house, which he hadn't seen since I'd restored it after the fire. I showed him the furniture I'd salvaged—possessions he and my grandmother had given my mother from the small château they owned outside Paris so she'd have furniture from home for her new life in Virginia. But he also admired the newer things I'd added to replace what had been destroyed—the hand-colored prints of Virginia wildflowers, the Shaker chairs, the carpet handmade by a woman in Georgia.

"The house has your charm and your stamp on it now, *ma belle*. Chantal would be proud of what you've done here, especially the way you are running the vineyard."

Pépé didn't often speak of my mother ever since her death seven years ago when Orion, her horse, inexplicably threw her as she and my sister, Mia, jumped one of the low stacked-stone walls on our farm. I knew he still grieved deeply.

"We could visit her while you're here, if you'd like," I said. My mother's grave was next to Leland's in the family cemetery. I'd also placed a small cross at the site where she died.

He laid a hand on my shoulder and for the first time since he arrived I felt his fatigue. "I would like to go there," he said.

We did not speak about her again, but later I saw him take a snow-white handkerchief from his pocket, when I'm sure he thought I wasn't looking, and dab his eyes. My heart ached for him.

On our way to dinner at the Goose Creek Inn I told him about Joe and Dominique calling off their engagement, betting my cousin hadn't mentioned it. He looked startled. She hadn't.

"They have been engaged for such a long time," he said. "What happened?"

"I think her workaholic habits finally got to him," I said. "But I suspect there's more to it because Joe started going out with another woman right away. A few days ago his new girlfriend's car went off the road into Goose Creek and she died. Somebody removed the lug nuts from one of her tires and she apparently lost control of the car. The sheriff is investigating but so far they haven't arrested anyone."

"Do they suspect Dominique?" Pépé asked.

"Good God, no! I never even thought of that. But I know they're talking to Joe. He, uh, spent the night with the woman—Valerie Beauvais—before she was killed."

"How is your cousin handling all this news?"

"Not well," I said. "And, to be honest, I'm not sure she knows yet about Joe staying with Valerie."

"Then we must protect her," he said.

"And you must act like you don't know anything until she tells you."

"*Ma puce,*" he said, "I have spent my entire career in the diplomatic service. I have pretended ignorance in front of kings and generals and dictators when it was necessary. I can handle your cousin."

I smiled. "I'm sure you can."

But he did look predictably annoyed when Dominique fussed over him as we arrived at the restaurant, fretting that he looked too tired to be out so late and promising we'd be served immediately so he could go home and right to bed. The first chance he got when she wasn't looking, he rolled his eyes at me and winked. Then no sooner did she bring us to her table and seated us when she flew off to solve a crisis in the kitchen.

"She needs a holiday," Pépé said to me. "She will kill herself if she doesn't take some time off. I don't think she looks well at all."

"She's chain-smoking again. I think she started when she and Joe broke up."

We ordered after she returned to the table. Dominique handed our grandfather the wine list.

"Are you going to choose a Burgundy, Pépé?" she asked, smiling.

In the 1930s two Frenchmen from the town of Nuits-Saint-Georges in Burgundy founded a society known as the *Confrérie des Chevaliers du Tastevin*—the Brotherhood of the Knights of Winetasters—in order to help the wines of that region survive an economic crisis. After the war my grandfather had become a member of this elite group and he knew his wines.

"I think we'll have a Clos de Vougeot with dinner," he said after consulting with us about our main courses. "And *une coupe de champagne* as an aperitif." He glanced at Dominique over the top of his reading glasses. "Dinner is on me."

"It's my restaurant—" Dominique said.

"I know that. But I am taking you both out to dinner."

"You can't—"

I kicked her under the table. "Thank you," I said. "That's very kind. We're delighted to accept."

He beamed. "My pleasure. I don't often have the opportunity to dine with my beautiful granddaughters anymore."

Ryan Worth showed up as the sommelier arrived to uncork our dinner wine.

"Evening, all," he said. "Celebrating something? Excellent choice of wine."

Dominique introduced Pépé, who stood and shook Ryan's hand. "My grandfather, Luc Delaunay," she said. "Visiting from Paris."

"Didn't mean to interrupt a family gathering," Ryan said. "I'm here to have dinner with Shane Cunningham and that delicious-looking California wine buyer he's going out with."

"I saw her when she came in with Shane," Dominique said. "She's stunning."

I looked from Dominique to Ryan. "You're talking about Nicole Martin?" My voice rose and the couple at the next table stopped talking to stare at us. Dominique touched a finger to her lips and frowned. I lowered my voice. "She's a wine buyer?"

"Since you seem to have met her, I'm surprised you didn't know," Ryan said. "She's in town to buy the Washington bottle."

"Are you serious?"

"Dead serious." He looked puzzled. "I can't believe she didn't tell you. She's a private buyer for über-rich collectors, mostly from California. Some client with pockets all the way to China told her not to come home from your auction without it. She's quite the barracuda when she goes after something from what I hear." He straightened his tie, suddenly self-conscious. "Shane said she'd like to pick my brain about that bottle."

"I bet she would," I said.

"Sorry to dash, but they're waiting. Excuse me, folks." He switched to French and said to Pépé, "You seem to have excellent taste in wine, sir, so perhaps you'd be interested in knowing that I'm the wine critic for the *Washington Tribune*. It's one of our better-known American newspapers. My column is syndicated in more than two hundred papers throughout the country. A connoisseur like yourself might be interested in some of my reviews."

I avoided making eye contact with my grandfather. Dominique had a brief fit of coughing.

"I'm sure I would learn a lot from you, Mr. Worth," Pépé said. "I'll ask my granddaughters for copies so I can read them while I'm here."

"Don't worry. I'll pull together a few recent ones and give them to Lucie. She can pass them along to you," he said. "At the risk of sounding immodest, they're quite good."

He left and Dominique and I grinned. "You were very polite," Dominique said. "You've probably forgotten more about wine than he knows."

"I hope his reviews are better than his French," Pépé said. *"Il parle français comme une vache espagnole."* I covered my smile with my hand at a uniquely French insult. He'd said Ryan spoke French like a Spanish cow. "As for you, *ma chère* Dominique, just since I've been here you are too busy to stay at the table with us for longer than a few minutes and you look exhausted. I'll have you know the old man has forgotten nothing. And you, Lucie, what Washington wine? What auction? You've said nothing to me about this."

He raised an eyebrow, waiting for explanations. Our grandfather may have feigned polite ignorance with dictators, but his own flesh and blood didn't get off so easily.

"I'll go first," I said to Dominique, letting her off the hook.

The auction intrigued him, especially Jack's donation of the Margaux. I avoided mentioning Valerie's remark about its provenance in front of my cousin because I didn't want to involve Joe. I'd tell him about it later. But I did say that Jack had no idea where the bottle came from.

"Jack Greenfield said he found it in a wine cellar belonging to his family's import-export business after his father passed away," I said. "In Freiburg. He told me the bottle is in such poor condition because whoever possessed it before he did didn't take care of it."

Pépé shrugged. "I find that quite plausible. A lot of the wine-producing châteaus didn't keep records of where their wines were sold until recently, nor modernize the way you Americans have done. Don't forget, until the 1950s some vineyards were still using cattle to plow their fields."

He paused to let that sink in.

"Wherever it came from," he said, "it's an extraordinary donation, even if the wine has turned. The person who acquires it will possess a memory bottle connected with two of your most famous Founding Fathers. The value is inestimable."

"A memory bottle," I said. "I've never heard that before."

"Every year on our wedding anniversary your grandmother and I drank a bottle of Clos du Vougeot from the year we were married. It's what we drank at our wedding reception. We called it our memory bottle."

"You never told us that," Dominique said.

"I think it's very romantic," I said.

"It was." Pépé smiled. "And of course there is such a strong link between wine and memory. I'm sure you both know that. Most of what people think they taste in wine is actually what they smell. Because scent is the strongest of the five senses, it can trigger memories we'd scarcely remember otherwise." He picked up his wineglass. "Who knows when we'll be together again, *mes enfants*? I think we should drink our own memory bottle tonight."

We touched glasses. I drank, but there was a lump in my throat. Dominique brushed something out of her eye. Though he seemed hale and hearty, I knew that it had been my grandfather's gentle way of reminding us he was slowing down and would not always be with us.

I closed my eyes and breathed in the scent of my wine, willing myself to memorize that link to this night and to him. When I opened them, I saw Dominique was doing the same. Our eyes met across the table.

Hers, like mine, were filled with nostalgia and melancholy.

When we got home, Pépé went directly to bed. I'd given him the room Dominique had lived in when she came to help take care of Mia after my mother died. After the fire, I'd gotten rid of the swimming pool–sized chafing dishes, sixty-cup coffee urns, and door-sized platters Dominique had stored in there for her catering business, turning it into a proper guest room.

The Jefferson diary lay open on my bedside table next to Valerie's book. I picked it up and leafed through the Foreword, which discussed Jefferson's tour in the vineyards of France, Italy, and Germany, and a brief trip to Holland, explaining that the trip was partly to quell an insatiable curiosity in everything around him and partly to indulge a lifelong passion for wine.

The diary itself was an almost encyclopedic catalog of everything Jefferson saw and did. I turned to the section on Bordeaux. He'd spent five days in the region from May 24–28, 1787, after passing through Italy. By then he was on his way back to Paris, wrapping up the first of his two voyages.

Jefferson wrote about the countryside in Bordeaux, naming four vineyards in the region which he said were "of the first quality"—Château Haut-Brion, Château La-tour, Château Lafite, and Château Margaux. More than two hundred years later, it was clear Thomas Jefferson had known his stuff. In 1855, at Napoleon III's insistence, the French instituted a classification system for French wine still used today. The four vineyards Jefferson listed in his diary were awarded *premier cru* or "first-growth" status, making them the top wines in France.

Jefferson's last Bordeaux entry dealt with wine merchants. After listing the principal English and French wine sellers, he wrote,

> Desgrands, a wine broker, tells me they never mix the wines of first quality but that they mix the inferior ones to improve them.

He was talking about blending—a practice used by forgers who mixed wines from different regions and even different countries, occasionally throwing in a little port, to produce a cocktail that could fool someone into believing they were drinking a first-class wine. All the wines Jack had donated were first quality, except the Dorgon. Had that one been blended, as Jefferson implied? If it had, how would I ever know?

Valerie had hinted that what she knew was significant. Whether or not the Dorgon was a mishmash of several inferior wines didn't seem that earth-shattering. I put the diary back on my bedside table.

I slept badly again. My nightgown chafed the cuts on my back, my skin felt like it had been stretched taut over my bones, and the bruises, now purple and green, were a lurid reminder of Valerie's death.

Something about what Jefferson had written in his diary bothered me, but I couldn't put my finger on it.

And the only two people who could help me—Thomas Jefferson and Valerie Beauvais—were dead.

Chapter 10

———❦———

The next morning when I woke, I heard snoring through the door of Pépé's bedroom. At home in Paris he never rose before mid-afternoon. With the jet lag—and how little sleep he'd gotten yesterday—I wondered if he'd stay in bed all day.

I made breakfast and set another place for him at the kitchen table, leaving a note that he could find croissants in the bread bin and cheese in the refrigerator. Usually he fasted for breakfast and lunch, making dinner his main meal, but maybe he'd make an exception since he was adjusting to the time change.

I drove to the winery and parked next to Quinn's El. The door to the villa was locked, so he was probably in the barrel room. I found him there, punching down the cap with Manolo and Jesús. The two workers smiled and said hello. Quinn barely looked up, mumbling "good morning" before going back to his task. I stood and watched, growing angrier by the second as I waited for some sign from him that we had some air-clearing to do. Instead he doggedly pushed the sludgy mass of grape skins below the surface of one of the fermenting vats with a large flat paddle and ignored me. I saw Jesús's uneasy glance in Manolo's direction. Manolo shook his head lightly.

No need to keep them in the middle of this.

"I'd like to see you in my office as soon as you're done here, Quinn." All three of them were bigger and taller and older than I was. I sounded like a student teacher in over her head, trying to discipline an unruly pupil. No one looked at me.

"In case you've forgotten, I own this vineyard," I said. "When I say something I don't expect to be ignored."

This time they all stopped what they were doing.

Manolo and Jesús nodded nervously. Quinn's head jerked up and his eyes locked on mine. I couldn't tell if he was embarrassed or furious I'd spoken to him like that in front of the men, but his machismo was his problem and too damn bad if he'd lost face. When I left the barrel room I closed the door harder than I needed to.

I still hadn't cooled off when I got to the villa. Gina flew out of the kitchen, holding a pot of coffee. Her eyes were huge.

"Oh, it's you, Lucie. I heard the door bang shut. Guess a gust of wind must have caught it." She stopped and stared at me. "What happened? Are you all right?"

If it had been Frankie with her calming, compassionate ways, I probably would have spilled everything. But not to lively, gossipy Gina, who began far too many sentences with, "I'm not supposed to tell you, but . . ."

Sharing a confidence with her wasn't quite as bad as telling Thelma Johnson over at the General Store or the Romeos, but it would still make the rounds. The only difference was that everybody in two counties wouldn't know by the end of the day. More than likely it would take a week or two.

"It's nothing," I said. "Just a gust of wind, like you said. Scared me, too. Sorry."

She poured me a cup of coffee and I told her I'd be at my desk. I glanced in Quinn's office on the way to mine. Kind of a cross between a low-rent motel room and a place where someone had nearly moved out. No photographs. Nothing personal. His cottage was the same. Maybe that's how he'd been able to keep his marriage a secret—acting like he had no past. I would never understand that about him.

An hour later the heavy wooden door between the library and our offices opened and closed. He went first to his office. A few minutes later, he showed up in my doorway and pulled the door shut.

He jerked a thumb behind him. "We've got customers. Gina's with 'em. If you're going to yell, might be better if they didn't hear."

"I'm not going to yell."

"But you want to."

"Yes." My voice shook. "I want to. What the hell happened yesterday?"

"I got stinking drunk, ma'am, and I shouldn't have. Reported for work totally inebriated and that's grounds for firing me. You can have my resignation on your desk, if that's what you want. I'll just go next door and write it." He was staring hard at me but his eyes were haunted and bleak. Like he was going to push this conversation to the absolute limit, test us both . . . see who cried uncle first.

It felt like I was talking to a stranger.

"Don't call me 'ma'am,'" I said, hurt. "Just . . . don't. And you know I don't want your resignation. But I do think you owe me an apology."

He bowed with mock formality. "Then I apologize. It will never happen again."

"Quinn . . ."

"What?"

"What happened?"

"I just told you." He wasn't going to back down.

"No," I said. "You told me nothing. I've never seen you do something like that before. Ever. I know you're upset about seeing her . . . and the fact that she's with Shane now—"

He cut me off. "You don't know *anything*!" he shouted.

"Then tell me! Just tell me!" I shouted back.

"You wouldn't understand."

That hurt, too. "Why?"

"It's complicated."

For a long moment we just stood there and stared at each other. I knew, just as sure as I knew he loved her, that he wasn't going to tell me how she had hurt him or what she had done to be able to still torment him like this.

I looked away before he did, picking up the first piece of paper I found on my desk. An unsolicited letter from another local limousine company who wanted us to use their services so our guests could sightsee without worrying about drinking and driving.

"I've got to take care of this right away." I indicated the paper. "I think we're done here. Apology accepted but I'll hold you to your word it won't happen again."

The fire in his eyes changed to ice and all his interior chambers slammed shut. "And I've got business in the barrel room, if we're finished. Don't worry, Lucie. It'll never happen again." He opened my door. "You want this open or closed?"

"Closed. Please." I managed to say it and still meet his eyes.

But the moment he left I reached blindly for the sweat-shirt I'd left on the back of my chair and buried my face in it until I no longer felt like the wind had been knocked out of me.

Amanda Heyward called mid-morning and asked if I could meet her at Mick's place to discuss the tent and a few other things about the auction. I hadn't seen or talked to Mick since the evening at Mount Vernon. Amanda didn't men-tion whether he would be there today or not.

Another complicated relationship with another compli-cated man. I seemed to collect them. Maybe Mick would be busy with his horses, but I didn't want to ask Amanda. Then she'd ask whether it was on or off with Mick and me and I didn't feel like discussing it with her. Especially since I couldn't answer the question myself.

"Sure, I can meet you," I said. "What time?"

"Four work for you?"

"See you at four."

"Are you all right, Lucie?" she asked. "You don't sound too good."

"I'm fine," I said. "Sorry to cut this short, but I've got somebody in my office."

"Sure, sure. Didn't mean to interrupt. See you later."

I hung up and swung my chair around, resting my bad foot on the credenza. For a long time, I stared at the wall.

Shortly after twelve someone knocked on my door. Not Quinn. Gina.

She poked her head inside. "I brought you lunch. Hope you don't mind." She opened the door all the way and set down a plate. A croissant filled with sliced avocado, sprouts, and Brie cheese.

She knew.

"Did you talk to Quinn?" I asked.

At least she didn't beat around the bush. "I didn't talk to anybody. Didn't have to."

"Oh God. Did those customers hear us?"

"Not everything. They left before you two were finished." She sat across from me in a wing chair covered in a pretty flame-stitch fabric. My mother had upholstered that chair. In all the years she and Jacques had occupied the offices Quinn and I now used, I don't think I ever heard them raise their voices at each other. "Want to talk?" she said.

"Not really."

She traced the fabric's design on an arm of the chair with her finger. "You had every right to yell at him."

"What do you mean?"

"Showing up for work drunk like that."

I closed my eyes and rubbed a spot in the middle of my forehead that had started to throb. "How did you hear about it?"

"Well, I didn't exactly hear about it from anybody," she said. "Just put two and two together after what happened just now. My boyfriend works at a bar over in Leesburg. Quinn came in so drunk he wouldn't serve him. Charlie took his keys and called a cab for him. I guess Quinn was in pretty bad shape for harvest yesterday, huh?"

Sometimes I should just keep my big mouth shut. "Yes," I said, "he was. Look, Gina, please don't say anything about this, okay?"

She stood up, her dark eyes big and serious. "Don't worry. I won't breathe a word." She made a zipper motion across her lips. "You can count on me."

After she left I stared at the sandwich. In two weeks, everyone from here to Richmond would know about our shouting match and my drunken winemaker. I had just started eating when I saw one of the phone lines in the tasting room light up on my phone.

Nah, not two weeks. It'd only take one.

After lunch I went back to the house to check on Pépé. I found him perched on the sofa in the library, smoking a Boyard, reading a battered copy of yesterday's *Le Monde*. He'd probably brought it with him from Paris.

I kissed the top of his head. "Did you eat?"

"I had a coffee. You know I never eat until dinner," he said. "I hope you don't mind, but I'll be going out shortly. One of my friends is coming to pick me up. I'll be at the International Monetary Fund for a meeting this afternoon, then dinner at the embassy. Don't wait up for me, *ma belle*. I'll probably be late."

He could still amaze me. "No grass grows under your feet, does it?"

Pépé smiled through a cloud of bad-smelling smoke. Boyards were unfiltered and had the highest tar and nicotine content of any cigarette on the market when they were still being produced. My grandfather's doctor told him to knock off smoking or it would kill him, but Pépé told him that at eighty-two he was going to die anyway and it may as well be doing something he enjoyed. The unmistakable acrid smell would be embedded in the house for weeks after he left, a lingering reminder of his visit haunting me like a ghost.

"Eh, bien," he said. "One likes to keep occupied, *n'est-ce pas?*"

The IMF meeting probably wasn't a courtesy call arranged for his benefit by a friend. More likely, they'd invited him to ask his counsel on some matter of trade or finance—and he was too modest to say.

"I have an appointment at four," I said, "but I'll be here when you get back."

Outside, tires sounded on the gravel drive. He folded his newspaper and set it on the coffee table.

"That should be my colleague and his companion. Until tonight, *mon trésor.*"

I walked him to the door and said hello to his friend, a man in his early nineties who had been one of Secretary of State Marshall's aides. I was happy to see that the companion—an attractive woman who looked to be in her sixties—was behind the wheel.

The phone rang in the foyer after they drove off. I picked it up and sat in a blue-and-white toile Queen Anne chair next to the table. A bust of Thomas Jefferson—one of Leland's prized possessions—watched me from an alcove across the room.

"Lucie, Jack Greenfield here." He sounded tense and businesslike.

"Hello, Jack."

"Probably best if I get right to the point."

"Sure," I said. Whatever the point was, it already didn't sound good.

"I've decided to withdraw the Washington bottle from the auction."

I sagged in the chair and closed my eyes. "Sorry, what did you say?"

"I said I've decided to keep the bottle. When all is said and done, it belongs in my family. I've had some time to think it over and I apologize for the inconvenience I might have caused. Don't worry, I'll give you something else. You'll still raise a lot of money."

What the hell was he talking about? Had someone gotten to him? Nicole Martin, maybe? She'd told Ryan she wasn't going back to California without that bottle.

"It's a lot more than inconvenient, Jack. Are you selling that wine to someone else?"

"Of course not!" He sounded insulted. "I just told you I'm keeping it."

"You're not selling it to Nicole Martin?"

"Who is Nicole Martin?"

He really didn't know? "Look, Jack, would you please reconsider—?"

"Don't make this difficult, Lucie. I feel bad enough already. But that bottle has been great for my business. I've been inundated with calls from all over the world ever since Ryan's column ran the other day."

Sure. So had we. People were coming out of the woodwork to attend our little auction. Now he wanted his prize donation back. How were we going to explain *that*?

I pinched the bridge of my nose. The headache that had begun after Quinn and I blew up at each other this morning now pulsed behind my eyes. There had to be some way to talk him out of this.

"You know how thrilled we were when you donated that bottle. Everyone at Shelter the Children has been beside themselves once they realized how much money it could raise and—"

He cut me off. "Stop right there. Don't make me out to be Scrooge. I won't stand for it. Besides, I'm not going to leave you with nothing. I'm swapping the Margaux for a jeroboam of Pétrus. You'll do extremely well with that."

Château Pétrus was another of the legendary Bordeaux, but we wouldn't do nearly as well as we would have done with a bottle destined for George Washington. All the magic that had enveloped the auction would vanish like smoke. But he wasn't going to change his mind and nothing I could do would persuade him otherwise. If he wanted the wine back, he wanted it back.

"I'll bring it by your house tonight. I have a meeting with Amanda Heyward at four so I can drop it off afterward and get it over with." I knew it sounded ungracious but I was mad and hurt.

He was as short with me as I'd been with him. "You can 'get it over with' tomorrow, please. Sunny and I are out this evening. And bring it to the house, not the store."

"Of course."

"One more thing."

I closed my eyes as lightning bolts stabbed the back of my eyes. What now? "Yes?"

"I'd like the Dorgon back. You'll thank me for that. I drank another bottle from that vintage last night and it had turned."

"You didn't find out until last night?" I asked. So he wanted me to return both Bordeaux.

"I would not purposely give you a bad bottle of wine." He sounded surprised. I had offended him again. "Please bring it with the Margaux."

"I'll bring them both tomorrow evening."

"Thank you."

"By the way," I said, "I was wondering if you knew Valerie Beauvais."

He hesitated a second too long before answering. "You mean that woman who was in the car accident the other day?"

Damn right I did and he knew it, too. I doled out rope. "That's right. The author. She followed Thomas

Jefferson's route through the European vineyards. Wrote a book about it."

"I know her by reputation," he said. "Knew her, that is. Never met her in person. Sorry, Lucie, I've got customers who just walked in. I'll see you tomorrow."

He hung up and I contemplated the bust of Jefferson for a while. Jack Greenfield just lied about knowing Valerie and I wondered why.

Did the reason he'd asked for the Margaux back have anything to do with her death? Jack's arthritis was so bad he had trouble corking wine bottles. He could hardly have loosened the lug nuts from Valerie's wheel, could he? Besides, why would he want to harm her?

Unless he'd found out what she knew about the Washington wine. Which I was about to give back to him so it could disappear into his collection, away from public scrutiny.

Forever.

Chapter 11

I took more ibuprofen and lay down for a few hours before my meeting with Amanda. When I woke my headache had subsided but my anger had not. I still thought Valerie Beauvais was mixed up with Jack's decision to withdraw the Washington wine, but I didn't know how or why. And then there was Nicole Martin and her client with pockets that went all the way to China. They say everyone has a price. I wondered what Jack's was. If Nicole offered him the moon and the stars for that bottle, would Jack sell his family's prize possession and reap a huge profit—or would he keep it like he told me he intended to do?

Amanda's Range Rover was already in Mick's driveway when I pulled up behind her and parked. Even though Mick and I shared a common property line, between us we owned more than a thousand acres, so it wasn't like we swapped cups of sugar across a backyard fence. It was nearly a mile between the entrance to my place and his.

Unlike my home, which had always been a working farm, Mick's place, with its parklike grounds, reminded me of an English manor house. Saucer magnolias and dog-woods lined the private road leading to his home. In the spring drifts of daffodils and tulips bloomed alongside the trees. The previous owner had a professional horticulturist put landscape labels on all the trees surrounding the formal gardens. Mick contacted the horticulturalist, offering him a job as full-time groundskeeper. Then he asked Sunny Greenfield to take on redecorating the house, giving her carte blanche so he could focus on his real love—renovating and upgrading his extensive stables. He'd also supervised the planting of thirty acres of vines.

Before he moved to Virginia, Mick owned Dunne Pharmaceuticals, a Florida-based mom-and-pop business he'd transformed into a multinational conglomerate, which he'd sold in a deal that made the front page of major financial newspapers. If he never worked again for two lifetimes, he'd still be richer than Midas. I wondered how long someone so restless would be content racing Thoroughbreds and growing grapes. I'd often wondered whether he was more captivated by the romantic notion of a gentleman farmer from Virginia than the reality of that life. One day would he wake up and discover he was bored?

A maid met me at the front door. "Mr. Dunne is in the stables, miss. He asked you to stop by when you've finished your meeting with Mrs. Heyward. She's waiting for you in the drawing room. You know the way, I believe."

I passed an enormous silver urn filled with several dozen red and white roses. If the Queen of England ever came for tea, she'd feel right at home. Sunny had knocked herself out redecorating the place and Mick had put no limits on what she could spend. The result was too grandiose for my taste but I knew Mick liked that kind of stately baronial splendor, even reveled in it.

I hadn't seen the drawing room since Sunny finished re-doing it in masculine shades of rust and royal blue. Persian carpets covered the floor, setting off the fine European and American antiques. The art looked like she'd borrowed a few treasures from a major museum.

Amanda stood by the fireplace, staring at a portrait of George Washington. She was dressed hunt country casual in a tweed blazer, silk blouse, and well-cut jeans. I joined her.

"That painting," I said. "Isn't it—?"

She nodded. "Yes. A Gilbert Stuart."

Maybe Sunny really had borrowed it from a museum. "Where did Mick get it?"

"Sunny wouldn't say. But Mick paid a bundle for it. Did you know Stuart painted over a hundred portraits of Washington? I had no idea there were so many out there."

"Me, neither. This one's fabulous."

"That's why I really want to hold the auction in the house, rather than a tent. This place is gorgeous."

"The tent might not be a problem anymore."

"What are you talking about?" Her eyebrows knitted together. "What's wrong?"

"Why don't we sit down?"

We sat on a large camelback sofa covered in pumpkin-hued brocade. Amanda's overstuffed planner and her paisley folder, now thick with papers, lay on the coffee table.

"Jack Greenfield is withdrawing the Washington bottle from the auction."

Amanda put a hand over her mouth like she was going to be ill. She closed her eyes, and when she opened them again, she looked tragic. "Sunny never said a word. I was just with her at the kennels."

"Maybe he didn't tell her."

"Well, shit!"

"I know."

"Why did he do it?" She picked up the folder and opened it. Then she closed it again. "Dammit, he *can't!*"

"He can and he did. He's giving us a jeroboam of Château Pétrus instead."

She looked like I'd said he offered us a bottle of hemlock. "That Washington wine was the centerpiece of the auction. Without it, we'll be lucky to fill the guest bathroom with whoever shows up."

"I tried talking to him, but he's made up his mind," I said. "We'll just have to live with it. Now we need to figure out how to let people know it won't be part of the auction."

Amanda threw herself back against the sofa. "We can't do that! I've been calling and e-mailing everyone on the planet crowing about that wine, for God's sake. We'll look stupid saying, 'Hey, guess what?'"

"We'll look more stupid when people show up and we can't produce it," I said. "Not to mention how angry everyone will be. They'll think we lured them into coming under false pretenses."

She glared at me. "God, what a mess! Have you told Ryan?"

"I haven't told anybody. Not even Quinn."

"Quinn." She tossed her head. "I heard a rumor about him."

"Oh?"

"I heard Shane Cunningham's hot new girlfriend is Quinn's ex-wife."

"From a long time ago." At least she didn't know about him showing up for work drunk.

"And he was drinking in Leesburg the other night. Got completely plastered."

"We're off the subject of the auction," I said. "And Quinn's love life is his own business."

Amanda's eyes narrowed. "Love life, huh? I thought they were divorced. Are you saying he's still in love with his ex? How interesting."

"Poor choice of words. Can we get back to the auction? I still think we need to tell people."

"Before we do anything, let me talk to Sunny. She might be able to persuade Jack to reconsider."

Sunny and Amanda were best friends. What did we have to lose?

"Good luck," I said. "He wants me to bring the bottle over to his house tomorrow evening. Can you talk to Sunny before then?"

"Oh, don't you worry," she said. "I'm on my way to see her as soon as I leave here."

We walked outside together. Amanda pulled out her car keys. "I'll follow you out," she said.

"I'm, uh, going to stick around for a while."

She smiled. "Really? Seeing Mick? You two still together?"

"He asked me to drop by the stables, that's all." I hoped she'd leave it alone, but I was blushing.

"He's quite a catch." She climbed into the Range Rover. "I heard you stuck it to the Orlandos the other day when they came by and asked you to close your farm to the hunt. They've got their nerve. Good for you for telling them to go to hell."

What, in my life, didn't Amanda know about? One thing about a small town, we lived in each other's back pockets—though that was part and parcel of the way people looked after each other around here. Neighbors who'd show up to help dig a garden, take down a tree, pull a car out of a snowbank, or drop off a meal because someone was ill. I knew I could never live in a big city where my next-door neighbor might be a total stranger. Maybe that was the problem with the Orlandos. They underestimated the bonds between families who had lived here since before the Civil War.

"I don't like being pushed around," I said.

She started her engine. "What did they say?"

"What you'd expect."

Amanda's glance flickered down at my cane. "You're just like your mother, Lucie. She had guts, too."

She drove off and I walked to the stables. Even if Amanda persuaded Sunny to talk to Jack, I still didn't think he'd change his mind about the Washington wine. In fact, less and less did I believe he'd told me the truth about why he wanted it back.

The wind had shifted during the day bringing in cooler air that sharpened the sky to a lacquered cerulean blue I had not seen for months. The Indian summer heat was gone for good.

I liked the ordered serenity I felt each time I walked into Mick's stables with their pleasant smell of hay and leather. His horses lived a regimented life—especially the ones being schooled. Ultimately, though, it was the animals that decided what they would and wouldn't do, and the trainers knew better than to try to force them otherwise. Mick raised Thoroughbreds, which he planned to race, some foxhunters, and two strings of polo ponies. To care for them, he had a staff of six grooms and exercise riders who reported to Tommy Flaherty, his Irish head trainer. Mick and Tommy had spent all spring and summer supervising the renovation of the farm's sprawling network of barns, stables, run-in sheds, paddocks and fields, as well as the repainting of miles of post-and-board fences, which divided his land like a giant checkerboard. Now that the work was finished, the place looked magnificent.

I glanced at my watch as I walked into the main stable. Just past four-thirty. Feeding time. Tommy had a rule about not letting anyone in the barns until after four o'clock during the months the Thoroughbreds were in training.

"These horses are athletes," he told me once, in his lilting, musical voice. "They train hard, darlin', and they need to get their shut-eye. I won't have anyone disturbin' them."

I checked first on my favorite—Black Jack—a Thoroughbred whose glossy coat fit his name. His feeding tub looked full, but he still came to the stall window when I called him and nuzzled my hand, looking for an extra treat. One of the grooms pulled a carrot out of his pocket and handed it to me.

"Got any apples?" I asked. "He loves apples."

"Give him an apple and he'll drool all over himself. He's just been groomed."

"Sorry, buddy," I said to Black Jack. "You heard what the man said."

"And what would that be?"

I whirled around. Mick stood there, looking amused.

"That apples are off-limits for Black Jack." My face felt hot. I should have asked the maid to tell him that I needed to return to the vineyard after my meeting with Amanda. I should not have come here.

"We'll make an exception for the pretty lady, all right, Jackie boy?" Mick nodded at the groom, who went to fetch an apple. "We'll clean you up again after that messy apple, won't we?" He rubbed Jack's nose as the groom handed it to me.

"How'd your meeting go with Amanda? She's running this auction like a bloody military campaign," he said.

I fed Black Jack, holding the apple while he ate. Gentleman that he was, he avoided chomping on my fingers, though he enjoyed his treat with teeth-baring gusto and a glint in his lovely, liquid brown eyes.

"Jack Greenfield decided to withdraw the Washington bottle this afternoon. He wants to keep it," I said.

Mick ran his hand down the horse's neck, studying him. "Sorry to hear that, but it makes sense. The intrinsic value of that bottle is out of this world. I'm sure Jack reconsidered now that it's getting so much attention."

"It doesn't make sense to me. Or the disabled and homeless kids who lost out."

He stopped patting Black Jack and considered me. "I'm sorry you're upset but you're thinking with your heart, Lucie. Jack's a businessman. I would have done the same thing."

"Then you're both cynics." I walked down to the tack room, leaning on my cane, and found a towel to wipe the apple juice off my hand.

When I came back, Mick pulled me close and brushed a lock of my hair out of my eyes. "I'm not a cynic, I'm a realist. Have dinner with me tonight. I'll cook for us. You'll be dazzled by my culinary skills."

"No." I didn't want him teasing me when I was angry. "No, thanks."

"You have dinner plans already?" He cupped my chin so I couldn't look away. "I thought not. It's settled. You're dining with me. I behaved appallingly the other night and I want to make it up to you."

"Mick—"

"Please." His voice was soft in my hair. "Say yes."

I knew I would regret this. "All right," I said. "Yes."

I finished making the rounds of the stables with him before we went back to the house. Our last stop was the stallion's barn and the stall which contained Dunne Gone, a bay with a white blaze on his face. Tommy was sifting through straw with a pitchfork, mucking the stall when we got there.

"You're keeping an eye on that hock?" Mick asked.

"Doc Harmon's comin' here first thing tomorrow when he does his daily rounds."

"Good. Get the farrier in, too. He needs to reset Casbah's rear shoe."

"Already taken care of."

Mick nodded. "See you in the morning, Tommy."

"'Evening, sir. Good evening, Miss Montgomery."

We walked back to the house holding hands. "Casbah's racing on Saturday at the Point-to-Point," Mick said. "Along with another of my maidens. I'd like you to come. Amanda's having her usual tailgate. We could meet there."

I knew—though he didn't say it—that he expected his horses to win at the Point-to-Point and he wanted me to see that.

"I'll bring my grandfather," I said. "He's visiting from Paris. I think you'd like him."

We had reached the terrace by Mick's swimming pool. When I'd been here last spring, he and I had spent many evenings watching the animals' beautiful silhouettes from this spot until the sun set behind the Blue Ridge and everything faded to black. When a horse is a champion he shows it. Even from a distance I had seen that regal elegance in Mick's horses. They knew their destiny and what they were meant to do. With the weather cooling off, he and Tommy had swapped the horses' routines so they now spent days outside and nights inside. Tonight I missed seeing them.

His housekeeper had already prepared dinner—steaks, baby vegetables, and a salad for two. All he had to do was throw everything together.

I looked over at the plates and cutlery already stacked on a silver tray. "When am I supposed to be dazzled by your culinary skills?" I said. "Is it when you set the table, or when you take the wrapping off that gorgeous salad?"

He grinned. "It's when I open the wine. Come on. I've got something I want you to try. Shane got me a couple of cases."

A bottle of Gevrey-Chambertin and two Biot wine-glasses sat on another tray on the drawing room sideboard. A Burgundy, this one from a *grand cru* vineyard in a part of France known as the Côte d'Or—the Gold Coast. It would be like drinking silk and velvet together.

I watched him uncork the wine. "Your drawing room looks lovely. Sunny did a wonderful job."

"She knows what I like," he said. "You'll have to see what she's doing to the guest suite upstairs. It'll be ready in a few weeks when Selena moves in."

One of his sisters? A cousin? "Who's Selena?"

"My goddaughter. Youngest child of an old family friend from the U.K."

"Why is she moving in?" I didn't like it that I sounded like a jealous girlfriend.

He didn't seem to notice. "She's been winning a lot of prizes in Europe riding show jumpers." He handed me a pale blue wineglass and touched his glass against mine. "Her father, Lord Tanner, thought perhaps she should get some experience in the States. I offered to let her stay here, though she'll probably also spend time in Kentucky. She just finished up at Cambridge and planned on taking a year off before working, anyway."

So she was about Mia's age—twenty-one.

"It sounds like a great opportunity for her." I drank some of my wine.

He took my glass. "You are so transparent," he said, and kissed me on the mouth. "I think of her as a daughter."

"I hate being transparent," I said, kissing him back. "And it's nice you're doing this for her. I mean it."

"Come on," he said. "There's something else I want to do."

He brought me to his bedroom and we were rough undressing each other. No tenderness or caresses or words. Our lovemaking was primal and intense, perhaps because it had been months since the last time. I could not tell what drove him, but my own fierce need came from an ache that had burrowed so deep inside me I'd almost managed to forget it existed. The need to be loved—no, to be *in* love—flared up like a dull pain each time he entered me, because I knew he didn't want to make any promises. Maybe didn't even need to.

What he gave in the moment was as good as it got. Sincere but not constant. Passionate but not besotted. In lust, not love. In the end, it was about flesh and comfort and nothing more.

When we finished for the last time he lay next to me, leaning on his elbow, trailing a finger from my forehead down my nose, my lips, my neck, between my breasts, then lower, hovering just before he brushed my sweet spot. Like he was dividing me in half. I shivered. He stopped. "What?"

"Nothing. That was wonderful," I said. "It always is with you."

"Stay tonight and it will be wonderful again."

"I wish I could, but I need to sleep at home. My grandfather."

"You need to sleep at home because of your grandfather?" He looked incredulous. "Can't he take care of himself?"

I pulled him down and kissed him. "Of course he can. But he's eighty-two and he just got here yesterday. I feel like I should be with him."

"You mean you'd rather be with him than me—"

"That's not true and you know it."

"Come on." All of a sudden he sounded all-business. "Let's eat. I'm starved."

He got up and put on his clothes. I picked up my things where he'd flung them and retrieved my cane.

"Give me a few minutes to pull myself together."

"Of course," he said. "Come outside on the terrace when you're ready. I'm going to start the grill."

We ate in his splendid dining room at a table that seated twenty-four. He moved two silver candelabras so they were at one end of the table and we sat across from each other. His dining room chairs reminded me of thrones. The paintings on the walls seemed to recede and the moss green curtains were drawn across the windows so the room was dark except for the flickering candles, which danced in an occasional current of air. We sat in a golden pool of light and talked quietly.

"I'll get another bottle of wine," he said.

"I've got to drive," I said. "That's enough for me."

"Your grandfather will be fine. Stay the night."

He opened the second bottle and I let him fill my glass. "If you're not careful we'll drink your entire cave."

"I rather doubt it."

"Buying that much, are you?"

He grinned. "And enjoying it. I've started buying futures, too. From Shane."

"When did Shane get into futures?"

"It's been a while. He told me he'd spent the last few years cultivating relationships with *négociants* in Bordeaux and a few of the boutique vineyards in California," Mick said. "He went to France last March for the *'en Primeur'* tastings. Raved about what he drank so I bought a few contracts in July."

Wine futures—like futures for any other product traded on the market—lock in a price of a vintage while it's still in the barrels. The purchaser bets the wine will be worth more down the road, after it's aged and bottled. If things go the other way, at least with wine there's always Plan B—drinking it. But while futures, especially Bordeaux futures, had been around for a while, it was an unregulated practice. Gambling with no one to police what went on.

"Futures are risky," I said. "You can lose a bundle."

"I like taking risks. And I can afford to lose." He looked me in the eyes and I was glad I never had to stare him down across a conference room table. In business, I bet he'd been merciless when he wanted something. He, too, had pockets that went all the way to China. He could match any price to get what he wanted.

"You sure Shane knows what he's doing?" I asked.

"Why wouldn't I be?" he said. "He's got great contacts. He introduced me to a wine buyer he's been working with. I'm thinking of hiring her."

I moved my wineglass to the side and leaned across the table. "You're going to hire Nicole Martin?"

"You know her? Yes, I think so. Why?"

"Do you know who she is?"

"You seem to think I don't."

"Quinn's ex-wife."

He spun a teaspoon on the table and watched the silver flash in the candlelight. "Does that disqualify her for some reason? I heard she was the best."

"No, it doesn't," I said, "but I don't trust her."

"So far I have no reason not to," he said. "But I'll keep that in mind."

I stood up. "I should go. Thank you for dinner."

He reached out and caught my hand. "Please don't."

"Mick—" But he was already pulling me into his arms, whispering that I needed to stay and that he wanted me again.

The Greek poet Aeschylus once said that wine is the mirror of the heart. With all the wine we'd drunk surely I should have been able to see into Mick's heart. But tonight I saw only shadows. Still I let him lead me back to his bedroom and the tangled sheets we'd left before dinner.

The last coherent thought I had before our lovemaking obliterated all other thoughts from my mind was that we were both doing this for the wrong reasons. When I looked into the mirror of my own heart I saw that in the not-too-distant future I would pay a price for my recklessness.

As for Mick, he wouldn't find what he was looking for in me. He was a gambler and a risk-taker. The more audacious, the better. Now he was into the occasionally gray area of buying wine futures from Shane, not caring if he got burned. And Shane had introduced him to the ruthless Nicole Martin, a woman who was apparently as addictive as heroin.

No good would come of his relationship with her. I was sure of it.

Chapter 12

I got up at two and dressed in a shaft of moonlight shining in through the bedroom window. Mick didn't stir. Mosby's Highway was deserted and the drive home uneventful. Good thing, since I didn't want to bet on passing a Breathalyzer test.

I climbed the spiral staircase in the dark so the hall light wouldn't disturb Pépé. But when I got to the second floor, his bedroom door stood open and the bed hadn't been slept in. My octogenarian grandfather was still out carousing on the town. I took two ibuprophen to ward off the effects of the alcohol in the morning and fell asleep in my clothes.

When I woke, Pépé's door was closed. What time had he come in? I scrawled a note and left it by the coffeepot, asking him to call me when he got up. On my way out the door to the villa, Kit called my cell. The display showed her office number in Leesburg.

"Someone's at work early," I said.

"Up getting the worm," she said. "I've got business in

Middleburg later. What if I make it around lunchtime and we grab a bite somewhere? I've got something to tell you."

Had she already decided about the Moscow job?

"Good news or bad?" I said.

"Neither."

"How can it be neither? What is it?"

"You'll just have to wait until lunch."

"You're no fun. Meet me at the Red Fox. Noon. I'll make reservations."

"I'm loads of fun. See you at noon," she said and hung up.

Shane Cunningham's Porsche was parked next to Quinn's car when I pulled into the vineyard parking lot. The villa was still locked which meant they were together in the barrel room. I walked through the courtyard. The early morning breeze was cool and the overcast sky obscured the Blue Ridge.

What business did Shane have with Quinn? The only thing they had in common right now was Nicole. One had her. The other wanted her.

But it was Nicole who was with Quinn, not Shane. I wondered if he'd loaned her the Porsche or if she'd borrowed it without asking. Shane was like Eli when it came to cars. If they had their way, they'd shrink-wrap passengers so they couldn't touch the leather seats or leave a stray fingerprint on any surface.

Quinn and Nicole were together at the far end of the room, engrossed in conversation. Neither looked up when I closed the door, though the thrumming noise of the fans, like the engine on a small plane, would have drowned out the sound. They stood directly under a spotlight near the winemaker's table, facing each other. The white concentrated light made them seem like heavenly apparitions.

I watched as Quinn leaned against one of the arches at the entrance to the bays and folded his arms across his chest. Nicole sat down in a chair so she faced Quinn. Her face was tilted toward his and her hands clasped together. She gestured as though she were praying—or pleading. He nodded as she talked. Reconciliation, maybe? An olive branch?

Whatever she said, he seemed to accept it and held out his hand. It was too late for me to leave or move or pretend I hadn't been doing anything but watching them. Quinn's eyes grew dark as they walked toward me.

"What are you doing here, Lucie?" In French there is an expression, *c'est comme des cheveux sur la soupe,* which means something is as welcome as hair on soup. He asked like I was the hair.

I decided against the obvious answer, that I owned the place and could be anywhere I damn well pleased. Nicole Martin watched me, sly amusement in her long-lashed dark eyes. For the first time, I had a chance to study her, too. Exotic-looking with high cheekbones and a heart-shaped face. Only her mouth, which, in an unguarded moment, settled into a sneer, ruined her beauty.

"The Porsche was in the parking lot so I thought Shane was visiting. I came by to talk to him." I looked at Nicole. "What brings you here?"

Quinn answered for her. "Nic wanted to see the Washington bottle before the auction. I'm taking her on a tour of the vineyard. We'll be back in a while."

I could tell by the way his eyes held hers that I'd been right and they'd made some kind of peace with each other. She smiled at him and his eyes grew soft.

"Enjoy yourselves," I said. They were still holding hands.

"I'm sure we will." Nicole turned the smile to me but her

eyes said to keep out of her business with Quinn. "Ready?" she asked him.

He nodded and I wished I hadn't decided to come by here after all.

"One thing before you go," I said.

Her delicate eyebrows arched. "What's that?"

"I'm surprised Shane didn't tell you Jack withdrew the Washington bottle yesterday. He wants it returned to his private collection."

I caught the flash of surprise in her eyes. "Of course he told me. The bottle's still here, so where else would I go to look at it?"

She'd come up with that retort fast enough, but she was lying. Either Shane knew about the wine and kept it from her, or Jack hadn't told Shane. I wondered which it was. So, probably, did she.

Quinn looked at both of us. His eyes were hard and I watched Nicole belatedly realize her error. "So how come neither of you ladies bothered to tell me?"

"Because Nicole didn't know and I only found out late yesterday." Maybe it was churlish to expose her, but it had been a dumb lie. Now maybe Quinn would think twice about believing what she'd just told him in the back of the barrel room. I said, "And you and I didn't get much chance to talk yesterday."

The shouting match in my office seemed like it had been a week ago, rather than less than twenty-four hours.

"No," he said, "we didn't, did we?" He looked at Nicole and hooked a thumb at me. "She right?"

She nodded like a child caught lying to a parent, but sure of forgiveness. "When are you returning the bottle?" she asked me.

"We're trying to get Jack to reconsider, so it's up in the

air." I had no intention of helping her plan her strategy for going straight to him so she could buy it.

"He won't reconsider. Get real." Nicole didn't bother to hide her scorn.

I wondered how I'd ever thought of her as fragile. Maybe that mistake was part of the reason she was so successful. People underestimated her and figured she was spun sugar instead of battery acid.

"The money was supposed to go to charity," I said.

Her shrug said who cared. "Things happen. That bottle is priceless."

"I heard you've got a client who told you not to leave here without it."

She smiled, showing the sneer, and her eyes were challenging. "Did you, now?"

"So it does have a price," I said.

"Which I'm prepared to pay." She looked at Quinn. "I have a way of getting what I want."

"I'll bet you do," I said.

"Maybe we ought to take that tour, Nic." Quinn made a cut-it-off sign in my direction. "Let everybody cool off a bit. Come on. The Gator's out by the barn. Let's go."

He tugged on her hand, pulling her toward the door. Before they left he turned around and stared hard at me. I shook my head and it seemed to seal things between us—Nicole and I had drawn battle lines and he didn't like it.

After they left, I brought the Margaux out to the long table and, with a light touch, set it down and stared at it. Tonight it would be back in Jack Greenfield's wine cellar—temporarily, that is, until Nicole Martin showered him with money and he parted with the bottle he'd said meant so much to him. I wondered if I'd ever hear how much Nicole paid and for whom she was buying it.

And what about the scene I'd witnessed between Quinn and Nicole? Had he fallen for her all over again? Surely he'd know what a mistake that would be—though who was I to give advice to the lovelorn, considering what I'd just done last night at Mick's place? Even though we were both probably going to get our hearts broken, to turn back now would be like trying to pour raindrops back into a cloud.

Shane's Porsche was still in the lot when I left to meet Kit at the Red Fox Inn just before noon. Where had Quinn taken Nicole on this tour? Charlottesville?

I walked by the Porsche on my way to the Mini, glancing through the windshield. A copy of Valerie Beauvais's book lay on the passenger seat. A piece of paper, like a bookmark, stuck out of the top. Nicole hadn't bothered to lock the car. Shane had installed a state-of-the-art alarm system and was so obsessed about that car I would have bet money he even locked it in his garage. If he found out Nicole left his precious baby unlocked and unalarmed, there'd be hell to pay.

I opened the door and picked up the book. The paper held her place at the beginning of the chapter on Bordeaux. I flipped to the title page. The dedication, surprisingly, was written in French.

> *Pour Nicole, en souvenir d'un temps sublime en France. Merci pour tout!*
> *Valerie*

Thanking Nicole for the fabulous time they'd spent together in France. When? During a tour of Jefferson's vineyards? A summer holiday together on the Riviera?

Was it just a coincidence that Nicole showed up in

Atoka with Shane a few days after Valerie's death, now that I knew they were friends? I doubted it. Maybe Valerie had told Nicole what she knew about the Washington bottle. Although if she did, Nicole would never share it with me. Instead she'd probably use the knowledge as leverage to make sure Jack sold her the Bordeaux.

I put the book back where I'd found it and drove to Middleburg, parking around the corner from the Red Fox. As I crossed the street at the lone traffic light at the intersection of Washington and Madison, two men walked toward me. One wore a baseball cap with a logo on it. "The Hunt Is On." The word *on* was a bull's-eye.

I decided to track down Nicole Martin after lunch.

The hunt was definitely on.

The Red Fox Inn had been around since colonial days—or at least, there had been a building on that site for nearly three hundred years. The sign hanging out in front of the building read "ca. 1728." The inn, which was now listed on the National Register of Historic Places, had been the heartbeat of Middleburg ever since the stagecoach days when it was a midway stop on the road from Alexandria to Winchester. During the Civil War, Colonel Jeb Stuart met the Gray Ghost here. One of the pine bars had once been a field-operating table for an army surgeon serving with Stuart's cavalry.

I got there before Kit did and was seated at a table next to the stone fireplace in the Tap Room. The fireplace still worked and, like the hand-hewn ceiling beams and the stone and plaster walls, dated back to the 1700s as part of the original structure.

Kit showed up fifteen minutes late, windblown and out of breath. She dropped her satchel on the red leather banquette where I was sitting and sat in the Windsor chair across from me.

"Sorry. I got stuck at the office." She looked me over. "What happened to you? You get any sleep last night? You look terrible."

"Thank you. Of course I got some sleep. You know how busy it gets at harvest." If I told her about Mick, she'd be all over me for details. Kit thought my sex life was like walking on the surface of the moon. Treacherous and full of craters.

We waved away menus and ordered the crab cakes, as usual. Kit asked for peanut soup and a beer. I had a glass of house red.

"I thought we might be breaking out the vodka to celebrate your imminent departure for Moscow," I said.

She stared at the collection of pewter tankards on the shelves next to the fireplace. "If we break out the vodka, it's because I could use a little liquid courage to help me decide. One minute I'm fed up with writing about the school board meeting and I feel like life is passing me by. I want to go somewhere and write about something important. A civil war or a world summit. Stuff that matters." She shifted her gaze and met my eyes. "Then I chicken out and figure I'll stay because it's just too damn far from my mom."

"Just because school board meetings don't make national headlines doesn't mean they aren't important. What they decide matters to lots of people."

"Yeah. Anyone with a kid in the school system. No one else cares."

"You finally tell Bobby?"

"I did. He said, 'You gotta do what you gotta do.' That's a direct quote."

"Sounds like Bobby. Not profound but nevertheless deep."

"He could have said, 'Baby, don't go.'"

"Maybe he knows how you feel about school board meetings and he wants you to be happy."

"I don't know anymore. Let's not talk about it. It's all I've been thinking about and it's driving me nuts."

Her soup showed up.

"So what's the news?" I said. "You said you had something to tell me."

She picked up a spoon. "You're not going to believe this. A couple of deputies from the sheriff's department came by. They confiscated Ryan's laptop and brought him down to the station for a little chat. At least they didn't cuff him."

"The sheriff thinks Ryan killed Valerie?"

"Right now they're just talking to him. He told me Bobby found an e-mail he'd written her that she'd saved on her computer. Unfortunately he wrote it the night before she died. Sometimes you should hit the delete button after getting something off your chest."

"What was in the e-mail?"

"A threat. Dumb, huh? You'd think he would have called. No paper trail."

"A threat like he was going to remove the lug nuts from her wheel?"

She rolled her eyes. "Sure. That's just what he said. Did you know he's considering insuring his nose because he uses it professionally? Ryan's body is his temple. If he'd wanted to kill her, it wouldn't have involved physical activity. He'd be too worried about cutting up his hands or something. What he did say was that when he got through with her the only thing she'd be writing would be her grocery list."

"I don't understand why he showed up at Mount Vernon to introduce her a few hours before he sent that e-mail if he hated her that much."

"I bet he was being paid."

I thought about it. "You're right. He was. Mentioned something about wishing he weren't such a whore and hadn't accepted."

"Because he's broke." Kit took a roll out of the bread basket and helped herself to butter. "Or at least, he's got money problems. I answered his phone yesterday when he stepped out. His landlord. Told me to tell Ryan his rent check bounced. Again." She raised her eyebrows and I could see her peach and green eye shadow. Kit applied eye shadow the same way she slathered butter on bread.

"What did he say when you gave him the message?"

"Are you kidding? At first I didn't want to pass it on because then he'd know I knew, but this guy sounded like such a bad-ass I figured I better do something," she said. "So I taped a note on a bottle of wine that was on his desk. He didn't bring it up, and I didn't either."

Our crab cakes arrived, steamy and fragrant, and we dug in.

"I wonder how he got into money trouble," I said. "He drives an old car, doesn't wear flashy clothes—where does he spend it?"

"Wine. Where'd you think?"

"That's a business expense."

"He buys *a lot* of wine," she said through a mouthful of coleslaw. "I'm always listening to him talk about how much he paid for some rare bottle of Château Whatever. I'm sure he's got a cash-flow problem. Plus he's buying stuff that's still in the barrel."

"Futures?"

"I guess. There's something else. You were right. Clay was actually thinking about letting Valerie work for us."

"No fooling? Wonder if Clay read her book. I tried to get through it. It was terrible."

"Clay's been lonely since his wife died. I don't imagine it was a decision he made with his head, especially after I saw her author photo. Blonde. Tan. Young. Clay probably ate her up with a spoon."

I stabbed a piece of crab cake with my fork. "I don't think Ryan killed Valerie. He came by the winery the other night to look over the donations for the auction since he's writing the notes for the catalog. We talked about her. He admitted he was glad she was dead but told me flat-out he didn't do it."

"Do you think he would have told you flat-out if he did?"

"Okay. But I still don't think he's guilty."

Our waiter seated two women at the next table. As he handed them menus he accidentally bumped my cane, which clattered to the floor. He picked it up, apologizing.

I took it and tucked it into the alcove near the fireplace. "My fault. I shouldn't have left it in your way."

He smiled and cleared our dishes. I ordered coffee and Kit asked for a cappuccino with a slice of chocolate torte.

After he left Kit leaned forward. "Sounds like you have an idea who *is* guilty."

"I know this might sound off the wall, but I think Jack Greenfield might be involved."

"No way. Jack Greenfield has arthritis. He could never have done it."

"He withdrew the Washington bottle from the auction

yesterday. Whatever you do, don't tell Ryan. Amanda is going to ask Sunny to lean on Jack to let us keep it."

Her eyes narrowed. "Jack asked for that wine back? Why?"

"He says it's too valuable to let go."

The waiter set down our coffees and Kit's dessert.

"How do you connect that to killing Valerie? Sorry, kiddo. This time I agree you're off the wall."

"Think about it," I said. "Valerie knew something about the provenance of that wine and died before she could tell anyone. Now Jack's taking the bottle back and he's either going to keep it in his wine cellar or sell it privately. If he sells it, I bet it will be to someone who wants to remain anonymous."

"So the bottle more or less disappears." Kit dumped three packets of sugar into her cappuccino and stirred so the spoon made clinking sounds against the mug. "Where would he find a buyer like that?"

"Nicole Martin knows someone."

"Shane's girlfriend. The wine broker."

"And Quinn's ex-wife."

"I heard about that over at the General Store. Everyone in Atoka's talking about it. They must have hated each other's guts when the divorce rolled around for him never to mention someone who looks like that."

"She came by this morning to see the Washington bottle. Afterward he took her on a tour of the vineyard. They left holding hands." I lined up her empty sugar packets in a neat row.

Kit watched me. "That bothers you, huh?"

"I don't like her very much."

"Is this about the green-eyed monster, Luce?"

"Don't be an idiot. Why would I be jealous of her?"

"You tell me," she said. "You know, I used to think you and Quinn cared about each other. At least a little."

The waiter set down the bill. "It's a professional relationship." I reached for the leather folder. "We're keeping it that way."

Kit rolled her eyes as I set down a credit card. "If you say so," she said. "Thanks for lunch."

When we got outside she glanced at her watch. "I'd better get back to work. You know how the place falls apart without me. You going back to the vineyard?"

"Not right away. I've got an errand to do."

"What are you up to? What errand?"

"I thought I'd track down Nicole Martin and have a chat with her without Quinn around."

"So you can talk about him?"

"No. So we can talk about the Washington bottle."

"I'll bet you talk about Quinn, too," she said.

After she drove off in her Jeep, I got in the Mini. Now that I knew Nicole and Valerie were friends, maybe I'd get some answers to my questions about Jack Greenfield and what Valerie knew about the Washington wine.

But Kit's words bothered me, too, like a dull ache that I knew wasn't going to go away any time soon. Was my animosity toward Nicole really petty jealousy?

Or was I right that Nicole Martin was nothing but trouble?

Chapter 13

————— ∞∞∞∞ —————

Nicole hadn't returned the Porsche to Jeroboam's after Quinn's tour. I drove past the store and down the alley to the small parking lot. Where else would she go with the car? Shane's place?

He lived in a rented cottage in Paris—Virginia, not France—the last town on the highway in what was known as Mosby Heritage Area. The name came from the city in France as a tribute to Jefferson's good friend the Marquis de Lafayette, but our Paris, unlike the City of Lights, was a tranquil village.

I turned west onto Washington Street, which soon became Mosby's Highway. Dead ahead, the Blue Ridge Mountains looked solid and comforting. Already ancient when the Indians lived here a thousand years ago, they had never been scoured by glaciers like the mountain ranges farther north, which accounted for their gentle speed-bump contours.

A few cumulous clouds speckled shadows on the foothills. I didn't know for sure why the mountains were blue— I'd heard it had to do with the pine trees releasing a chemical compound that caused a permanent bluish haze—but whatever the reason, the hue varied depending on the light, time of day, and season. Here the scenery turned to farmland as horses and cattle grazed in pastures and farmers mowed their fields for the last time this year. It looked as though summer had finally faded like an old watercolor.

The Porsche was just outside Paris, parked in front of a small convenience store. I pulled in as Nicole came outside, phone pressed to her ear, engrossed in conversation. Her eyes widened when she saw me.

"I've got to go," I heard her say. "Don't worry, I'll handle it. No, I haven't booked it yet. I'll call you later."

She snapped the phone shut and walked over to my car. Minis, by definition, are low-slung. Nicole wasn't tall, but she did have the psychological advantage of looking down on me.

"What are you doing here?" she asked.

"Looking for you."

I could tell I'd caught her off-guard, but then her blasé self-confidence returned. "Is this about Quinn?"

I kept my eyes on hers. Was I that transparent? "No. It's about you."

Her eyes roamed over me and my cane propped against the passenger seat. I'd seen that look plenty of times in the faces of people who believe those of us with disabilities asked for it or somehow deserved what we'd gotten. Her look said it all. It could never happen to her. I almost felt sorry for her arrogance and stupidity. Almost.

"You want to talk about the Margaux, don't you?" she said.

I moved to open my car door and she stepped back.

"Buy you a cup of coffee or a cold drink?" I said.

She squinted, appraising me like she was trying to figure out my angle. "You want to have coffee? Here?"

"Coffee's pretty good. They get it from a place in Lees-burg."

She shrugged. "Yeah, sure, I'll have a cup of coffee."

She came inside while I bought two coffees. When we were back in the parking lot I said, "Unless you want to talk here, I know a place that's not too far away. It's nicer and more private."

"Why all the secrecy?"

"No secrecy. It's just an interesting place. You might like it."

Another shrug. "I've got nothing else to do right now."

She followed me to the old Goose Creek Bridge. In high school, Kit and I used to sit on the stone parapet and watch the creek while we drank unlabeled bottles of wine I'd stolen from the barrel room. The bridge dated back to Jefferson's presidency but had been abandoned in the 1950s when Mosby's Highway was rerouted. Now the garden club looked after it. We parked on a nearby dead-end road and walked over to a rusted gate at the entrance that kept cars out, but not people.

"What is this place?" Nicole asked as we walked down the gravel path to the bridge.

"The site of a Civil War battle. In late June of 1863, Jeb Stuart's troops fought Union soldiers, hoping to delay them so Lee's army could get to Pennsylvania."

She looked around at the quiet hills and surrounding woods. "And did they?"

"No. Gettysburg was ten days later."

"The Civil War," she said, "is ancient history."

"Not around here. Gettysburg was one bloody campaign in Pennsylvania, but most of the war was fought right here on Virginia soil. Lee-Jackson Day is a state holiday."

She brushed a strand of hair off her face and stepped

up onto the parapet, staring down into the creek. "I'm sure that's fascinating for you, but I just can't relate to any of it."

I sat on the bridge and swung my feet so they dangled above the creek. "Have a seat," I said.

"Looks dirty. I'll stand."

"It's not dirty." I took the top off my cup and turned so I could look up at her. "Why did you go with Valerie Beauvais to the vineyards Thomas Jefferson visited in France, if you're not interested in history?"

She blew on her coffee. Mine was already tepid. Hers was, too. She was stalling.

"Valerie tell you that?"

"Valerie didn't get a chance to tell me anything before her car went off the road into this creek," I said. "A few miles farther upstream."

Nicole wrapped her hands around her cup. "Shane told me what happened. You're the one who pulled her out."

"I did," I said. "It was too late."

She sipped her coffee. "I was sorry to hear about her death."

She didn't sound that sorry. "It's a murder investigation," I said. "The sheriff doesn't think it was an accident."

"Somehow I'm not surprised."

"Why not?"

"I'm just not. Valerie didn't always get involved with the best people." I wondered if she included herself in that group. Nicole continued sipping. "You didn't tell me how you knew we were together in France."

"If I do, will you answer a question?"

"Depends. What's the question?"

"What you know about the provenance of the Washington wine."

"Sure," she said. "Be happy to."

As easy as that. "Your copy of her book was on the passenger seat of Shane's car. My apologies, but I looked at the inscription."

"You've got a hell of a nerve."

"Valerie was on her way to see me when she died. She was going to tell me something about that bottle," I said. "I figure you're the only other person who knows what that was."

" 'Fraid not," she said. "I can't help you."

She threw what was left of her coffee into Goose Creek and it disappeared into the water below, along with my hopes.

"Can't or won't? You were there," I said. "You were with her in Bordeaux."

Her lips curved as she seemed to take stock of my logic and where this conversation was going.

She shook her head. "You've got it wrong. Not Bordeaux. I bumped into Valerie in Epernay. The Champagne region. I was with a few friends who liked to party. She joined us."

"What about her book?"

"She sent it to me. Wanted me to show it to some of my clients because she hoped they might be interested in buying it."

It still didn't mean Nicole hadn't talked to Valerie about the Bordeaux. I wasn't ready to give up.

"Either you heard about the Margaux from Valerie after she read Ryan Worth's column or Shane told you when he found out Jack was donating it—even before Valerie would have known. So maybe you went back and had a conversation with her."

"You seem to think we were best friends," she said. "It was a business relationship. We talked about her book."

"What about the Margaux?"

"What about it?"

"Did she say anything about its provenance?"

"Not to me." Nicole tapped her index finger against her mouth, as though she were debating something. "I examined that bottle this morning, remember? As far as I'm concerned, it's real enough. More important, the right people *believe* it's genuinely a bottle of wine bought by Thomas Jefferson for George Washington." Her expression was scornful. "Come on, Lucie. A lot of wine collecting is done off the books between buyers and sellers once it leaves the château. There is no paper trail. Who can say for sure where it originally came from?"

"Or bother to try finding out," I said. "Right?"

She smiled with a trace of a sneer. "Right."

"What are you going to do now?"

She shrugged. "Go back to Shane's place."

"I meant about the wine. You work out a deal with Jack yet? Or is Shane helping you with that?"

"Shane." She rolled her eyes. "He'd be the last person I'd ask."

"Trouble in paradise?"

"Paradise. What a laugh." She wasn't laughing. "The sex is good enough, I suppose, but I'm done with him. Thanks for the coffee. I've got to go."

"You never said whether you've made a deal with Jack yet."

"Me to know and you to find out, sweetie." Another derisive smile. What had Quinn ever seen in her?

"Maybe you shared the news with Quinn." I leaned on my cane and stood up. "By the way, how did your tour of my vineyard go?"

She looked away. "It was nice."

"Leave him alone, Nicole. Leave him in peace."

She squeezed her Styrofoam cup and it split open.

"That's none of your business." Her façade suddenly seemed to be cracking. Right along the fault line.

"He never told anyone here he'd been married," I said. "He never talked about you."

I should not have said that, but in a day or two she'd walk out of his life again and I'd be left watching him go through whatever private hell he still lived in when he thought of her.

She placed a hand over her heart like she was covering a wound. "You have no right to judge me. I was young. He was my oldest brother's best friend. I was just a kid." Her voice shook. "He knew me since I was ten, watched me grow up. We eloped the day I turned eighteen. I had to get out of the house and he—" She stopped as the tears fell down her face.

"I'm sorry." I meant it.

"I have to go." She smeared her eyeliner and mascara when she wiped her eyes, so they looked like two bruises. I watched her walk toward the gate as though she was leaning into a strong wind.

She turned around. "You don't deserve to know this, but he cares about you, Lucie. Why, I'm not sure."

She slipped through the gate and ran to her car. After she left I sat back down on the parapet and watched the waters of Goose Creek flow toward the Potomac, feeling somehow shamed by Nicole Martin who had—in the end—been kinder to me than I'd been to her.

She did not have a deal with Jack Greenfield—yet. At least I didn't think she did. She probably wouldn't leave town until she did. I did not want to see her again while she was here and I hoped that she would not meet up with Quinn.

As it turned out, I did not get either of my wishes.

Chapter 14

When I got home Pépé was in the library sitting in his familiar place on the sofa reading *The Economist*. A Boyard sat in an ashtray and his half-finished cup of coffee looked cold. He never could get used to American coffee but then I couldn't drink the high-octane brew he loved without feeling my heart slamming against my chest. He smiled when I came into the room.

"Any good news in the world? Where did you get *The Economist*?" I kissed him on the cheek and sat next to him. The legendary animus between the French and the British—"the frogs" and *"les rosbifs"*—went back to Joan of Arc, but my grandfather was broad-minded. He read the British press.

"The usual. The world is falling apart but at least intelligent people are writing about it, which makes it seem more palatable." He closed the magazine. "One of my colleagues drove me to the General Store in Atoka but we did not find it there, so we went to Leesburg."

"I'm afraid Thelma only stocks local papers," I said.

"And the tabloids, because she's addicted. I'm sorry you had to go all the way to Leesburg."

"I enjoyed it. We passed in front of Dodona. I see they've made General Marshall's home a museum." He shook his head and reached for his cigarette, relighting it. "I had dinner there a couple of times when I was at the embassy. I feel like a dinosaur, *ma belle*."

"You are *not* a dinosaur."

"Apparently one now needs an appointment to see the house." He puffed on his cigarette. "I also had a nice chat with your Thelma. She was asking about you. And my visit here. And anything else I could tell her."

The General Store was a chokepoint for all local gossip and Thelma, who'd been around since God was a boy, did the gentle choking. Maybe it was her vampy, flirtatious ways, or her dress-to-kill wardrobe, but she had an almost mystical ability to wangle information out of everyone who dropped by. Very little got past Thelma's trifocals and bat-antennae hearing.

"Did she bleed you dry?"

Pépé grinned. "We could have used her in the Resistance. Don't worry, I didn't say much. I think she likes me."

"That's because you're such a charmer. I guess that means you've replaced her previous boyfriend. Some hunky doctor from one of her soap operas."

"Not such a dinosaur after all, eh?"

I leaned my head on his shoulder. "Want to go for a ride? I'd like to show you around the vineyard. And there's something I want to ask you."

I got his jacket from the closet in the foyer.

"I see you still have Leland's guns locked up," he said. "I saw the gun cabinet in the library."

"I probably ought to sell them," I said, "since no one uses them now."

He slipped on his jacket. "And what about you?"

"You know I don't hunt or shoot."

We took the Mini instead of the Gator, because it was more comfortable and Pépé could use the ashtray when he smoked. Since Hurricane Iola back in August, we'd had almost no rain and had been warned to be careful with matches and open fires. My grandfather listened as I told him about this year's harvest while we drove through the established vineyards. Next I showed him the new fields and the vines we'd planted last spring.

"Your mother would have been pleased that you are expanding," he said. "You are like her. Both so ambitious."

We had stopped at the split-rail fence, which surrounded the larger of our two apple orchards. In the fall we opened it to the pick-your-own crowd, who had been coming steadily for the past few weeks. After last weekend, the trees were nearly bare of fruit.

Pépé smoked quietly and stared at the Blue Ridge.

"Are you all right?" I asked. "Is it about my mother—?"

"A little. But I have also been thinking about the past on this visit—the old days," he said. "There are not so many of us left for this reunion, I'm afraid."

"That must be hard," I said. "You miss your friends, don't you?"

"Yes." He smiled but his eyes were sad. "Did you know that some of the money from the Marshall Plan helped the French vineyards get back on their feet after the war?"

I knew the stories of how the Germans had moved into the premier wine-producing regions of France and commandeered production. Thousands of cases of the best French wine had been shipped to Germany to sell on the international market to help pay Hitler's crippling war expenses. Lesser vintages went to their troops on the front.

"I knew the vineyards were in a bad way," I said.

"You cannot possibly imagine how much wine the Nazis stole—how they looted the vineyards and châteaus." His eyes grew dark and his voice was suddenly strident. "What they took was as bad as plundering art from the Louvre. Do you know when the French finally arrived at Hitler's hideaway on that mountaintop in Berchtesgaden they found over half a million bottles of our best wines? And that was only for Hitler, a man who did not drink." My grandfather's normally serene face contorted with anger. "They took whatever they needed—even using it for industrial alcohol when they were desperate."

"Did you have anything to do with getting the Marshall Plan money to the vineyards?" I wanted to get him off the subject of Nazi thuggery. His face had turned an unhealthy shade of red.

"No, I was in Washington during that time. But some of my colleagues were involved." He sounded calmer.

"You never really told me what you did during the war." Family lore was that he'd been a spy in the Resistance. I suspected my grandmother knew the truth, but as far as I knew she was the only one.

I wondered if he would tell me now.

"I was in France—well, Occupied France. And Spain." He stubbed his cigarette in the ashtray, grinding it until it was nearly dust. "We got Allied airmen who had been shot down across the Pyrenees to Spain. Our escape trail was called 'the Comet' because we moved so swiftly."

More than half a century later, that's all he would say. "You must have some incredible stories."

"We did what we had to do. It was a time of man's

worst inhumanity to his fellow man. It must never happen again." He placed his hand on mine. "Enough sad talk. You said you had something to ask me, *ma chère*?"

"Let's go to the barrel room," I said. "I'll get a thief so we can sample last year's Cab. I'd like your opinion of how it's developing. After that I want to show you the Washington bottle."

"I would like to see that wine," he said. "And an aperitif would be nice."

The parking lot was empty. Frankie and Gina had closed the tasting room since it was after four. Quinn's El was gone. A few days ago Frankie asked what I planned to do about planting fall flowers in the border gardens and in the barrels and hanging baskets in the courtyard. Sera had always taken care of it, but now that she was in Mexico nothing had been done. The summer impatiens, petunias, salvia, and geraniums looked tired, thinned out, and faded.

"I don't know what to do," I'd said to Frankie. "I haven't really thought about it."

She'd waved a garden flyer under my nose. "Leave it with me. Okay if I make some changes, or do I have to do what Sera did?"

"You can do whatever you like."

She must have taken care of it this afternoon because when Pépé and I walked into the courtyard, the hanging baskets spilled over with yellow and white winter pansies and the halved wine barrels were brilliant with yellow, rust, and burnt orange mums. The surprise was the scarecrow, dressed as a farmer, except for the Hawaiian shirt, which she'd obviously pinched from Quinn. He sat on a hay bale next to the old Civil War cannon that was said to have been fired in the Battle of Middleburg. At the base of the cannon and the hay bale, Frankie had placed more pumpkins and mums. I could have kissed her. The courtyard looked wonderful.

I turned on the fans as soon as Pépé and I entered the barrel room. Already the primary fermentation, begun at harvest, was showing signs of slowing down. The cauldron-like bubbling and foaming had diminished to a simmer.

I got out the thief and two wineglasses. Pépé opened the bunghole of one of the barrels while I placed the glass thief—which resembled a chubby open-ended thermometer with a handle—inside and sucked a small amount of last year's Cabernet Sauvignon into the chamber. Pépé reclosed the cask immediately to keep out fruit flies as I released wine into our glasses.

My grandfather swirled the contents of his wineglass, then put his nose in and sniffed deeply. I watched as he let the wine roll around in his mouth. The Cab still had one more year to mature in its barrel before we bottled it, but nevertheless we both would have a good idea of the wine it would become. I tried not to think of Pépé among his colleagues in the *Chevaliers du Tastevin,* tasting and evaluating some of the world's fabulous wines as I waited for his verdict on my one-year-old Virginia Cabernet.

Finally he said, "Good nose. Nice structure. The finish is developing nicely. You make good wine, Lucie."

"Do you mean it?"

"Would I lie to you?" he said. "Now let's see that famous bottle."

I brought out the Margaux and set it down in front of him at the winemaker's table. He reached into his breast pocket and pulled out his reading glasses.

"Formidable," he said. *"Un vrai Margaux.* I have never seen one of this age but I have seen others that were well along in their years."

"Do you think there's anything wrong with it?"

"Wrong—how?"

"I don't know. Valerie Beauvais learned something about this bottle when she was in Bordeaux. I have no idea what it was."

He examined the lettering, touching a finger to the date—1790. "Perhaps, even though the wine is old, it is not from that year. Maybe the lettering was etched later."

"Then how can we tell how old the wine is?"

"You would need to open the bottle and test it. Carbon-dating. The process is expensive. You would need a special laboratory."

"I wonder if Valerie saw another bottle just like it in France?"

"Or a similar one."

"That could explain why Jack wants it back. To keep it from further scrutiny," I said, "because he knows what she saw."

"You realize it would still be difficult to ascertain the precise year, even with carbon-dating," he said. "The most you can prove is that the wine was not made in the late twentieth century. If it were, the amount of Carbon 14 would be higher due to the nuclear atmospheric tests of the 1950s and 1960s." He shrugged. "Otherwise all you know for sure is that it dates from sometime between the late 1600s and the mid-1900s."

"Three hundred years! That's no help."

"Unfortunately, no."

"Would you kill to keep information like that a secret?"

Pépé looked startled. "*Mon Dieu,* of course not. Besides, anyone could be fooled. There have been many scandals involving fake Bordeaux over the years because the wines are so sought after."

"I have to return this bottle tonight. Along with a bottle of Château Dorgon. Why don't you come with me? I can introduce you to Jack."

"I'm sorry, *ma belle,* but I have a dinner engagement. Perhaps I could meet him another time." He polished his glasses on the sleeve of his jacket. "You have a bottle of Château Dorgon? May I see it?"

"Of course."

I got the Dorgon. Pépé put on his glasses again and examined the bottle.

"I haven't seen one of these for many years. The château stopped making wine after the war. Why are you returning it?"

"Jack drank another bottle recently and said it had turned."

"Quel dommage."

"I know," I said. "A real pity."

We drove back to the house with Jack's wine bottles, which I had repacked in the original shipping cartons from Jeroboam's. Pépé went upstairs to change.

While I waited for him, I called Amanda to see if she'd had any luck persuading Sunny to talk to Jack.

"She's on our side," Amanda said. "She thinks Jack made a big P.R. faux pas donating it, then asking for it back. But she won't talk to him."

"Why not?"

"I don't know. She just clammed up and said, 'You deal with him.' So I did."

"What did he say?"

"Well, I talked to him, but he finally hung up on me."

"I guess that means I'm driving over there and returning it."

"We're in a hell of a mess."

"Why don't you call Ryan," I said, "and tell him what happened. He'll get the word around that the wine will no longer be at the auction and we'll just deal with the consequences."

"Before I do I'm going to pour myself a very tall glass of Johnnie Walker Blue," she said, "and spend the evening trying to figure out why Jack Greenfield is being such a son of a bitch."

"Enjoy yourself."

"Only if you promise that when you see him you'll kick him in the shins for me."

I hung up as Pépé came down the stairs, dapper in a charcoal suit with a red and gold paisley tie and matching pocket handkerchief.

After he left, I drove over to Jack's. I was not looking forward to this errand.

Sunny met me at the front door, cocktail glass in hand, a pleasant but questioning smile on her face. "Lucie, what a surprise. What can I do for you?"

"I should have called," I said. "But Jack did say tonight."

She glanced at the carrier in my hand. "Did we invite you to dinner?"

She looked serene and elegant in a long Indian-print caftan. Her shoulder length hair, which she usually wore pulled back or in a French twist, hung loose around her face, making her look younger than a woman in her mid-fifties.

"Your husband asked me to come by tonight and return these. The auction bottles. Is this a bad time?"

She waved me in with her glass. "No, no, it's not. And I'm sorry about the misunderstanding over these wines. I'm having a vodka tonic. Jack's still at the store going over something with Shane. Join me?"

"Thanks, but I can't stay." Misunderstanding?

The Greenfields lived in a converted stable that had once been part of a larger estate. When the original owners fell on hard times in the late nineteenth century, they divided the land and sold it in three parcels. Jack's and Sunny's property came with several outbuildings from the larger place, including a small one-story tenant cottage they'd converted into Jack's wine cellar.

"At least come in for a minute," she said. "For your trouble."

I relented and stepped inside.

A plain glass vase filled with dusky orange hypericum berries, coral Gerber daisies, and dark peach sweetheart roses sat on a table in the foyer.

"You probably want to get this over to your wine cellar right away." I set the carrier on the floor next to the table. "Unless you want me to do it?"

"We've got a small temperature-controlled cellar downstairs." She smiled at my surprised expression. "Yes, I know. Two cellars. A real extravagance. I'll put these bottles there myself. Thanks for offering."

"No problem." I gestured to the floral arrangement. "Your flowers are lovely. Did you do that?"

"Yes, for Jack. He gets such pleasure from the simplest things. I never fuss with making big professional-looking arrangements. My clients' homes may end up in *Architectural Digest* but Jack likes his own home to be gemütlich. Good old down-home German charm."

Sunny had made a fire in the stone fireplace. Schubert's Trout Quintet came through two speakers in the bookcases on either side of the mantel. Her needlepoint—something floral—lay on the sofa.

"Sit, sit. Take Jack's chair by the fireplace. I know it's not really that cold outside but it felt good to make a fire," she said. "Can't I pour you something? How about a glass of wine? Come on. There's some Cabernet Sauvignon open. French. I'm not drinking alone now that you're here."

I sat. "All right. One glass. Thanks."

She handed me the wine and took up her needlepoint as she sat down on the sofa. "I hear you got some pressure from the Orlandos to close your farm," she said. "Amanda said you told them to go to hell."

"Something like that."

"They're serious about trying to outlaw foxhunting, you know." Sunny reached for a pair of glasses and put them on, focusing on her canvas. "Stuart Orlando had a meeting at his house the other day to jump-start the whole thing. They're going to try to slam us in the media, fight it out in the court of public opinion." She looked up. "Place articles about how cruelly we treat the hounds. What we do to the poor fox."

"How do you know about the meeting?"

She slipped her feet out of ballet flats, tucking her legs gracefully beneath her on the sofa. "A friend of mine got wind of it and asked if she could go along. The Orlandos don't know everyone in town yet." She pulled rose-colored floss through the canvas, looking pleased with herself.

"Can I change the subject?"

"Not if it's about that Margaux."

I watched her stab the needle again, this time with a jerky motion, and asked anyway. "Do you know if Jack met with Valerie Beauvais before she had that accident? The historian who was murdered."

"I know damn well who Valerie Beauvais was. I read the papers. I would have known if he met her." More stabbing.

"So he didn't."

"I just said so."

"Then why is he withdrawing the wine?"

She set down her needlework and took off her glasses with some care. The gesture seemed to age her. "I'm going to tell you something. And it better not go any farther than this room. Jack told me that his father got that wine from a friend as a thank-you gift after the war. My father-in-law was sent to France in a Nazi uniform but he was sympathetic to the French because he had so many friends in the wine business. You can imagine what would have happened to him if word got back to Berlin about some of the things he did. Jack's father took tremendous risks to help old friends and former business associates."

"Did Valerie know about this?"

"She chose to believe lies. That he betrayed the French during the war."

I wondered if Sunny realized she'd just contradicted herself about Jack knowing Valerie. She massaged her forehead with her fingers and reached for her drink.

She realized.

"Look, Lucie, you and I have no idea what it was like during the war. My father-in-law did the best he could under impossible circumstances. He still had to obey his superiors. Who are we to judge some of the choices he made—and who was *she* to judge? Valerie was going to drag Jack's family through the mud. Bring up their Nazi past and humiliate my husband for no good reason other than to further her book sales. Can you imagine what it would do to his business? Let it go, can't you?" Sunny finished her drink and got up to refresh it. This time she didn't add much tonic.

I waited until she sat down. "I could," I said, "if somebody hadn't killed Valerie. You know, don't you, that this gives Jack a motive for wanting her dead?"

She sat up ramrod straight. "How dare you? I was with Jack all evening. We had dinner at the Goose Creek Inn with Shane, then came home and went to bed."

"Somebody killed her," I said.

She looked like I'd slapped her. "Not my husband. You can see yourself out, Lucie. Thank you for dropping off the wine."

I set my partially drunk glass of Cabernet on her coffee table. As I left the room, I glanced at her needlework. In the middle of a yellow flower she had taken a few stitches with rose-colored floss.

"I think you've made a mistake." I pointed to the canvas.

She was watching the fire and didn't turn her head. I let myself out. The needlework wasn't her only mistake.

Chapter 15

A pickup truck with a flatbed trailer showed up in my driveway the next morning while I was still drinking my coffee. The driver was a young, athletic deputy sheriff.

"I'm here for your car," he said when I answered the front door.

"You're what?"

He pulled a folded paper out of his pocket and looked at it. "Montgomery? Donating a Volvo station wagon to the sheriff's department?"

"Of course. Sorry," I said. "Let me get the keys. And the registration."

One night last summer as I was driving home from the Goose Creek Inn, the front end of Leland's ancient Volvo collided with the back end of a deer as it emerged from the woods and tried to cross Atoka Road. In all my years of driving it was the first time I'd ever hit anything. I wasn't hurt—Volvos are built like tanks—but my mechanic took one look at the car, which had more than two hundred thousand miles on it, and told me to put it out of its misery, like Animal Control had done with the deer.

I'd nearly forgotten I promised to give the car to the sheriff's department after Bobby Noland told me they were always looking for vehicles to use on their training track to add realism to simulated high-speed chases. The SWAT team liked to try out new ammo on something besides a paper target and the fire department sought out opportunities to practice extinguishing vehicle fires or using the Jaws of Life. If the Volvo—the car I'd learned to drive on as a kid—had nearly come to the end of its days, at least it would go out with style.

"It's not that road-worthy anymore," I told the deputy. "Are you sure you're going to be able to use it on your track?"

"Don't worry," he said. "I work at the CRU. Our mechanics are tops. We'll go over it before we run it. Can I take those plates off for you?"

"Sure. Thanks." So he worked for the Crash Reconstruction Unit.

He got a screwdriver from a toolbox in the truck. The front plate, which had been on the car since Leland bought it, was rusted to the holder.

"Did you work on the SUV that went into Goose Creek about ten days ago?" I asked as he knelt by the front bumper and tried to unscrew the license plate.

"Yes." He gave up and went around to the back of the car. "Why? Did you know the victim?"

The back plate came off with no trouble. He got a different screwdriver and worked on the front plate again, this time concentrating on the holder.

"I pulled her out of the creek."

He stood up and his glance strayed to my cane. "I heard about that. Pretty gutsy." He handed me my license plates. "Sorry I couldn't get that front one out of the holder for you."

"It's okay. Thanks."

"Detective Noland told me he'd take care of getting you a donation letter. I'll call him and let him know we finally picked up the car. I apologize for taking so long to get to you. I think I caught you off-guard when I showed up this morning."

"A little," I said. "By the way, did you find anything else when you went over that SUV besides the wheel coming off?"

If he was surprised by my question, he didn't let on. "We gave our report to the guys who are handling the case, but it's still an ongoing investigation so I can't comment," he said. "And one more thing."

"Yes?"

"Don't forget to turn those plates in to DMV."

Bobby called later that afternoon when I was in my office and thanked me again for the Volvo.

"Much appreciated, though it's going to be weird seeing it out on the track," he said. "I remember being in it with Eli when we were in high school. And some of the stuff we did—"

For a moment I remembered the high school boy who used to be a regular in detention hall and how I'd tutored him to earn honor society service hours because he was flunking algebra. He was smart enough, but back then he thought algebra was, as he used to tell me, as useful as tits on a bull.

"Tell me about it," I said. "Eli never would."

"Better not," he said. "The statute of limitations isn't up yet."

"That's a joke, right?"

His heh-heh laugh was all I got. "I can drop your letter off this afternoon since I need to come by."

"Buying some wine?"

"Talking to your winemaker."

"Is he in trouble?" I asked.

"I just want to talk to him."

"About what?"

"This and that."

"Come on, Bobby, it's me. What's up?"

"I need to ask him about an acquaintance of his."

"Oh," I said. "Nicole Martin."

I heard him let out a breath. "I understand she's Quinn's ex-wife. Also that she's here in town."

"That's right. Is *she* in trouble?" Maybe Bobby'd figured out how to connect her to Valerie and the Washington wine.

"Sounds like you know her, too."

"I've seen her a couple of times. She dropped by here yesterday."

"What for?"

"To look at a bottle of wine Jack Greenfield donated for our auction. Actually, donated, then asked for it back."

"I heard about that. That wine is supposed to be worth a bundle," he said. "You talk to the Martin woman yourself?"

Knowing Bobby, he already knew the answer to that question and all the others he'd just asked.

"Yes."

"Yes, what? Don't play games with me, Lucie."

"Okay, okay. Nicole was friends with Valerie Beauvais,

so I asked Nicole if Valerie talked to her about the provenance of Jack's wine," I said.

"Provenance?"

"History of its ownership."

"Why would Valerie talk to Nicole about that?"

"Because they met up in France when Valerie was doing research for her book," I said.

"Is that so? What'd Nicole say?"

"That as far as she was concerned the wine was genuine." I left out her comments about the muddiness of documenting the trail of ownership of a two-century-old wine. "And that she and Valerie didn't discuss the subject of provenance."

"Huh."

Something about his noncommital tone made me realize he knew they'd spoken and he was trying to fit what I'd told him into what he could already confirm. The deputy from the CRU who picked up my Volvo said they'd just wrapped up their investigation on Valerie's car. They must have found something—her cell phone, maybe?

"You got the records from her cell phone, didn't you? So you know they talked to each other recently?"

"No comment." But he sounded irritated, which meant I'd guessed right.

I wanted Quinn to hear from me that Bobby would be dropping by and it wouldn't be a social visit. I knew I'd find him in the barrel room running the Brix tests on the Cabernet since we needed to determine whether or not primary fermentation had finished and the sugar had fully converted to alcohol. Once that happened, we'd press the wine and add bacteria to start the malolactic, or secondary, fermentation.

As I expected, he was in the lab recording test results. Now that the weather had cooled off he'd retired the

Hawaiian shirts until next spring. Today he wore faded jeans and a Henley shirt with frayed cuffs. The Hawaiian shirts were loose and baggy. I couldn't help noticing that the Henley, which looked like it had shrunk with wear, revealed how muscular and fit he was.

He threw down his pencil when he saw me. "What's up?"

We hadn't talked since he gave Nicole the vineyard tour yesterday. "You finish Brix?"

He squinted at me. "It's around thirteen. I want to take the free run juice before we press. So we have at least two or three more days before it goes to zero and we start ML fermentation."

"Sounds good."

"You could have called, if that's all you wanted to know," he said. "Something's up. You've got that bug-eyed look you always get when you're trying to pull a fast one. I can tell every time. What's going on?"

Sometimes I wondered why I bothered trying to spare his feelings since he usually ran over mine with an eighteen-wheeler. "Bobby Noland's coming by to see you."

"He say why?" He focused on something over my head. Who was he to talk about conning someone? He may not have known why, but he sure knew who.

"He wants to ask you some questions about Nicole."

He kept his voice bland. "Is she in trouble?"

"Bobby knows she knew Valerie Beauvais."

"How do you know that?"

My mother always said if you tell the truth then you don't have to remember what lie you made up. "She had a copy of Valerie's book. It was inscribed to her. I saw it on the seat of Shane's car when you two were taking your tour of the vineyard."

"You really have it in for her, don't you? Why can't you stay out of this?" He banged his fist on the metal lab table. A beaker that had been sitting next to his calculator bounced and hit the concrete floor. It shattered and glass flew everywhere.

"Stay out of *what*? Why did you have to break that beaker? She lied to you yesterday and and I'm pretty sure she lied to me, about what she and Valerie talked about before Valerie died. Bobby already knows, Quinn. So don't you go lying to protect her, okay?"

Quinn looked at the floor and then he looked at me. "I think it would be a good idea if you left. There's a lot of broken glass here and you might cut yourself."

The two feet between us could have been the Grand Canyon. Trying to keep him from getting dragged into whatever Nicole was involved in was like throwing dust into the wind. Either it was going to get thrown back in his face or it would blow away and he'd be left with nothing. Whichever way it went with Nicole, he was going to lose.

"You don't need to worry about me. I'm not the one who's going to get hurt." My voice shook I was so angry. I gestured to the floor. "You better be careful, when you clean up the mess you made. I'll see you later."

An hour later I watched through my office window as an unmarked Crown Vic pulled into the parking lot. Bobby got out and headed directly for the barrel room. He left about forty-five minutes later.

I wondered what he had asked and what Quinn had told him. But I did not go back to the barrel room to ask.

That night Quinn went to the summerhouse. I saw the red flashlight as I finished putting away my dinner dishes. Pépé was out with friends for the evening once again.

I got my jacket and a flashlight. As I crossed the lawn, I shone the light to make sure he'd know I was coming. Once I passed the rosebushes I switched it off to preserve his night vision.

He was setting up his telescope next to the Adirondack chairs, with the red light propped on an arm of a chair so he could see what he was doing.

"I knew you'd come," he said without looking at me. "You want to know what Bobby said."

I was tired of this war between us. "I came for you," I said. "We're barely speaking. I can't take it anymore."

This time he did turn his head. "Have a seat."

I sat and laid my cane on the ground next to my chair. The chilly night air had swept away the clouds that had hung over the Blue Ridge at sunset. The moon looked like a scuffed silver coin in a star-filled sky.

"Are you all right?" I said.

He threw himself in the other chair and pulled out a cigar from his jacket pocket. "I've been thinking about Pluto."

"Pardon?"

"Pluto. One minute it's the ninth planet in the solar system, the next it's bumped off the list and relegated to being a dwarf."

"That's what's on your mind?" I didn't smell alcohol on him. Why was he talking about that? "Pluto?"

"Despite the demotion it's still the same ice ball it always was. Still takes 248 years to revolve around the sun because of its wonky orbit. Nothing's changed except what people call it."

"That's too bad." I watched him light his cigar. The flare of the match illuminated his face. He, too, looked the same as he always did, even though he sounded like he'd temporarily lost a marble or two.

"In its planet days, it was the planet that ruled Scorpio."

"Really?" I read my horoscope for fun and believed it when it suited me.

"Nic's a Scorpio. She's really into all that voodoo junk."

I waited.

"Did you know," he said, "that Pluto's moon—Charon—is bigger than it is and they orbit in a kind of dumbbell formation like they're permanently locked in a power struggle to see which one can dominate?"

"I did not know that."

"Kind of a metaphor for our marriage," he said.

"I'm sorry."

He expelled a cloud of smoke. "Don't be. It's over. You know what else? It's the goddamn planet of power and destruction and corruption. That is my beautiful ex-wife to a T. Almost makes you believe all that horseshit."

"This is about what happened with Bobby today, isn't it?"

"You know it is." He was angry. "And you can stop pretending you're not glad you were right about her."

"I am *not* glad about anything and I am *not* going to be your whipping post again!" I was mad, too. "Until four or five days ago I never even knew you'd been married. How the hell would I know, anyway? You don't talk about your past—your life in California—anything. You came to Virginia like you dropped in from—" I waved my arm above my head. "Someplace up there. No history, no nothing." I picked up my cane and stood up. "I'm going inside. I'm sick of you jumping down my throat no matter what I say. I understand why you don't want to talk about Le Coq Rouge but—"

"Don't go." He wrapped his hand around my wrist like a vise. "Sit down and I'll tell you. You don't understand anything."

I sat but his voice scared me.

"She was screwing Alan." He sounded hoarse with anger, shame, and remembrance. "On top of everything else he did to me. She was in that whole scheme with him but I covered up for her so she could walk away free and clear without doing jail time. I left town with a goddamn cloud over my head because of the scandal and the trial. You have no idea what it was like—the way people looked at me."

Alan Cantor was the winemaker at Le Coq Rouge. So Quinn's old boss and his wife had had an affair, on top of the wine fraud and embezzlement, which finally forced the vineyard to close. I waited for Quinn to continue.

"When I left, I never wanted to see her again. Then she showed up here." He expelled a long breath of smoke. "Shit, I just about died."

"I'm sorry. I know it's been rough for you since she's been here."

His mock-laugh almost sounded like a sob. "Rough. Yeah. That's one way of putting it."

"Does Bobby think she has something to do with Valerie's murder?"

He rubbed his forehead with his thumb. "I don't know. Wouldn't surprise me if he did."

"What did he ask you?"

Quinn looked at me. "I knew you wanted to know."

At least in the darkness he couldn't see my face burning. "Please tell me."

"He asked about our relationship. When I was with her, whether I had any contact with her before she came to Atoka."

I'd never thought of that. "And did you?"

"Jesus, Lucie. No."

The wind had picked up. I shivered and pulled my legs

up into the chair, wrapping my arms around them. "It's cold out here. Come on. Why don't we go inside and have a drink?"

"You go," he said. "I'm not cold. I'd like to stay right here."

"Then I'll stay, too. I don't mind."

"No, thanks. I'd rather be by myself. No offense."

I stood up and reached for my cane again. The chasm between us was beginning to narrow, but it was still there.

"See you in the morning," I said.

"Tomorrow's Saturday," he said. "I'll be in to check the Brix and make sure the cap's punched down but otherwise I plan to get lost this weekend."

"Oh. Well, sure. See you Monday, then."

"Yep."

I left him and walked back to the house. Nicole was ruled by the planet of death and destruction and corruption, he'd said.

And here we were, right in the middle of her maelstrom.

Chapter 16

I woke up early Saturday and went downstairs in my bathrobe to make coffee. On the way to the kitchen I looked through the parlor window to see if Quinn's car was still in the driveway, though I doubted he'd spent the night in the summerhouse with the temperature dipping into the forties. The car was gone but a bright red trail of something led up the gravel driveway toward the house.

I opened the front door. If I hadn't looked down, I would have stepped on the bloodied, gutted animal on the doorstep. I cried out and moved back. A dead fox.

Or meant to be. A stuffed animal. I'd seen him in a couple of shops in town—Freddie the Fox, bright-eyed, tail pointed straight as an arrow, feet positioned as though he were on the run, and a goofy, sly smile on his face.

Someone had ripped Freddie open and poured red paint on him, leaving his "entrails" for me to find. I listened at the bottom of the staircase in case my shriek had wakened Pépé but there was no sound from the second floor. Thank

God, because I didn't want him to see someone's twisted idea of a prank.

I went back upstairs and got dressed. Freddie's final resting place was a black plastic trash bag, which I left in the old carriage house we used as a garage. It seemed like a good idea to hang on to Freddie, at least for a while. A few minutes with the garden hose, the nozzle turned to a hard spray, washed away the paint until the pale pink rivulets disappeared into the border gardens and bushes.

That was the end of the fox, except for the image still in my mind. Somehow such a juvenile act didn't seem like something Claudia and Stuart Orlando would pull to get their point across about foxhunting. But if not them, who else was angry that I planned to let the Goose Creek Hunt ride through my farm in three days? This afternoon Pépé and I planned to watch a couple of Mick's maiden horses run in the GCH's fall Point-to-Point. Whoever left Freddie on my doorstep probably expected me to be upset enough to react—maybe even call off the meet at Highland Farm.

I put away the hose and decided to keep my mouth shut.

From an oak-shaded ridge overlooking 112 acres of green velvet hills that tossed and rolled, spectators gathered to watch Thoroughbreds gallop across the vast, sweeping panorama of Glenwood Park. On the far stretches of the four-mile course, the horses and riders would look like toys as they cleared fences of brush or timber. I liked coming here for the spring and fall races. For all the breathtaking beauty of Glenwood, the atmosphere was less formal and less pressured for the horses, owners, and jockeys than the big-purse races like the International Gold Cup held nearby at The Plains.

The relaxed mood spilled over to the tailgate picnics where people with kids and dogs in tow sauntered from group to group to mingle, chat, drink, and eat. It was possible to feast royally at these events—smoked salmon, caviar, pâté, champagne served in Waterford flutes, fine wine in Riedel stemware, and handmade chocolates and exquisite cakes for dessert. The drinks were kept on ice and served off the tailgate of a Range Rover or Mercedes station wagon. The food—sometimes catered, sometimes homemade—was arranged on tables with pretty tablecloths and matching napkins. Fox- or horse-themed decorations and elaborately arranged flowers in antique silver urns or crystal vases were centerpieces. I liked the grace and easy flow of these parties and the chance to see so many friends and neighbors on a cool sun-spattered afternoon.

Amanda always had a betting pool at her tailgate, asking guests to make dollar wagers on each race. The maiden races were pure fun because the horses were unknown and untested in racing, which meant bets were often placed because someone liked an interesting name or the color of the jockey's silks. The winner always donated the money to one of Amanda's charities.

Her position as secretary of the Goose Creek Hunt gave her the clout to secure a railside space next to the finish line for her picnic. Although post-time wasn't until one o'clock, I knew from experience that her party started at eleven when the gates opened. It was twelve-thirty when I parked the Mini on the grass field behind the paddock where dozens of cars and trucks had already lined up in ragged rows. Pépé and I walked toward the enclosed area reserved for patrons, past a line of empty horse trailers. Today all the horses that were racing were foxhunters since the Point-to-Point was the GCH's annual fund-raiser.

Mick, I suspected, would be in the owners' tent near the stables and the jockeys' area though he'd promised to join us once the races began.

As we got closer to the paddock I saw Shane Cunningham on a chestnut Thoroughbred, talking to Sunny Greenfield. He wore his foxhunting Pinque, the red jacket that supposedly got its name from the British tailor who first made them, and a black hunt cap. Though he wouldn't be racing, he'd be out in the field once the races started, working as an outrider to bring back any horse that got away from its jockey. He waved an arm over his head when he saw me and Sunny turned around. When we got to the paddock I introduced them to my grandfather.

Sunny was cool but polite. "You'll have to excuse me. I'd better get going," she said. "I have an appointment with a client in Charlottesville."

"You're missing your own Point-to-Point?" I asked.

"Can't be helped. I think it may turn into a big job." She glanced at Shane. "I'll talk to you later."

She nodded to Pépé and me. After she left there was an awkward silence and I wondered what she and Shane had been discussing.

"I hear your neighbors are trying to get you to close Highland Farm to the hunt," he said to me. "Are they giving you much grief?"

I thought about Freddie. "Nothing I can't handle."

"Good for you. So we're still on for Tuesday?"

"Of course."

"Okay if I come by before that and check the jumps and fences?"

Shane was one of the Goose Creek Hunt's whippers-in, which meant he not only helped the Master of the Hunt but also was responsible for controlling the hounds—catching stragglers and making sure the pack stayed together as they chased the fox. Though the name sounded savage, a whipper-in didn't abuse the hounds. Instead he rode ahead with the pack, often alone, before the other members of the hunt joined him.

I was glad he was conscientious enough to check in advance that nothing was damaged or broken before the meet, especially after what happened this morning. If whoever dropped Freddie off at my door decided to do some real harm out in the field, a rider or horse could get hurt.

"Of course you can come by," I said. "When would you like to do it? We've been letting one of Quinn's friends hunt deer lately since we're overrun. I need to make sure no one's out shooting that day."

"How about Monday morning?"

"Monday's fine."

He touched his hand to his cap. "Thanks. I'd better go. They're calling the riders to the starting line."

"We'd better go, too," I said to Pépé.

We got to Amanda's crowded tailgate as the race, a novice flat, was about to begin. The horses, four-year-olds and up, had never won a race on the flat and would run for a mile and a half on turf only—no jumps or hurdles.

"You're too late to bet." Amanda sounded disappointed as we joined her at the fence where a dozen jockeys and horses waited for the starting gun.

"We'll bet next time," I said. "Sorry we're late. I had to take care of something at the vineyard."

"The riders are up." The voice, which came over the speaker from the tower next to us, spoke soothingly. A moment later the same calm voice said, "And away they go."

Amanda watched the course through binoculars as the

horses moved farther away. "Good Lord," she said. "I think I bet on a dud. Well, forget that race."

"It's only a dollar. And you give it to charity," I said.

She lowered her binoculars and clutched her wide-brimmed hat as a gust of wind rustled the leaves in a nearby oak tree and blew others that had already fallen to the ground in a small whirlwind around us. "I still like to win," she said. "Come on. Let's get some champagne."

We made our way through a crowd of her friends and family who clustered around the buffet tables or congregated in small groups with their food and drinks. A few older guests sat in the camping chairs, which had been arranged in rows facing the racecourse. People dressed up for these parties—women wore dresses or skirts and jackets with jewelry or scarves with foxes or horses on them. Men dressed in blazers, buttoned-down shirts, and khakis; the horses and foxes showed up on ties, cuff links, and belts.

The fashion exception was a teenage girl who leaned sulkily against Amanda's car with the martyred expression of someone who'd been ordered to show up or else. Black makeup and clothes—lips, eyes, and nail polish on chewed fingernails went with tight, ripped jeans, high-topped black laceless sneakers, and a ratty jacket. Her lower lip and nose were pierced and she wore a studded leather collar around her neck that looked like it belonged on a dog. It took me a moment to recognize Amanda's daughter Kyra. The last time I'd seen her, a few years ago at a landowner's party given by the Goose Creek Hunt, she'd been a pretty, sweet-faced girl with honey-colored hair. Now the hair was midnight black and streaked red like bloody stripes.

Amanda noticed her, too. "Excuse me a moment," she said and walked toward her daughter. She kept her voice low but Kyra, who looked as though she'd come to prove a point and embarrass her mother, did not.

"I told you I didn't want to be here." She folded her arms and looked away. "There's nothing wrong with the way I'm dressed. I look fine."

"Kyra—"

The girl bent and picked up a dirty satchel from the ground. "Can I go now? I have to meet someone. I showed up, didn't I?"

Amanda looked as though she were trying to salvage whatever she could from the situation. "I want you in by midnight."

Kyra slung the satchel over her shoulder and gazed at her mother with a look of contempt and incredulity. "I'll be in when I feel like it." She turned to leave. "Stupid cow."

"Kyra!"

Her daughter walked away, head down and satchel bouncing on her back, but with a spring in her step that said she wasn't sorry she'd just humiliated her mother in front of her friends. I felt sorry for both of them but I knew what I'd just witnessed was probably nothing compared to what went on at home.

After my mother died, Mia decided to pay God and everyone else back for her loss by getting into as much trouble as possible as fast as she could. Her downward spiral and the screaming matches with Leland over boys, school, booze, and drugs scared and exhausted all of us. No one knew if she was prepared to go past the point of no return when there'd be no saving her. I used to lie in bed at night and wonder whose life had become the living hell— Mia's or the rest of the family's? Then I would try to recall the past and which cracks she'd slipped through that I'd missed seeing, until finally one day I woke up to find my sweet baby sister had become a raging, rebellious stranger. Though Mia had calmed down since then, we still weren't out of the woods. Last spring she'd nearly gone to jail after a drunk driving accident had resulted in a death.

Amanda stood with her back to us, watching Kyra walk away. When she joined us, two bright red spots flamed on her cheeks.

"I apologize for my daughter and her bad behavior." Her voice was stiff with embarrassment.

"No apology necessary," I said. "You probably won't believe this, but she'll grow out of it. Mia did."

Amanda looked at me like she was trying to focus on my words. "Not if I don't kill her first. There's no reaching her, nothing we can do or say." She gestured around her. "All this—she says it's materialistic and pretentious. Says she loathes the way we live. Of course it didn't stop her from taking the car we bought her. Or her horse. Or spending the summer backpacking in Europe when we paid for her."

As she spoke, Pépé left and went over to the drinks' cooler. When he came back he handed us two glasses of champagne.

Amanda's hand shook when she took it. "Thank you, Luc."

"Are you all right?" I asked her.

She sipped her champagne. "I will be. Sorry. I shouldn't be talking about any of this. Look, the race is nearly finished. Let's see who won."

Mick arrived just before the third race to watch Sweet Emma, one of his three-year-old mares, run in the maiden flat race. It was the first time I'd seen his colors—blue and white squares with a red stripe in between and red trim on the collar and cuffs. The jockey's red, white, and blue cap reminded me vaguely of a Union Jack.

He kissed me on the cheek and shook hands with Pépé. After a few pleasantries he moved on to the rest of the crowd—more social kisses for the women and a genial arm around the shoulders of the men. His kiss had been cool and dry and seemed devoid of affection. It was one of the many things I didn't understand about him—his ability to turn his emotions on and off—and it kept me off-balance. Maybe he wanted it that way or maybe he was trying to keep our relationship private, but the second-guessing and uncertainty about where I stood with him on any given day was growing tiresome.

"I'd like to invite your friend to dinner," Pépé said in my ear as Sweet Emma won and Mick opened a new bottle of champagne with a loud pop that sent liquid fizzing all over his hands.

Mick laughed and his eyes met mine. He blew me a kiss and a few women standing next to him noticed.

"It's a nice idea, Pépé, but I don't know—"

"I would like to become acquainted with this man who flirts with my granddaughter in front of everyone."

"He's not flirting—"

He clicked his tongue. "Lucie," he said, "a man knows when another man is flirting with the woman standing next to him. Give an old Frenchman some credit."

I smiled. "Okay, you can invite him to dinner."

But Mick already had dinner plans. "I'd love to," he said. "Unfortunately it's business and I just can't get out of it."

"If it's not late when you finish, come join us for dessert and coffee," I said. "Or a brandy. We're taking the last seating at the inn since my grandfather prefers dining after eight."

Mick caressed my arm with the back of his hand. "I'll

try, but I think it's going to go all evening." He looked at Pépé. "Thank you for the invitation, Luc. Some other time, I hope. Lucie has spoken so much about you."

"Mick!" Amanda called. "Are we betting on Casbah in this race or not? The riders will be up in a few minutes."

Mick had entered Casbah, a black gelding with a white snip on his nose and two white socks, in the next race, which was three and a quarter miles over timber.

"Of course we're betting on him. He's going to win." Mick pulled out his wallet and handed Amanda a hundred-dollar bill. "Here you go."

"The bets are a dollar," she said. "Though I'll take it since the money is going to the Loudoun Hospice."

But when the jockey riding Casbah came up to the starting line, the horse balked and didn't want to take his place. Mick looked tense as the jockey trotted Casbah in a small circle, talking to him quietly. Finally the horse seemed to calm down. When the gun went off, he bolted ahead of the others, holding on to a lead of at least ten lengths for the first two miles.

"He looks good," Amanda said to Mick.

"I don't know," Mick said. "Alberto is having trouble holding on to him."

As he spoke one of Casbah's hind legs caught a timber jump and the horse stumbled. He managed to recover but Alberto lost his seat and tumbled to the ground. The jockey did not get up, remaining motionless as the rest of the field bore down on him. Unless the others coming up the hill realized what had happened and changed course, Alberto would be trampled to death.

The normally calm voice over the loudspeaker now sounded alarmed. "It looks like Casbah's jockey has taken a fall. He's not getting up—"

"Get up, Alberto, get up," Mick said next to me, like a prayer. "Jesus, please. Get up."

I saw one of the outriders go after Casbah, who was veering wildly, then suddenly Shane seemed to fly out of nowhere, galloping at full speed toward Alberto, who had gotten to his feet.

"Shane's going after him," Amanda said. "I don't think he has enough time—" She put her hand over her mouth.

"They're both going to be killed," I said. "The rest of the field is coming up too fast."

"Give me your binoculars!" Mick stood up on the fence for a better view and grabbed them from Amanda. "Come on, come on. Do it, Shane. Get him!"

I held my breath as Shane reached out a hand to Alberto, who grabbed it, and swung up behind him in the saddle just as the next horse cleared the jump, followed by the rest of the field.

I met Mick's eyes. His face was ashen but he managed to smile.

"Remind me never to play chicken with Shane when we're hunting." Amanda had crushed her racing program in her hands. "That was incredible."

"Bloody hell. It was close," Mick said. "I've got to go." He squeezed my arm. "See you."

"Your friend is very brave," Pépé said to me. "A superb horseman."

"You should see him play polo," I said. "He's fearless."

Pépé and I left after the race. As we walked back to the car, I saw Shane in the paddock being congratulated by the other jockeys, grooms, and owners. I wondered where Nicole was. Maybe she really was done with Shane, as she said.

I got my answer back at the vineyard. Frankie and Gina

had spent a busy afternoon selling wine along with two waiters from the Goose Creek Inn. Most of the tables on the terrace were still occupied but we were closing within the hour. The crowd would begin clearing out, though I knew many would linger as long as possible.

My octogenarian grandfather flirted with Gina while Frankie and I went over the day's sales in my office.

"You all right, Lucie?" she asked when we were done. "You seem distracted."

"I'm fine. Did Quinn stop by today?"

"No, and you aren't the only one looking for him. Nicole Martin showed up. You just missed her."

"She came to see Quinn? That explains why she wasn't at the Point-to-Point with Shane."

"If you ask me, she was just killing time. Said she had a dinner meeting with Mick Dunne later on." Frankie raised an eyebrow. "What's that all about?"

I felt something break apart inside me. "I saw him at Glenwood and he told me he had a business dinner this evening." I tried to sound nonchalant. "He's planning on hiring her. Wants her to find him some out-of-this-world vintages for his collection."

Frankie eyed me. I hadn't fooled her. "Sorry, hon. She wasn't dressed for business."

I gave up the pretense. "Thanks. I needed to hear that."

"Okay, she was wearing sackcloth and ashes and she looked like hell. Feel better?"

"No."

"I thought it wasn't that serious between you and Mick. You both seem sort of loosey-goosey about your relationship. Besides, if you ask me, he's nothing but heartache. Too selfish to commit to anyone."

I picked up her stack of sales receipts and straightened

them so the edges were aligned to perfection. "Sometimes he reminds me of Leland the way he acts around women."

Although my father's indiscretions had been conducted away from home, I'd found out about them after he died. When I looked back, his laissez-faire attitude toward his wife and children probably explained why my mother had thrown herself into working so hard at the vineyard. And why she'd filled the void in her marriage with a close—and romantic—relationship with my late godfather.

As Tolstoy said, every unhappy family is unhappy in its own way. Mine had parents who remained married and in love—except they were in love with other people.

Frankie shrugged. "I didn't know your father, but you deserve better than a guy whose leitmotif is that it's all about the thrill of the hunt. On and off a horse."

That night at dinner Pépé ordered a spectacular bottle of Château Lafite Rothschild to go with our meal. "When I drink wine my pain is driven away and my dark thoughts fly to the ocean winds," wrote Anacreon, one of the ancient Greek lyrical poets.

I ate and drank with my grandfather and enjoyed myself. For the rest of the evening I banished all thoughts of Mick, dark or otherwise, to the ocean winds.

Chapter 17

———— ⊱≋⊰ ————

The phone woke me Sunday morning. I switched on the light and looked at the clock. Six A.M. The caller ID display showed Eli's home number.

I picked up. "What's wrong, Eli? Everything okay with Hope and Brandi?"

"Luce. Glad I got you. The girls are fine. At my in-laws for the weekend." He sounded tense. "I just got a call from Sunny Greenfield. Someone broke into Jack's wine cellar last night and tore the place apart. Jack heard something and went out to check on it. Whoever it was knocked him over the head and they had to take him to Catoctin General."

I swung my feet over the side of the bed and reached for my cane. "Oh my God. Is he all right?"

"He'll be okay but he's got a huge bump on his noggin and a mild concussion, according to Sunny. They just got back from the hospital. Sunny said the sheriff's deputies left a while ago but would be back later. She asked if I could drop by and look at the damage. I thought maybe you could come, too."

"You mean, right now?"

"Why not?" he said. "She can't get the door to close so I'll try to fix it temporarily, but I could use you to see what's what with his wine collection. Jack's in no shape. Besides, you're up, aren't you?"

Thanks to him I was. "Give me half an hour to change and get over there. Maybe afterward you could come back for breakfast. Pépé's been here since Tuesday. You really ought to see him."

He made a noise like air leaving a tire. "I know, I know. It's been on my calendar to call or drop by, but I'm just so damn busy all the time."

"Well, you can drop by this morning. I know I can tempt you with breakfast, especially if you're on your own."

"Is that a dig about my weight?"

"No, it's a dig about your calendar. I've got to get dressed. See you there."

Eli's Jaguar was already parked in the Greenfields' driveway when I arrived just after six-thirty. We'd had the first hard freeze last night and the landscape, before the sun came up, glittered like diamonds.

The door to Jack's wine cellar was ajar, as Eli had said. It looked like an animal had chewed it where it had been pried open. Sunny and Eli sat facing each other on stools at a new redwood bar. My impeccably dressed brother had his hands wrapped around the largest size of a coffee-to-go. Sunny nursed a glass of red wine. I saw the bottle. Château Haut-Brion. She was drinking first-class stuff.

Eli turned around. "Hey, Luce. Join us."

"Want a drink?" Sunny asked. She was dressed in a maroon velour tracksuit and white turtleneck under a Burberry trenchcoat.

I'd been expecting a cool reception from her since our last few encounters hadn't gone so well, but just now she seemed to have forgotten the rancor she felt toward me. Probably the result of exhaustion and a couple of glasses of wine before breakfast, if the level on the bottle was anything to judge by.

"Uh—no thanks." I swiped Eli's coffee. "I could use a little caffeine." I sipped it and gave it back. Something with lots of whipped cream and a shot of something cloyingly sweet. "Any coffee in that?"

"Bring your own next time." He used his finger to wipe the place where I'd drunk. "We'd like you to have a look and see if you can get any idea about what's been taken."

I glanced around. My brother hadn't been kidding about a first-class renovation. Redwood paneled walls and wine racks, slate flooring, and recessed lights twinkling like dimmed stars. It was laid out like a library with long rows of shelves, but wine bottles instead of books filled the diagonal alcoves. Except for the damage to the door, the place looked fine. The way Eli had described it over the phone I'd been expecting a mess.

"I'll try," I said. "I'm not sure how much help I can be."

"Jack's the only one who can really say what's been stolen but from what I can tell so far, it looks like they went after only the most expensive vintages," Sunny said. "Cases and individual bottles."

"That must have taken some time," I said. "Not like breaking a store window and grabbing whatever you get your hands on." I met her eyes. "They got the Washington bottle, didn't they? I bet that was what they came for."

Sunny smiled tiredly and lifted her glass. "A small triumph. We never brought it back out here. It's still in the house. In the downstairs cellar."

"Thank God for that," I said.

"Do you think Lucie's right and that bottle was what they were after?" Eli asked. "When they couldn't find it, they took all the other stuff?"

"I don't know. This seems like it was well planned. Almost like they had a list. Most people wouldn't know the difference between a California cult wine like Screaming Eagle and a bottle of Château Mouthwash. These guys did. One of them must have been a wine expert," Sunny said.

Or maybe someone who bought rare wines for wealthy clients. Hadn't Quinn said Nicole was involved in Alan Cantor's embezzlement scheme? Where had she been last night after her dinner with Mick?

"Did Jack get a chance to see any of the robbers? Any idea how many there were?" I asked.

"No and no," Sunny said.

"Do you know how it happened?" Eli asked.

"Sorry." She shook her head. "Jack stayed downstairs to watch the news at eleven and I went to bed. All of a sudden I woke up and he wasn't there. When I went down to check on him, he wasn't in the house. So I figured maybe he'd come here. I found him lying by the door." She picked up her glass and drank with an unsteady hand. "Unconscious but still breathing."

"What time was this?" I asked.

"I guess around midnight."

"You called 911?" Eli said.

"An ambulance and a couple of deputies from the sheriff's department came right away."

I got up and walked over to the door, running my fingers over the new keypad that was part of what Eli had said was a state-of-the-art security system. "How did they get in with all this high-tech stuff?"

Sunny sighed. "It's not hooked up yet. Isn't that the ulti-mate irony? For years all we had was an old-fashioned lock that Jack bought at the hardware store. Then a few days before we get a new security system put in, we're robbed."

"Eli said Jack was worried about some wine thefts out in California," I said.

"That's not all. Jack pays a king's ransom in insurance for this collection," she said. "The problem is that over the years, we've been drinking some of it and he's been buying more wine. At some point he lost track of how much it was all worth at today's prices since he used an old composition book to record what he bought and it just got too time-consuming to continually update it. Shane finally persuaded him to put everything in a computer database."

"So you'd know what you had and what it was worth," I said. "That's smart."

"Yes, except you know Jack and computers. He still prefers a quill and parchment. Fortunately Shane offered to handle it for him. He told Jack maybe we could finally lower that huge insurance premium. Having the security system would also help."

"How complete is the database?" I asked. "It'd be a lot easier to figure out what was stolen if I could look at that."

She shrugged. "You need to ask Shane."

"Where is he?" I asked. "I'm surprised he's not here."

"No idea," Sunny said. "I called his house, his cell—even the store. Left messages everywhere."

"Last time I saw him was yesterday at the Point-to-Point. He saved the life of one of Mick Dunne's jockeys who got thrown from his horse."

"I heard about that. I'm sorry I wasn't there but the job in Charlottesville turned out to be as big as I'd hoped." She flicked a finger at the room as an irritated expression crossed her face. "Look at all this. Stained-glass murals. Redwood paneling. Expensive flooring. Jack spent a fortune."

"Mind if I look around?"

"Help yourself. Eli, I need you to figure out how to seal this door until we can get a new one. Otherwise, the wine will freeze with these outdoor temperatures and then we've lost everything."

My brother took off his Italian leather jacket and laid it on the bar. "Can you get me a hammer, nails, and any scrap wood you've got lying around? If there's some plywood left over it'll do for a couple of days. I'll put in a rush order for a new door tomorrow."

I left them and made a slow tour through the cellar. Thirty thousand bottles was a lot of wine. Some had tags hanging around the necks; others did not. I examined the wines that were next to the empty spaces on the shelves. They were always expensive vintages. What surprised me, though, was that no bottles were partially pulled out. As Sunny said, it seemed the thief or thieves already knew where to find exactly what they wanted.

I wondered how late Nicole's dinner meeting with Mick had gone. Had it ended with a businesslike handshake at the end of the evening, or had she spent the night in his enormous bed as I had done a few nights earlier? If she'd stayed over then she couldn't have been here at midnight clearing out Jack Greenfield's wine cellar.

I could either ask her or I could ask Mick. Or I could stay out of it because my real reason for wanting to know had little to do with her alibi and a lot to do with my complicated relationship with Mick and the fact that I did not like Nicole Martin very much.

On my way out, Eli was still repairing the door. I told

him I expected him for breakfast as soon as he was done and promised Sunny I'd call later to check on Jack.

I suppose the old saying's true that what the eye can't see the heart can't grieve for. But I no longer wanted to be blind about the kind of man Mick Dunne was—that women were expendable in his life and our relationship was based on convenience.

I got in my car and headed over to Mick's place.

I didn't see his car at the house so I drove down to the stables. Since it was Sunday, none of the horses were being worked though a groom hand-walking Casbah passed me.

"Is he all right?" I asked.

"Looks to be. Just checking to make sure there's no soreness or swelling after nicking his leg yesterday."

I found Tommy Flaherty in the tack room sorting out medications. He looked surprised to see me but said that Mick had just left for the house a few minutes ago.

Mick's farm, like mine, was based around a private circular road that linked his house and the main stable complex. But his operation was much larger so there were other roads that led to the new winery, Tommy's house, and an indoor training track for the horses. Since Mick hadn't driven past me, he'd taken one of the back roads to the house.

This time the Mercedes was there when I pulled up. I saw a flash of a red jacket in the garden beyond the swimming pool. Though it was late in the season, a few roses still bloomed. Mick had told me once that this garden reminded him of a rose garden in Hyde Park, where his mother often took him as a boy. I walked through an arbor that, in spring, would be thick with violet clematis.

He didn't see me so I called his name.

"What are you doing here?" He walked over, holding a coffee mug in one hand. "Is anything the matter?"

"Someone broke into Jack Greenfield's wine cellar last night. Whoever did it took a lot of wine—cases, bottles. Only the best stuff." I leaned on my cane, trying to steady myself and my nerves. I was babbling. Not a good start. "I was just there with Eli and Sunny. The thieves knocked Jack out and he's got a concussion."

He took my arm. "Slow down. I can hardly understand you. Let me get you something. Would you like to come in for a cup of tea? Coffee?"

"No, thanks. I'm fine. I've got to get home anyway."

"I'm sorry to hear about Jack." He still looked puzzled. "Is there anything I can do . . . ?"

The perfect opening. "I was wondering what time Nicole Martin left after your dinner last night."

His mouth opened and closed. He dropped my arm and wrapped both hands around his mug. "First of all, what does that have to do with Jack Greenfield, and second of all, what business is it of yours?"

My cheeks burned. "Because whoever broke into his wine cellar knew what they were taking. Sunny said it's almost like someone had a list."

"I see." His voice hardened. "So you believe Nicole had something to do with the break-in. That she's a common thief. My understanding is that she *buys* wine for her clients. She doesn't steal it for them. Unless you know something I don't?" His eyes were flat and expressionless.

I couldn't tell him. What Quinn told me he'd done for Nicole in California had been a private confession. "No. I'm sorry. I can't talk about it."

"Can't talk about *what*?" Now he was angry. "Look, you come here more or less asking me if I slept with the woman to give her an alibi for a robbery. What the hell's going on with you, Lucie?"

"Nothing. Nothing. I'm sorry, Mick. I've got to go."

I stumbled on the uneven path as I tried to move away from him but he grabbed my arm again and this time jerked it so I faced him. Even through my jacket his fingers dug into my flesh and it hurt. He was angrier than I'd ever seen him.

"We finished dinner around nine. She left straightaway. Satisfied?" He dropped my arm in disgust and walked back to the rose garden.

I drove home, my cheeks burning with shame and humiliation, but at least I had the answer to my question. Nicole Martin could have gone to Jack Greenfield's last night after she left Mick.

I'd been evasive with him in order to protect what Quinn told me in confidence. In turn it had earned me Mick's scorn and contempt. Indirectly, I'd also protected Nicole—the very thing I'd warned Quinn not to do. She had already betrayed his trust, letting him take the blame for something she did, and he was still paying for it.

Why was it that all roads led back to Nicole? Perhaps it was the feeling in the pit of my stomach—like nausea—that made me think she was as dangerous now as she'd been then. And that it wouldn't be long before her whole house of cards was going to come crashing down on all of us.

Chapter 18

Quinn was in the lab, working on more calculations, when I showed up in the barrel room first thing Monday morning. His eyes were dark and hooded and he hadn't shaved in a couple of days. Wherever he'd been and whatever he'd done, it hadn't brought him any peace if his face was anything to go by. He'd probably spent a fair bit of time with his drinking buddy, Johnnie Walker.

"You all right?" I said.

His look said he appreciated my fine sense of irony. "Brix has gone to zero. I'm going to pump out the free run juice, then press."

Since we apparently weren't pulling our punches I said, "Someone broke into Jack Greenfield's wine cellar at his home on Saturday night. Jack showed up in the middle of the robbery and got knocked unconscious."

Quinn finally showed some genuine emotion. "Are you serious? Is he okay?"

"Mild concussion but he's home. Eli and I went over there yesterday morning to help Sunny." I picked up the paper with his calculations on it. Without looking up I said, "Whoever did it knew exactly what they were looking for. They took only the best vintages."

He took the paper out of my hand. "She didn't do it, Lucie."

"She was with Mick Dunne until nine o'clock," I said. "The break-in was sometime between eleven and twelve."

"What was she doing with Mick?"

"Having dinner. He's hiring her to buy wine for him."

His tight smile said it was news to him. "I wondered how long it would take before they hooked up. Mick Dunne is Nic's kind of client." He pointed out the lab window at the fermenting vats. "As long as you're here, you can help me with the free run juice. We'll put it in the number-six tank for now."

He left the lab before I could say anything and wheeled the pump over to one of the vats. I still wasn't done with our conversation.

I joined him. "What makes you so sure she didn't leave Mick's place and drive over to Jack's?"

"Because she spent the rest of the night with me." His tone was matter-of-fact but there was still an edge to it. "Get me some clamps, will you?"

I got the clamps. It gave me a few seconds to compose myself even though it felt like he had just wrapped piano wire around my heart and he was pulling it tighter the more we talked. Nicole hadn't slept with Mick. She'd slept with Quinn.

"If she was with you all night then I guess she couldn't have broken into Jack's place."

He plunged a hose into the fermenting vat. "Guess not."

"Wonder who did it, then."

"I'm sure the sheriff will figure it out."

He put a hose from the other end of the pump into the number six stainless-steel tank. "You think I'm covering for her again, don't you?"

"I never said that."

"You didn't have to. Come here." He left the hose where it was and led me to the winemaker's table. "Look at this."

An elaborately carved pumpkin of a witch flying across a harvest moon. He pulled matches from his jeans pocket and lit the votive candle inside the pumpkin. The flickering orange glow made rippling shadows on a rack of wine barrels. He dimmed the lights and the effect was even spookier.

"Nic did it. And this one." He got a second pumpkin from his workbench and brought it back to the table.

He lit the candle and suddenly an angry Freddie the Fox glowed eerily at me. I froze momentarily, staring at the menacing eyes and fanged teeth. "My God, Quinn. Why did she carve Freddie the Fox?"

"What are you talking about?" He turned the pumpkin carefully so he could look at it. "That's no fox. It's a werewolf. Anyone can see that."

The blood pounded in my temples. "Are you sure?"

"Of course I'm sure. What's wrong with you?"

"Nothing."

"Come on, Lucie. You look like you're about to pass out. You want me to get you some water?"

"No, thanks. I'm fine." I stepped back. He was right. It was a werewolf, not Freddie. "Sorry. Of course it's a werewolf. It's very good. They both are. I had no idea she was so talented."

He smiled ruefully. "Ever since she was a kid she loved Halloween. She bought these pumpkins at the farm market and brought them over to carve Saturday night. Figured I'd have the knives and tools she needed to do it."

"You mind if I ask what time she arrived?"

He stared at me, but answered readily enough. "Ten. Ten-thirty. I don't know. She just showed up." He moved the pumpkins so they were next to each other. "She slept on my couch. Apparently it's over between her and Shane."

The wire around my heart loosened and I wondered why I seemed to care more whether she had slept with my winemaker than with my sometimes lover.

"What's she going to do now?" I asked.

"Talk Jack into selling her that bottle of wine and wipe the dust from her feet on her way out of Atoka."

"You sorry she's leaving?"

We walked back to the pump. "Hold on to that hose, will you? Am I sorry? You must be joking. Nic still knows how to punch my buttons." He flipped the switch on the pump and we watched the juice flow from the fermenting vat to the tank. "Hell, I'd buy her ticket home except I know she's flying first-class. The only way she travels now."

"Nice of you to put her up for the night." I had to speak up over the noise of the pump.

"Yeah, well, I'm a nice guy."

"Sometimes." I smiled at him.

Or maybe he'd been a pushover for her again. Now he was her alibi for the burglary at Jack's. Was Nicole using Quinn one last time? Wherever she'd been, I still thought she was somehow involved with that robbery.

"What made you think that werewolf was a fox?" He shut off the pump, interrupting my thoughts.

"Someone disemboweled a stuffed animal, poured red paint on him, and left him on my front doorstep Saturday morning. Freddie the Fox—maybe you've seen him in the shops in town."

"I have. Jesus, that's sick."

"Whoever did it was probably trying to get me to cancel the Goose Creek Hunt's meet here tomorrow. Scare me, I guess."

"Did you tell Amanda or Shane or anyone from the hunt?"

"No. I didn't want to upset them. By the way," I said, "Shane's coming over later this morning to ride their territory. Make sure the fences and jumps are all in order. You didn't tell your friend he could come by and go deer hunting today, did you?"

He moved my hose to the next vat. "No. Look, Lucie, you should have told Shane. Or someone. What if this nutcase tries to sabotage those jumps? Putting barbed wire around them or digging holes where no one expects them? Someone could really get hurt. Riders. Horses. The hounds."

The color drained from my face.

"Call Shane," he said. "Get hold of him before he gets over here. I can handle the rest of these vats. Manolo will be here in a while, anyway."

But I couldn't find Shane and he still wasn't answering his cell phone.

"I'll call Amanda," I said. "Maybe she can reach him."

"Tell her everything," Quinn said. "She needs to know."

I got her just as she was getting ready to leave her house for a hospital board meeting. She didn't speak at all while I told her about Freddie. When I finished she still said nothing.

"Amanda? Are you there?"

"Yes. Yes, I am." She sounded distracted. "Sorry. Just checking something."

"Did you hear what I said?"

"Of course I did."

"Can you reach Shane?"

"Don't worry, I'll get hold of him. And I'll do better than that," she said. "I'll be over there myself checking things out."

"Be careful."

"Count on it," she said.

I hung up and told Quinn what Amanda had said.

"Your cousin called while you were on the phone," he said. "She wants you to call her back. Something about lunch with her and your grandfather."

"I just talked to Pépé," Dominique said when I reached her, "and woke him up. I thought you two might come by for lunch. Or at least he could have his morning coffee here. I couldn't get an answer out of him that made sense."

"His big dinner with his friends from the Marshall Plan is this evening," I said. "I think he wants to get his beauty sleep before he parties all night."

"Probably burning the midnight oil at both ends as usual," she said. "Well, let him sleep. Why don't you come?"

"Sure," I said. "What's up?"

"Nothing's up. I haven't seen you in a while."

When the English slipped, something was up.

"I'll be there," I said.

I left the vineyard shortly before noon. If Amanda or Shane were out riding somewhere on our land, I hadn't seen a sign of either of them as I left the vineyard.

Out of habit I glanced in my rearview mirror as I got ready to pull onto Atoka Road. Red paint covered both stone pillars marking the entrance to the vineyard.

More blood.

Chapter 19

I shut off the engine and reached for my cane. The fox had frightened me. This made me mad. When I found out who did it, they would pay.

The paint continued for about twenty feet along the left wall. It ended abruptly as though someone had come to the bottom of the can—or fled before getting caught in the act. It looked like the same red used for Freddie's blood. I went over to the pillar and touched it. Dry. If it was the same paint, at least it was water-based and would wash off.

The pillars had been here for more than a century. The garish smears meant to look like a wound on the weathered stone were as repulsive as a bully beating up a grandmother for the lousy couple of bucks in her purse. I leaned my cheek against one of the pillars and wondered who was that sick. Less and less it seemed like the Orlandos.

I called Quinn. "Someone found a use for the paint left over from Freddie. Meet me at the front gate."

He showed up almost immediately. "I'm calling the

sheriff," he said when he saw the mess. "Good thing you kept that stuffed animal."

He pulled out his phone.

"Wait," I said. "Don't call yet."

"Why not?"

"Maybe I ought to drop by and talk to the Orlandos first."

Quinn looked disgusted. "And do what? Check their garage for empty paint cans?" But at least he snapped his phone shut.

"Whoever did this knows Claudia and Stuart are trying to stop the Goose Creek Hunt from riding through my farm. That's not a large circle of people."

"And?"

"I think the Orlandos are law-abiding citizens. If someone is trying to capitalize on their efforts to shut down fox-hunting by making threats and defacing my property—and like you said, possibly even booby-trapping some of the jumps and fences—they'll be as upset as we are."

He opened the phone again. "And they'll say just what I'm saying. We should call the sheriff."

"As long as my family has lived here we've always been on good terms with our neighbors," I said. "I don't much care for Claudia and Stuart Orlando but we live next door to each other. Right now we're not even speaking. At least this will give me a chance to try to remedy that."

"We still need to report this."

"We will. But you know as well as I do they'll be the number-one suspects. I'd rather be the one to tell them to expect a visit from a deputy sheriff than have a cruiser show up in their driveway and blindside them. Then it really will be all-out war between us. Because they didn't do this."

Quinn traced the outline of red on one of the pillars with his finger. "You have a point."

"There's something else," I said. "Whoever is responsible is going to clean it up. I don't care if they have to use a toothbrush and dental floss. When they're done, it's going to look like nothing ever happened."

He went back to the winery and I called Dominique on my cell, letting her know I was running late. I put the top down on the Mini, hoping the cool breeze would clear my head. The sky was Williamsburg blue and the sunlight, flickering through the branches of the trees, made stripes on my windshield like gentle lightning. Here and there a few leaves were brilliant yellow like Christmas ornaments on a tree. One morning I knew I'd wake up and suddenly everything would be flame-colored and I'd wonder how I missed the transition.

I got to the Goose Creek Inn just after twelve-thirty. The maître d' spotted me through the lunchtime crowd, waving me over to his stand and kissing me on both cheeks. "She's in the kitchen. Told me to let you know she won't be long."

"Some crisis only she can handle?"

He rolled his eyes. "*Chérie,* they're all crises only she can handle."

"Doesn't it drive you nuts?"

"I am used to her. Maybe you forget I have been here since your godfather was cooking in the kitchen. Now I have the pains in my legs and varicose veins from so many years of standing. I am used to those, also."

I smiled. "I assume we're at her table?"

"She thought you might enjoy eating outside. Is that all right?"

"Yes. Lovely."

"Your waiter will take you there. If you can wait *un petit instant?*"

Dominique showed up just after I was seated. She kissed me absently and set an ashtray next to her place, pulling a pack of cigarettes from the pocket of her black trousers.

It seemed to be my day for being with people who looked like they'd spent the weekend being run over by a tractor-trailer rig.

"I'm glad you came." She lit up and took a deep drag, closing her eyes.

My cousin hadn't chosen to eat outdoors because of the glorious weather. She needed to smoke and it was off-limits in the restaurant.

"My pleasure. What's going on? No offense but you look rotten."

"I feel rotten. How about a glass of champagne?" She raised her hand and our waiter appeared at our table. *"Deux coupes de champagne, s'il vous plaît."*

After he left she said, "Joe and I have split up for good. He's leaving."

Napoleon once said that in victory you deserve champagne but in defeat, you need it. My cousin needed it.

"Leaving what?" I said.

"Everything. The academy. Atoka." Her eyes were anguished. "Me."

I reached for her hand as our champagne arrived. "I'm sorry."

She sucked on her cigarette like it was life-sustaining. "A couple of parents got wind that one of their daughters' teachers was involved in a murder investigation. They didn't think someone like that ought to be on the staff at the academy."

"He got sacked?"

Dominique nodded. "Two weeks' notice. By the way, I ordered our lunch before you got here."

Her world could be falling apart but she still had to be Superwoman, taking care of everything and everyone. "Great," I said. "And Joe's not guilty of killing anybody."

"Doesn't matter. He buttered his bread when he slept with that woman and now they're making him lie in it."

"I guess so," I said. "Though it seems pretty harsh."

She shrugged as the waiter set two plates of salmon tartare in front of us. I hoped she was going to put her cigarette down while she ate. Even outside, the smoke was annoying.

"What's he going to do?" I asked.

"Move to D.C. You know how desperate they are for teachers in that school system. He'll find a job right away, even in the middle of the school year."

"Why does he have to move there? Why can't he stay here and commute?"

She lit a cigarette off the end of the previous one. "He feels like he has crow all over his face if he stays in Atoka."

"You're going to give yourself lung cancer."

She eyed me. "We come from good genes. Look at Pépé. He's been smoking since the dinosaurs roamed the earth and he's fine."

She had a point. "How are you doing?" I asked.

"I'd like to strangle Joe for what he did. Otherwise, I'm fine."

"At least you're not keeping your emotions pent up. That's a good sign."

Our empty salmon plates vanished and a salad of bitter greens with herbed chèvre croutons arrived. Dominique asked for more bread.

"I made some calls," she said. "I found out about her."

"Valerie?" I looked up from my salad. "Why did you do that?"

Another drag on the cigarette. "I wanted to know." She glanced at me. "Don't look at me that way. In my place you'd do the same thing."

I thought about my questions to Mick yesterday and, this morning, prodding Quinn for information in the barrel room. We also came from inquisitive genes.

"UVA fired her and she was in debt. No permanent address after she came back from France. She lived with various friends in Charlottesville to avoid paying rent." My cousin stabbed her salad aggressively with her fork. "Promised everyone who loaned her money she would pay them back after she finished writing the Jefferson book, but she never did."

I watched her eat. "That's a lot to find out from a few phone calls. What'd you do? Hire a private investigator?"

She tossed her head. "I didn't hire anybody. You forget I have clients who have known me for years. Maybe I take care of a gentleman who wants a discreet dinner with a lady friend and maybe he'd like to show his appreciation that I provide a private dining room for him and his friend each time they show up and never say a word when he returns with his wife."

"Oh," I said. "Payback. A lesser form of blackmail."

"What goes around comes around." She smiled sweetly. "I wonder where Valerie thought she'd get the money."

"Not from book sales, that's for sure. Maybe she *was* trying to blackmail Jack Greenfield, though Jack wasn't the one who fooled around with her car."

"Who did?"

"I don't know. Nicole Martin is trying to get him to

sell her the Washington wine for one of her clients," I said. "Did you know she and Valerie were friends?"

"Isn't that interesting?" Dominique rolled her eyes as she sat back in her chair and crossed her legs. "Some friend. Now Valerie's dead and Nicole gets that bottle."

"Nicole didn't come to town until after Valerie died," I said. "But it's an odd coincidence."

"If it's a coincidence. It seems like there's still a missing piece to the puzzle," my cousin said. "Somewhere in the middle of this is a smoking mirror. All you need to do is find it."

"Sure."

Unless I was trying to put together the wrong puzzle. I was beginning to wonder about that.

Chapter 20

Claudia and Stuart Orlando lived in a large stone house that had been built in the late nineteenth century from stone quarried on their own property. As I turned in their driveway I noticed they had replaced the white metal mailbox that had been there for years with something large enough to hold mail for an entire condo complex.

Claudia answered the door when I rang the bell. Perfect makeup, impeccable clothes. In the middle of a conversation on a portable phone. She didn't look overjoyed to see me, but at least she gestured for me to come in.

She put her hand over the receiver and whispered in her raspy New York accent, "I'm just finishing up here. Why don't you have a seat in the living room?"

I followed the direction of her manicured ruby fingernail and nodded. She strolled into another room which looked like a study or her office.

"Call Hong Kong," she said into the phone. "Find out if they'll go along with it." The door to the room closed. Based on her tone of voice, Hong Kong needed to go along with it.

The living room was modern, with a palette that ranged from parchment to cream. More Claudia than Stuart. The neutral tones reminded me of a beach. Several small artifacts, oriental and quite ancient, sat on a lighted étagère. The paintings were modern, also in restful neutral shades. A black lacquered coffee table and two black-shaded lamps on the end tables provided counterbalance to all the whiteness. On the sofa were Shantung silk pillows with oriental designs in black, white, and scarlet. Not my taste, but I liked the effect.

Claudia entered the room while I was sitting on the cream-colored sofa, admiring her collection of bronzes. I noticed for the first time that she was dressed in black and white, like her room. An ivory and black medallion hung around her neck on a black velvet cord. Her perfume smelled of jasmine.

"Sorry," she said. "I've been trying to put this deal together for weeks."

"What do you do?"

"Import-export. Almost exclusively Asia. The time difference is a killer. Sometimes I'm up all night and sleep all day." She clasped her hands together as though she were praying and joined me on the sofa. "To what do I owe the pleasure? I have a feeling it's not a social visit."

After the hostilities the other day at the winery, the wariness was justified, but at least she made an effort to be civil.

"I wanted you to find this out from me," I said. "There's been some vandalism on my property. I haven't called the sheriff yet, but I will probably report it later today."

Claudia's hand went to her beautiful medallion. She knotted the cord around her fingers. "We left New York to get away from the crime, for God's sake."

"Well, it's—"

She wasn't listening. "Stuart *promised* me it'd be safe here. Now I suppose we'll have to get an alarm system put in." She looked around the room at her possessions as though they might vanish while we sat here. "At least in New York if you scream, someone will hear you. Here there's . . . no one."

"Claudia," I said. "Please let me explain."

She looked blank. "Explain what?"

"What happened at my farm."

"Oh."

"On Saturday morning someone left a stuffed animal on my front doorstep. Freddie the Fox. They sell him around here. He was torn apart and there was red paint all over him like blood."

Her hand moved from her necklace to her throat. "Oh my God," she said. "How horrible."

"Today we found more red paint on the pillars at the entrance to the vineyard. I think the same person or persons was responsible for both. Someone doesn't want the Goose Creek Hunt riding on my property is the way I figure it. They're trying to scare me. Or possibly threaten me." I stopped and watched her face. It didn't take long.

"Have you come here to accuse—?"

"No," I said. "Absolutely not. But whoever did this knows you are campaigning against foxhunting here. And I bet they know you asked me to close my farm."

She looked stunned.

"Any ideas?" I asked.

"My God," she said again. "No, of course not."

"Once I call the sheriff," I said, "someone will probably be by to talk to you about this. I'm sorry, but I don't think I have much choice about whether or not to report it. My winemaker and I are afraid their next move might be tampering with the jumps and fences."

Her face turned the color of the bone-white fabric on a club chair opposite us. "Someone could get hurt."

"Yes. Or one of the animals."

Claudia moistened her lips with her tongue. "I'll call Stuart. Right away. He'll come home."

"Who else have you been talking about this to?" I asked. "I understand you've had some meetings."

She looked surprised that I knew. "We certainly don't advocate violence. And I don't think anyone involved with this movement would—" She fell silent.

"I'm sorry," I said again, "but it looks like someone did. I know foxhunting is an emotional issue for some folks. Like you and Stuart. But the people involved in hunting are some of the staunchest environmentalists and advocates for preserving open space. Why do you think it's still so beautiful here? No shopping malls, no apartment complexes—no kitschy-themed amusement park. I'm sure it had something to do with the reason you moved to this region, didn't it?"

Claudia studied her manicure and pursed her lips. "We will not change our minds about the brutality of what you people do." She stood up, signaling the end of our meeting. "But I appreciate you coming by to talk to me."

In the front hall I said, "I know it's a lot quieter here than New York and very different. But it's also a place where everyone helps everyone else out. We're a close-knit community. If you need something, your neighbors are there for you. We take care of each other."

She held the door open. "May I ask you a personal question?"

"You can ask."

She indicated my cane. "You can't run. Doesn't that scare you sometimes? What if you were attacked or you needed to get away from somebody?"

"You're right that I can't run." I looked her in the eye. "But you know what they say about losing one of your five senses, don't you? That the others become more acute. It's kind of the same thing with me. I've learned to compensate for what I've lost. And to answer your question, I don't scare easily."

She fingered the necklace again, though this time she rubbed the medallion like it was a talisman. "Maybe I underestimated you," she said.

"You wouldn't be the first," I said.

Quinn was in his office in the villa when I got back. "How'd it go with the Orlandos?" he asked.

"Better than I expected," I said. "I talked to Claudia. Stuart was at work. She was pretty horrified but she understood why we need to call the sheriff. Said she had no clue who might have done it. Swore it was no one they've been meeting with to lobby against foxhunting."

"I got some good news." He looked pleased with himself. "A clue."

He opened one of the side drawers in his desk and took something out. "Look at this. I found it near the spot where the paint ran out. Whoever did it brought their dog with them."

I picked up the black leather collar with the silver studs on it. "She didn't bring her dog," I said. "She wears it as jewelry."

"What are you talking about—she?"

It was the collar Amanda's sulky daughter Kyra had worn at the Point-to-Point on Saturday.

The paint. The fox. What better way to get back at her mother—the secretary of the Goose Creek Hunt—than to attempt to sabotage one of their meets? I only hoped she hadn't taken her juvenile anger one step further and tampered with the trails or jumps her mother and the rest of the hunt might take tomorrow. What she'd done had been stupid and malicious but at least no one had been hurt.

So far.

Chapter 21

—⊗⊗⊗—

"I don't see any reason to call the sheriff anymore, based on what we know now," I said to Quinn after I explained about Kyra. "But I do need to call Amanda. And Claudia."

"Why'd she do it?" he asked. "The kid, I mean."

"If you met her, you'd know. She's like Mia used to be at her age. Maybe worse. In a permanent stage of rage."

"Glad I don't have kids. Never did want them."

I set down Kyra's ugly collar. It was the first time he'd ever said something like that. Unlike Quinn, I wanted children. But after my car accident, the doctor told me that the odds were against it, given the internal damage.

"I didn't know that," I said. "Never, ever wanted them?"

He shrugged and picked up a tennis ball from the corner of his desk, tossing it in the air and catching it, over and over. When he was really thinking, he'd bounce it off the wall opposite his desk. It had left scuff marks and annoyed the hell out of me.

"Long story." He threw the ball against the wall.

"I wondered if that might be another secret from your past," I said. "A son or daughter growing up in California?"

He looked at me so intensely I blushed. "Not that anyone told me," he said.

"Sorry. That was out of line. Guess I'd better make those phone calls. I don't suppose you'd stick around while I do it?"

He swished the tennis ball through a hoop attached to his empty trash can. It bounced a few times and he retrieved it. "I've got a better idea. Let's go out on the terrace and you can call there. The sunset's going to be nice tonight. How about if I get us a couple of glasses of Cab?"

It was the first time since his ex-wife had shown up in town that he seemed like his old self. Maybe he'd finally managed to free himself of whatever hold she had on him.

"I'd like that," I said.

I called Amanda first and kept it short and to the point. There was a long silence when I finished.

Finally she said, "While I was talking to you this morning, I went to Kyra's bedroom. She got Freddie the Fox as a gift from her grandparents a few years ago. He was gone."

"So you suspected her since this morning?"

"I'm so sorry, Lucie. You have no idea how embarrassing and upsetting this is for me. Her father and I will deal with her, I promise," she said. "I'll take care of having your wall professionally cleaned. I know a good company."

I shook my head and looked at Quinn, who frowned at me and mouthed, "What?"

"She wants to pay for the cleanup," I said with my hand over the receiver.

He shook his head. "No dice."

"Thank you but no," I said. "I want Kyra to come over

here this evening to apologize and explain why she did it. Then I want her to clean the wall and the pillars. She and anyone else who helped her deface them. She can take her fox back, too. I cleaned up my driveway from that one."

"Let me handle this, Lucie. She's my daughter."

"By covering for her and bailing her out? No. Sorry, but she has to take responsibility for what she's done."

"She won't come. She won't listen to me. Why should she listen to you?" Amanda sounded stiff.

"Because if she doesn't listen to me she'll have to deal with the sheriff. He's a lot less tolerant than I am."

"You'd call the sheriff?" She seemed stunned.

"I would. Look, if this goes any further . . . if she's done something out in the field and someone gets hurt tomorrow, she's in big trouble."

There was a silence on Amanda's end.

"God, Amanda," I said, "don't tell me she did something to the jumps and fences?"

Quinn set down his wineglass and stared at me, his lips compressed in a thin line.

"I took care of it." Her words were clipped. "Everything's fine. Don't worry."

"Took care of *what*? Why didn't you tell me about this right away?" Whatever else Kyra had done, it was far more serious than defacing the stone pillars. Worse, Amanda seemed to be trying to minimize it. I could feel my anger growing.

"Because I checked everything," Amanda said. "You don't need to worry." I pointed my index finger to my head like a gun and pretended to pull the trigger. Quinn looked grim.

"What'd she do, Amanda?" My voice was tight with disbelief. She really intended to let her daughter off the hook.

"She, uh, rigged one of the fences so it would come apart when a horse went over it."

I closed my eyes. That was how my mother had died. "I'm canceling the hunt."

"It's not necessary, Lucie. I talked to Kyra. It was only the one fence and it's fixed. She didn't do anything else."

"I absolutely want her to come over here tonight. We can talk about whether or not the hunt goes on after she explains herself and apologizes."

"I'll talk to her, but I can't guarantee she'll come."

"Then the sheriff will be by and it won't matter what she feels like doing."

"You've made yourself quite clear." Amanda sounded terse and unhappy as she hung up.

"She's mad at you, isn't she?" Quinn said when I snapped the phone shut.

"Yes, dammit. Stupid, stupid kid. Someone really could have gotten hurt. Amanda was acting like it was no big deal."

"We'll take care of that tonight." He still looked grim.

I called Claudia next. That conversation went better.

Quinn and I finished our wine as the sun turned into a hard orange ball that hovered just above the horizon. Higher in the sky a line of clouds like beads on a necklace changed from blood-colored to violet, then washed out into flannel gray as the sky darkened behind them.

Quinn picked up our empty wineglasses when all that remained was a line of gilded brightness separating the sky from the mountains. "What are you going to do now?"

"See my grandfather off for his big reunion tonight," I said, "then wait for Kyra and Amanda to show up."

"You think they will?"

"They'd better."

"You doing anything for dinner?" he asked.

"Probably something involving a can opener and the microwave. Or cheese and crackers. I'm beat."

"What if I bring takeout over to your place, say, in about an hour? Chinese, maybe," he said. "You might need some backup, especially if the kid refuses to admit what a jerk she was."

I sat up in my chair and looked at him in surprise. "That sounds nice—even if the kid doesn't admit she was a jerk. I can handle her on my own, you know. You don't need to worry about me."

"I'm not worried about you," he said. "I'm worried about her and Amanda. I'll bet you they start going at each other."

"I don't think it will get violent."

"I know it won't," he said. "That's what I'm there for."

My grandfather, looking like a gracefully aging matinee idol in his double-breasted dinner jacket, was waiting in the foyer when I walked through the door twenty minutes later.

"*Tu es magnifique!*" I said.

He grinned as though I'd just confirmed a well-known truth. "*Merci beaucoup.*"

"Someone's coming to get you?"

"My colleague," he said. "You met him and his friend the other day."

"I'll wait up for you. I'd like to hear all about your reunion."

"I'll be home after breakfast," he said. "You may want to get some sleep."

I heard a car pull into the driveway, the tires crunching on the gravel. "How do you do it?" I asked. "I know people who are twenty, thirty years younger than you and couldn't keep up with half of what you do. You're amazing."

He caressed my cheek. "I have always looked at whatever came my way in life and tried to find the good in it. It brings one energy and *joie de vivre*."

"Even during the war?"

"Especially during the war."

I smiled at him and felt like my heart would break. "I love you, Pépé."

"I love you too, *mon ange*," he said.

I walked with him to his friend's car, his posture as erect as a soldier's. As he climbed into the back passenger seat he said, "I have been thinking. Perhaps tomorrow we could visit your mother's grave?"

"Of course," I said. "Whatever you wish."

He held his hand up in a small salute as the car pulled out of the driveway. I went inside and tried not to think about how much I would miss him when he returned to France in a few days.

Quinn brought enough Chinese takeout to feed our entire crew when he showed up an hour later. We ate dinner in the parlor in front of a fire I'd made in the fireplace. Last spring when the men cleared additional acreage so we could plant more vines, a couple of the guys split the logs into firewood and everyone was told to take whatever they wanted. They stacked half a cord for me near the carriage house next to my dwindling old woodpile.

"Did you use that new wood for this fire?" Quinn asked as a log crackled and popped, sending a shower of sparks up the chimney.

"Most of it's the old, seasoned logs. Maybe I accidentally brought in one or two new ones."

"Still too green," he said. "You might end up with burns in your nice new carpet if more sparks shoot off in the wrong direction. You should know better, country girl."

"I guess I'm distracted about tonight," I said as I put the small white takeout boxes back in the bag he'd brought them in so he could bring home the leftovers.

"Don't worry, it'll be fine." He moved so he was lying on his side with his chin propped on one hand, watching the fire.

I sat on the rug across from him with my back against the sofa. "I hope so."

"Another two weeks and we'll be ready to blend the Cab," he said.

All evening we'd kept the conversation on neutral ground, talking mostly about work. Nicole's name hadn't come up once.

"Are we going to have three hundred samples until you achieve perfection?" I asked.

"No more than two-fifty. I don't like to go overboard."

I laughed. "You're spoiled here in Virginia, you know that. In California you make the same wine every year since your weather is sunshine and more sunshine. Here it's like Bordeaux and you can experiment your blending little heart out because every year the weather is different from the year before. Or the year before that."

"I'll ignore that highly oversimplified comment and chalk it up to ignorance," he said. "You make it sound like California is the land of homogenized wine."

"*Terroir* matters much less there," I said, "because of the climate."

"Not true," he said. "California winemakers may have a lot less variation in their harvests from year to year, but we must be doing something right. Remember the 'Judgment of Paris'?"

I did. Everyone in the wine world did.

More than thirty years ago a small wineshop in Paris sponsored a blind tasting of French and California wines. To everyone's astonishment—not least of all the French—the California wines won hands down. The event made worldwide news thanks to a *Time* magazine correspondent named George Taber, who was there. After that California's reputation as a world-class wine producer skyrocketed.

"Talking about judgments—" I said as the sweep of headlights coming into the driveway flashed through the front parlor window. "They're here."

"Yup." He stood and helped me up, handing me my cane. "Show time."

Chapter 22

———∞∞∞———

"Listen to me," Quinn said as the doorbell rang. "We're going to play this as good cop, bad cop. Okay?"

"Sure," I said. "Which one am I?"

"Go answer the door."

Kyra's fashion sense—and her attitude—hadn't changed since I saw her at the Point-to-Point. Dressed in black from head-to-toe, lots of metal. In need of a bath or a dose of flea powder.

I led her and Amanda into the parlor where Quinn waited and invited them to have a seat. Amanda sat on the sofa. Kyra stood where she was.

"You were asked to sit down," Quinn said to Kyra. "Do it."

I'd only heard him use that tone of voice a couple of times since I'd known him. She sat. Quinn leaned against the fireplace mantel and glared at her. I sat in the wing chair opposite them, hands in my lap.

Kyra resumed her sullen hostility while I questioned her about what she'd done. Finally Quinn, who'd been growing increasingly exasperated, said, "Do you know why you're here?"

"Yeah. Because if I didn't come she'd call the sheriff on me."

"Is that so?" A muscle twitched in Quinn's jaw. "The right answer, sweetheart, is that you came to explain why you did what you did—and apologize for it."

"Sorry."

Quinn looked like he wanted to flog her. I caught his eye. We weren't going to get anywhere with her.

"Kyra," Amanda said, warning her.

"I said, 'Sorry.'"

"Don't go into acting," Quinn said. "I don't think you've got much of a future."

I glanced at him again and shook my head slightly.

"Do you realize how much trouble you could be in if a horse went over the fence you tampered with and the rider took a spill?" I asked. "Seven years ago something spooked my mother's horse so he threw her going over a jump. She broke her neck and died in the ambulance."

That got through to her. Her eyes, raccoonlike with too much eyeliner and mascara, widened and, for the first time, she looked scared.

"Did you booby-trap another jump that your mother didn't find?" I asked. "Do anything else we need to know about?"

"No," she said.

Quinn pointed a finger at her. "If you are lying, my dear . . ." He didn't finish.

"I'm not. I didn't. I promise." Her words came out in a rush.

"All right," I said. "I believe you."

She nodded and I could see her start to relax.

"We're not done yet," I said. "I expect you to clean the

pillars and the stone wall. They need to look exactly like they did before you threw paint on them."

"Where'll I get the water?" she said.

"I'm sure you'll figure out something," I said.

"It'll take forever."

"No. But it will take a while."

"Why did you do it?" Quinn asked.

Kyra looked at him warily. "I dunno. I don't like fox-hunting, I guess." She glanced over at her mother and said, "I think it's stupid. People who do it are stupid."

Amanda had looked like she'd been biting her tongue ever since she walked into the room. Now her face flushed dull red.

"That's enough, Kyra. Time to go." If Amanda's words had been in a little balloon above her head, they would have been encased in ice.

"I don't foxhunt," I said.

"No, but you let them do it." She jerked her head toward Amanda. "Your farm's part of their territory."

"It's one of several farms. Why single me out?"

She cocked her head and shrugged. "I heard my parents talking about that woman who died when her car went into Goose Creek. And how you're trying to find out something she was going to tell you," she said. "I thought maybe you'd wonder if someone was after you, too. And you'd be scared enough to cancel the hunt."

Quinn and I exchanged glances. I cleared my throat. "I see."

Amanda's face was a mixture of anger and embarrassment. "I'll deal with her at home," she said to us.

"And we'll see her tomorrow," Quinn said. He glanced at Kyra. "Right?"

She nodded, with a trace of the old sulkiness.

"Oh, don't you worry. She'll be here as soon as school's out," Amanda said.

"Excellent," I said. "In that case, I think this conversation's over."

Quinn and I walked them to Amanda's Range Rover.

"We're not quite done," Quinn said. He walked over to the carriage house and opened the door. When he came out he was holding the plastic bag with Freddie's remains in it. "This is yours. And this."

He handed her the bag and her studded collar.

Kyra took them silently, her eyes downcast. She held the collar like it was made of something heavy. I knew she realized that was how she'd been caught.

"That stuffed animal was the last gift you got from your grandfather before he died, Ky," Amanda said. "Put the bag in the trunk and wait in the car."

She obeyed, still quiet.

"I apologize again for my daughter," Amanda said. "Like I said, her father and I will discipline her."

"I think she's been punished enough," I said. "Hopefully she's scared now, too. I'm sure it won't happen again. See you tomorrow for the meet?"

She nodded. "Thank you."

"I'll open the south gate first thing in the morning," Quinn said. "That way you and the rest of the hunt don't have to ride through the main entrance if you don't want to."

"No one knows about Freddie but us," I said. "As for the paint at the front gate, if anyone asks, it was probably someone's idea of a pre-Halloween prank."

"You don't have to do that but I'm grateful."

She got into her car and drove off.

"I think that put a definite chill in our friendship," I said.

"Well, she better get over it," Quinn said. "She's got her hands full with that kid."

"I know. Hey, you were good at that bad cop thing," I said. "You terrified me."

He looked pleased. "That was nothing," he said. "I wasn't even warmed up."

Pépé showed up at eight o'clock the next morning just as I was leaving for the villa. We met in the foyer. He looked a little worse for the wear, his bow tie charmingly askew, smelling of cognac and tobacco and someone's heavy, old-fashioned perfume. Thank God he hadn't been driving.

"You want a cup of coffee? I just turned the pot off, so it's still pretty hot," I said, kissing him on the cheek. "How was it?"

"Formidable," he said. "But I am a little tired."

"Maybe you should go to bed."

He nodded. "I think I will."

"I'll be back this afternoon to pick you up," I said. "Maybe around three or four? Unless you want to sleep longer and we can go to the cemetery tomorrow."

"No, no," he said. "I want to go today. If that's still agreeable with you."

"Of course," I said. "I'll see you later."

I watched him climb the stairs. He took his time. Eighty-two years old and out all night partying like he was twenty-eight. I blew him a kiss that he didn't see and left for the vineyard.

I was the first to arrive at the villa. Quinn came later after opening the south gate for the Goose Creek Hunt.

"Did they show up?" I asked.

"Oh, yeah. Blowing that foxhorn, doing all the stuff

they do. Came through the south gate like we figured they would."

"Many horse trailers?"

"A few. Most of them rode their horses. Hacking, or whatever it's called."

"It's called hacking. You see Amanda?"

"Yup."

"Shane?"

"Him, too. With all the hounds, yapping up a storm. He said it's going to be a good day with no wind and cool air. The fox's scent will lie right there close to the ground. Easy for the pack to follow."

"Good. Mick there, too?"

He put his hands on his hips. "Maybe I should have taken roll. Yeah, Mick was there, too. Sunny, Ryan. All the usual suspects."

"I just asked."

"You should have asked about Mick up front. Though I would have thought he would have told you himself. Especially since you're sleeping with him again."

"Don't you have work to do?"

"Not before I get a cup of coffee. Is it made yet?"

"I haven't had time."

"I guess I have to do everything around here, don't I?"

I followed him into the kitchen. "How'd you know about Mick and me?"

"Went by the General Store this morning. Thelma was feeling chatty."

I'd been filling the coffeepot with water. I turned sharply and water splashed onto the floor. "When Thelma doesn't feel chatty, she will no longer have a pulse. Do you mean to tell me it's making the rounds at the General Store that I spent the night at Mick's place?"

"You slept there? She wasn't sure who bunked with who." He took the pot from me and poured the water into the reservoir.

I wiped up the floor as the coffeemaker started to gurgle. "Don't share that, okay?"

He got a carton of milk from the refrigerator. "So you are back together?"

"No. And I don't want to talk about it."

He leaned against the counter and folded his arms across his chest. "Okay, fine."

I reached for the sugar bowl and spooned some into my coffee. "Any idea if Nicole's left town yet?"

His eyes narrowed. "I don't know. She called Sunday morning and left a message but I never called her back. You going to have any coffee with that sugar?"

"Huh? Oh. You make strong coffee. It needs extra sugar."

"You're mad Mick hired Nicole."

I picked up the carton of milk. "Okay, so I am. You know something? I've finally realized everything's about business with him—even when it seems like it's not. His whole life revolves around work and winning and owning the best of everything." I stirred my coffee until it became the color of liquid caramel. "Nicole's got a great reputation, so of course he had to hire her. The thing is, he never seems satisfied or happy. He's always restless. Bored."

I thought about what Frankie said about him the other day. It was all about the thrill of the hunt with him.

"That include you?" Quinn asked.

"Yes." I blew on my coffee. "How come you didn't call Nicole back?"

He picked up his mug and held the swinging door open for me. "I don't know." We both walked into the tasting room as the door swung so hard the hinges creaked. "Guess we both have things we don't want to talk about," he said.

The hunt, which had allowed the new puppies entering the pack and the younger horses to be tested in the field, ended just before noon. It was the more informal season known as cub hunting and lasted from September through November. Even the dress was more casual because the members wore lightweight tweed jackets instead of the formal black jackets they'd use once the regular season began in November.

Amanda called just after twelve to say thanks and let me know everyone had left after a short tailgate.

"Any good runs?" I asked.

"A couple of good ones," she said. "This time we stayed mostly in the western part of your farm. Beyond the pond."

"That's new for you, isn't it?"

"Shane wanted to keep the pack well away from the Orlandos' property," she said. "We've got some unruly pups. Didn't seem like it made any sense to tempt fate."

"Everything look okay when you were out there?"

"Fine." Her voice turned chilly. "Kyra will be by later today, of course."

"Thank you. Look, Amanda, I hope everything's okay between us. As far as I'm concerned, it's all settled."

"Why wouldn't it be okay?" she asked, but I could tell it wasn't.

Pépé was dressed and sitting in the library, reading old copies of the *Washington Tribune* when I got home around three-thirty.

"Ryan Worth's columns?" I asked, kissing him on the cheek. Ryan had sent me a package a few days ago. "You're finally reading them?"

"Eh, *bien,* I promised him I would."

"What do you think?"

He set them on the coffee table. "He seems to drink a lot of wine that is 'flirty.' Or 'muscular.' Also a wine that grabs you by the throat and won't let go." He looked at me over the top of his reading glasses and put his hands around his throat in mock strangulation.

I laughed. "I think he's trying to describe wine in ways that people can relate to."

He shook his head. "I guess I am old school. I like to know about the taste, the finish, the nose. I do not want to know if the wine wants to wrestle with me."

"Come on," I said. "I'll take you for a ride. Are you ready to go to the cemetery?"

"Yes. But first I must get something. It's in the kitchen." He returned with a bouquet of mums, daisies, and sweetheart roses in the rusts and golds of autumn. "I was keeping them in water until you came."

"They're beautiful! Where did you get them?"

"Your friend Thelma arranged it. She had them delivered a few hours ago."

"Thelma doesn't sell flowers."

"Oh . . . ? She does to me."

"I think you've definitely got yourself a girlfriend," I said.

He straightened his collar, looking pleased with himself. "What is the expression in English? A ladyslayer?"

"Ladykiller."

"*C'est moi.*"

"Come on, Casanova. Get your coat and let's go."

The weather had turned cooler in the last few hours so I put the top back up on the Mini and drove my grandfather to the brick-walled cemetery where my ancestors had been buried for more than two hundred years. My mother used to love to come here to paint because of the breathtaking view of the Blue Ridge and the light, which she said was magical. I often came with her as a little girl, playing among the gravestones. After she died, I used to sit by her headstone and talk to her. When I took over running the vineyard those conversations became pretty regular. Since harvest, though, I hadn't been by much because of all the work.

Pépé held the wrought-iron gate for me. The flowers I'd placed at my parents' graves on Labor Day were black with rot and the vases lay on their sides. I picked up the flowers and threw them over the wall, wishing I'd thought to come by and do that before bringing my grandfather here. He took a rose from my mother's bouquet before laying her flowers on the grassy spot where she was buried. If I knew him, he'd tried to place them above where he guessed her heart would be. Then he set the rose at Leland's grave. I admired him for doing it. He'd known that my father had given my mother a bad time during their marriage, what with Leland's eye for the ladies and his penchant for gambling and bad business deals, and I knew it grieved him still.

I left him at my mother's grave and walked among the tombstones of generations of Montgomerys, brushing away fallen leaves and pulling weeds. In the next few days maybe I could persuade Eli to come back with me and do more clearing up. Soon it would be the Feast of All Saints and the Feast of All Souls. We would leave flowers for everyone then—and flags on Veterans' Day for those who fought in wars.

Pépé joined me as I finished picking up stray leaves that had clumped against the headstone of Hugh Montgomery who had fought with Mosby during the Civil War.

"I would also like to visit her cross," he said.

I had placed a small cross at the site where my mother died in a meadow on the south side of the farm beyond the old vines. Last spring we'd planted new varietals nearby, so now there was regular traffic passing by the place, which had once been relatively isolated. Quinn had seen to it that the area around the cross was left pristine and untouched so it looked as it had when she'd ridden there, except for the footpath we'd worn from years of visits.

I drove down the service road, pulling off at the edge of the field near her marker. The wind had picked up in the last half hour and the light had turned milky at the end of the day. The crickets' serenade had quieted down, occasionally drowned out by the random cry of birds and the steady rush of the breeze in our ears. Several turkey vultures circled overhead, probably eyeing a deer carcass.

I slipped my arm through my grandfather's and walked with him to the memorial. He held a long-stemmed yellow rose in front of him like he was carrying a vigil candle. When we got there Pépé laid the rose down and his lips moved. I squeezed his arm and left him alone to pray.

Overhead the vultures wheeled and swooped, crying out that our presence interfered with their meal. I walked over to see what it was. Sometimes—not often—the people who came to pick apples at our orchard would heave a bag of picnic trash out the car window into the woods if they were too lazy to take it home and throw it out there. Quinn swore if he ever caught anyone in the act he'd make them eat the contents while he watched.

If we didn't clean it up, the vultures and other animals would scatter the trash, leaving a mess of inedible cardboard, plastic, and paper. As I got closer the stench of something rotting came at me like a wave. Human flesh.

Bobby Noland described it to me once in unforgettable terms. I pulled the lapel of my jacket over my nose and took a few more steps.

I could not see the face from where I was standing, but I did recognize the gorgeous russet suit Nicole Martin had been wearing the day I met her.

Chapter 23

I jammed my hand into my mouth, staring at Nicole's body as I processed the fact that not only was she dead, but she'd been murdered and dumped here on my farm. My stomach heaved and I leaned over and threw up in some weeds. Whoever put her body here must have figured it was no-man's-land and she wouldn't be found for a long time, if ever. Besides, Nicole supposedly left town. Who in Atoka would miss her?

Who in Atoka would do this?

"Lucie!" Pépé waved at me. *"Tu vas bien?"*

I couldn't speak so I waved back and started walking toward him. He should not see what I'd just seen. I had to get him back to the house and call 911.

And tell Quinn. God, how was I going to do that?

"What's wrong?" he asked. "You look so pale. What happened?"

"Nothing," I said. "We should go home now."

"Are you going to tell me or shall I look for myself?"

He waited. "There's something over there where the vultures are."

I shivered as one of the birds screeched above us. "It's Nicole Martin. Someone killed her and left her body there."

"*Mon Dieu.*" He put his arm around me. "Show me."

"I'm not sure you should see—"

"*Ma petite,*" he said, "I have seen more than you can imagine in my lifetime. Let's go."

Like me, he pulled the lapel of his jacket over his nose and mouth when we got close enough to the putrid smell. He knelt by Nicole and examined her.

"She's still fully clothed so it seems she was not raped," he said, "but she was certainly beaten."

I shuddered. Nicole was tough, though she looked like an angel. I bet she'd fought back at her killer. "We need to call 911. But first I have to tell Quinn."

"First you must call the sheriff." He sounded firm. "Before you tell anyone."

"Quinn's her ex-husband. He should know—"

"Lucie! You know as well as I do he will be a suspect."

"Quinn did *not* kill Nicole, Pépé. He did not! I have to tell him about this—in person. Otherwise he'll find out from the sheriff and he'll know I didn't come to him first."

Pépé moved his tongue around in his mouth like he was probing for a toothache. His eyes never left my face. "You care very much for him, don't you?"

"Of course, I do. He works for me."

"You know that is not what I meant." His stare was unwavering, but I wasn't going to budge. "All right. Tell him. But I will stay here with this poor woman while you do that. She should not be left alone as carrion for the vultures."

I called Quinn as I drove toward the winery. "Where are you?"

"Barrel room. Why?"

"Meet me in front of the villa, will you?"

"Sure, what's up?"

I hung up without answering. It was going to be hard enough to face him in person.

"What is it?" he said when he saw me. Something flickered in his eyes and for a moment, I wondered if he didn't already know what I was going to say and Pépé had been right to be suspicious.

I told him in simple words. His eyes grew dark but they stayed locked on mine. "My grandfather is with her. I wanted to tell you first but we need to call the sheriff right away."

I didn't know what reaction I expected from him—grief, rage, shock. Whatever he felt, he sealed it inside himself and said in a monotone voice that unsettled me more than if he'd been angry or violent, "Then let's call and get back to your grandfather." He took my arm. "I'll drive. You call. Let's go."

I hooked my cane on my free arm and pulled my phone out of my jacket pocket again. "You all right?"

"Yup."

I called 911.

When we got there he jumped out of the Mini and ran ahead of me to where Pépé still watched over Nicole. He knelt, then touched his fingers to his forehead like he was beginning to make the sign of the cross or else shielding his eyes from the horrific sight. By the time I reached the two of them, he was standing again and speaking in a low voice to my grandfather. Still emotionless.

"I appreciate you telling me before the sheriff shows up," he said. "I'm sure they'll have a few questions for me. The ex is always a suspect."

Pépé's eyes met mine briefly.

"You didn't do it," I said. "They'll find whoever did."

The wind had a knifelike edge to it in the waning day-light hours. Clouds whited out the mountains so they were nearly invisible against the colorless sky. Pépé tucked his hands under his armpits and I turned up my jacket collar. As near as I could tell Quinn, lost in his own world, wouldn't have noticed if it started raining locusts.

In the distance came the wail of sirens.

"This is not going to be good," Quinn said.

"No," I said, "it isn't."

It was nearly midnight by the time Nicole's body was lifted into the medical examiner's van. I watched it drive off into the darkness, taillights bumping and jouncing on the rutted dirt road. Earlier Quinn, Pépé, and I had been separated and questioned. It didn't take long before Pépé was allowed to return to the house. He wanted to stay with me, but he'd also been sneezing for the last hour and I worried that he could catch his death out here in the night air.

"Go home," I said. "An officer will drive you. Make yourself something hot to eat and I'll join you when I can."

Finally he agreed.

Bobby Noland showed up just as Pépé left and took me aside. "We'd like permission to search your farm," he said. "Including the winery. Barns, sheds, the whole ball of wax."

"Why the winery?" I asked.

"Killer probably did it here somewhere." He took a pack of gum out of his pocket and offered it to me.

I shook my head. To be honest, it hadn't occurred to me that Nicole might have been at the vineyard—alive—before she was murdered.

"You don't think she was brought to this place after she was dead?" I asked.

"Now why would someone strangle her, then lug her dead body all the way out here when they could dump her anywhere in the county?" He tucked the gum into his mouth. "Hell, yeah. I think it's a very good possibility."

"She was strangled?"

"Looks that way."

"You're saying someone who works here might have done it?"

"I'm not saying anything. Do *you* think someone who works here might have done it?" He blew a bubble.

"Quinn didn't kill her," I said.

He popped the bubble with a smack. "I didn't bring up Quinn," he said. "You did. Something you want to tell me?"

"Look, we have people in and out of here every day buying wine. On weekends during apple season they take this road to the orchard. The Goose Creek Hunt held a meet here this morning. That's a lot of cars and people coming and going," I said.

"We'll talk to everybody who came here to hunt, you can be sure of that. But I still think there's a reason her body was left here." He folded his arms across his chest. "Which is why I want to search your place. Are you gonna give me permission or not? I can always come back with a warrant."

"You've got permission," I said. "And you won't find anything."

"Maybe yes," he said. "Maybe no."

Pépé was sipping a glass of Armagnac and smoking a Boyard when I got back to the house.

"What happened after I left?" he asked.

"Bobby Noland thinks she might have been killed at the vineyard because we found her body here. They're going to search the place."

"That seems logical if that is what they believe."

"It means they believe Quinn did it."

"It doesn't mean anything until they find something. And if he is innocent he has no worries." He reached for the bottle of Armagnac. "A drink?"

"No, thanks."

"Go to him."

"What?"

"Go see Quinn, Lucie. It's what you want to do."

"Will you be all right if I go?"

"I think I can manage for one evening without you, *mon ange.*" His eyes were kind, but concerned. "I'll see you in the morning."

I kissed the top of his head and he patted my arm. "*Que le Bon Dieu te portes bien,*" he said.

I hoped God was listening to my grandfather because I was going to need all the help I could get.

A light shone in the living room window of Quinn's cottage as I pulled up next to the El Camino. I sat in my car and stared at the house. Coming here was a mistake. Maybe I should just go home and leave him—

He tapped on the car window and I jumped. I hadn't heard him come up.

He opened my door. "You waiting for a better parking place? Or did you think you'd sit out here all night and watch my house in case I make a run for it?"

"You scared the wits out of me. I never saw you come out of the house."

"That's because I went for a walk." I thought he slurred

his words slightly. "On your way home from the crime scene?"

"No. I came by to see if you were okay."

He laughed. "That's great. I really 'preciate that. Am I okay? Come on inside and have a drink with me."

"I think you've probably had enough."

He grabbed my hand and pulled me out of the car. "I would have to drink the ocean for it to be enough," he said. "Please come drink with me."

He climbed the stairs unsteadily. When we got inside I marveled, as I always did, how anyone could live for as long as he'd been in this house and leave no trace of himself.

"Can I offer you a Scotch?" he asked. "Or do you prefer wine?" He looked like he was having trouble focusing.

"Wine. I can get it."

"Naw, I got it. Right here." There was a collection of bottles on a scarred-up table next to the entrance to his dining room. He picked up a wineglass and frowned at it. I wasn't sure if the glass was clean or not and he seemed in no shape to make that determination, either. He glanced over at me. "What?"

"I shouldn't have come here," I said. "This wasn't a good idea."

He was across the room before I knew it, pulling me into his arms. His kiss tasted like fire and it felt like he was pulling the oxygen out of me. I wanted to kiss him as fiercely as he wanted me—but I wanted to be more than just the vessel into which he poured his grief and anger. He must have felt me go tense because he pulled back his head.

"I'm sorry." He buried his face in my hair. "That was stupid. I shouldn't have done it."

"It's okay." I stroked his hair, still reeling from that kiss. "You were going to get me a drink."

He dropped his arms and stared into my eyes. The depths in his were vast enough to lose my moorings.

"Do you still want to leave?" he asked.

"I'll stay if you want me to."

"I want you to." He led me over to the couch and got my wine, refilling his glass with Scotch. When he sat down, he pulled me close. This time more brother than lover. I leaned my head against his shoulder and closed my eyes.

"What are you going to do?" I asked.

"About what?"

"Everything."

"I called Nic's brother," he said. "He'll fly out here when they release her body and bring her home. I hadn't talked to him since she and I split."

"That must have been a tough phone call."

"Yup." He picked up my glass and handed it to me. "Now I'm asking. You want me to stay?"

"It's your house."

His smile was rueful. "I meant the vineyard. Even though I didn't do it, there's going to be a hell of a scandal."

"There'll be an even bigger one if you cut and run. It will look like you did it."

"I suppose."

"I'm sorry," I said, "about Nicole."

"Whoever killed her," he said, "it wasn't random. She was into something worth killing for. Something she had, something she knew."

"Do you think she was involved with the break-in at Jack's place?" I asked. "Even though she was with you that night?"

He shrugged. "I dunno anything anymore. Maybe she was mixed up in it. Set it up or something."

"Then she had to have a partner. Or partners."

"Like Noah, Nic believes the world should be two by two. Yeah, she had a partner all right."

"I guess she never got the Washington wine, after all," I said.

"If she did she sure wouldn't have left it lying around the Fox and Hound."

"What are you talking about?"

"She moved there after she left Shane."

"You were staying in touch with her? You said the other day she called you and you didn't call her back."

"I didn't call her back." He ran a finger around the rim of his glass.

The hair on the back of my neck prickled. If he was innocent, why so evasive?

"Did she leave a message when she called?"

He shook his head and I could feel things start to unravel. "She had something she wanted to tell me and it had to be in person."

"Did you tell Bobby this?"

He shook his head.

"Quinn," I said, "don't be dumb. You have to come clean about everything. If Bobby finds out—and you know they'll get her phone records like they did with Valerie—you're going to be in a hell of a mess."

He gulped his Scotch and set his glass on the table hard. "I already am."

"What are you talking about?"

"They'll find out I lied for her once and they'll figure I'm lying for her again."

"Because you are! That's why you have to tell the truth. You can't protect her anymore. She's dead."

"It's too late." He covered his face with his hands and moaned softly. "Years too late."

Chapter 24

Quinn finally fell asleep with his head on my shoulder, an arm thrown across my waist pinning me down. I must have dozed off, too, because the next thing I knew he was shaking my arm. It took a moment before I realized where I was and what I was doing here—and why there was a blanket covering me.

He stood over me, barefoot, unshaven, shirtless, and dressed in a pair of camouflage trousers. Last I remembered he'd been fully dressed and in other pants.

"Lucie? You awake?" He held a coffee mug in one hand.

"I am now." I sat up, feeling awkward, and surreptitiously checked my own clothes. I was still wearing them.

"Here. Drink this. You feeling all right?" He handed me the mug.

Our fingers touched as I took it and I remembered last night's kiss. The mug had "Somewhere between Forty and Death" stenciled on it. I wouldn't turn forty for more than a decade, but given the way I felt at this moment, death didn't seem that remote.

"I don't know yet." I sipped the coffee. It tasted like boiled tires. "What kind of coffee is this?"

"Yesterday's. I ran out, but there was some left in the pot so I stuck it in the microwave. I figured you could use it."

"Oh." Either he was being gallant or I looked as bad as I felt.

He sat on the far end of the sofa. I drank more bad coffee and tried to ignore how good he looked half-naked.

"I owe you an apology for last night," he said. "I said some things I shouldn't have said."

"Why don't we forget it? You were upset. We both were." I ran a finger down the side of the ceramic mug. Would he apologize for the kiss, too?

"I, uh, unfortunately don't remember much except I think I slept on your shoulder. I'm really sorry about that. I hope I didn't drool on you or anything."

He wouldn't apologize because he didn't remember it. I tried to smile. "Nope. No drooling. And it's all right."

"I couldn't get the sight of Nicole lying there in that field out of my mind. I appreciate you being there for me. I probably said a bunch of things you didn't need to hear."

So he'd been thinking about Nicole the whole time. "What are friends for?"

He stood and ran a hand through his shaggy hair. "I'd better shower and get over to the barrel room. I need to get to work, get my mind off all this."

"Sure." I stood, too. "Last night you were kind of rambling. If there's anything you held back from Bobby, I think it would be a good idea to get it out in the open and tell him, you know?"

He scratched behind one ear. "What kind of things? What did I say?"

"That Nicole contacted you after she moved to the Fox and Hound. And that she might have been involved—indirectly—with the break-in at Jack Greenfield's place."

"I said that? Jeez. I really must have been loaded." He shook his head. "I don't know anything about the break-in at Jack's. Guess I was running my mouth."

"You said Nicole left a message for you to call her back, but you didn't."

"That I remember." He began balling and unballing his fists. "Maybe if I had she'd still be alive."

"You don't know that."

"No," he said, "I don't. And that's why I got so stinking drunk last night. Because I'll never know if I could have saved her and I've got to live with that."

"Quinn—"

He held up a hand. "Look, I know I've been a complete asshole lately and I'm sorry. Once we get done with the Cab I thought I'd take some time off since it will be quiet around here. Get lost and get past all this. Past her."

"Sure. Fine." I set down my coffee mug. "I guess I'd better get going, too. I might be in late today."

"No problem. And, hey, thanks for being a good sport. I apologize for anything else I said or did that I don't remember."

"Don't mention it," I said and left.

I drove home and felt like I'd spent the night rubbing sand in my eyes. My head ached and, to be honest, my heart ached, too. The sooner I forgot last night, the better.

Pépé was still asleep. I showered and changed, then went downstairs to fix breakfast. Quinn wasn't the only one out of coffee. Pépé must have gone through both bags of the Ethiopian and Sumatran I liked to blend so that he could make the robust rocket fuel he craved. And we had no bread.

I got my coat and car keys and drove to the General Store. I needed something to eat and Thelma would have home-baked muffins and fresh coffee. She would also have her antennae up and ready to receive any gossip she could extract from me by fair means or foul. But I reckoned that she knew everything that had been whispered about Nicole Martin—and, for a change, maybe I'd be the one to glean new information from her.

I angled the Mini into a place on the chunk of cracked asphalt that Thelma liked to call "the parking lot." She'd been running the General Store for as long as I could remember; there had been some sort of store on this spot since Atoka was founded in the mid-1800s. Thelma swore Mosby had used the place as a hideout, which probably was true, but she also enjoyed dropping names of other famous people she claimed had frequented her establishment. FDR, when he came through to dedicate the Blue Ridge Parkway. The Kennedys when they'd lived here. Movie stars. Politicians. European royalty.

The silver bells on her door sounded like wind chimes when I entered. During the day Thelma stayed glued to the soaps when she didn't have any customers, but at this hour of the morning the tabloids, spread out on the counter by the cash register, had her undivided attention. Until she saw me. Her smile made me think of cats and canaries.

The General Store got stuck in a time warp a few decades ago, deciding to let the rest of the world pass it by. No computerized cash register, no bar codes, no mist watering the fruits and vegetables. Thelma fit right in with the bygone era of the decor, dressing for work with a vampy flair that was half Auntie Mame, half Roxie Hart.

She clapped her hands together like a child. "Why, Lucille! What a treat! I haven't seen you for an age. Come right on in. How about a nice cup of coffee or a muffin? You're lookin' a bit peaky."

She tottered over in stiletto slingbacks, dressed today in fire-engine red a few shades off the current color of her teased helmet of hair. She surveyed me with the practiced eye of a 4-H judge looking over prize livestock.

"Your eyes are all bloodshot," she said before I could answer. "You get any sleep last night, child? 'Course you didn't, all those doings out at your farm. I didn't like that woman much but what someone did to her was turrible. Just turrible."

"Yes, ma'am."

"Sit yourself down in that rocking chair over there and let me pour you a cup of coffee. On the house. You want a muffin?"

"Yes, please."

"Muffin'll cost you a dollar-fifty. You can pay me on the way out. I got blueberry or blueberry. The Romeos were in this morning and ate up most everything I had like a plague of locusts come through."

"Blueberry's fine."

She poured my coffee from a pot labeled "Fancy" and handed it to me. "It's got a little pumpkin and cinnamon spice in it, this one," she said. "On account of Halloween and all."

The coffee bordered on cloying but the muffin, filled with tart blueberries, offset the sweetness and the combination hit the spot.

"So tell me all about it." She sat next to me in another

rocking chair like a queen on a throne. The store smelled of fresh-brewed coffee, spices, and homemade pastries mingled with the slightly baked odor of her central heating. Sunlight filtered through an east-facing window making lattice stripes on the floor.

I knew she wanted details—the more lurid, the better.

"I'm sure you've heard everything already." I didn't want to relive finding Nicole's body, especially after last night with Quinn, and flattery was Thelma's weak spot.

"Well, a person does need to keep informed." Her faced twitched in a smile, accepting the compliment as her due. "Especially if we've got a serial killer running loose around here. First that writer, now the ex-wife of your winemaker. He must have taken it hard."

I ignored the wide-enough-to-drive-a-truck-through opening to talk about Quinn and said, "What makes you think the same person killed them both?"

Thelma leaned forward, elbows resting on her knees. Her eyes, behind thick glasses, showed surprise. "Why, I couldn't say. It's just one of my feelings. You know, Lucille, some people believe I have psychotic powers. A God-given ability to know things from . . ."—she paused for drama—". . . the Great Beyond."

Thelma, like Dominique, had issues with the English language. "You've often talked about that," I said.

"Oh my, yes. And, of course, I always watch those police shows and such on television. A person can learn a lot from them. The way things are really done." She straightened up. "How'd you happen to find her, anyway? I heard someone left her in a field in the middle of nowhere."

"Not 'nowhere.' Near the place my mother died."

Thelma worked hard at achieving eternal youth, but mentioning my mother—whom she'd adored—softened her features until the web of lines and wrinkles deepened with sympathy and memory. "I did not know that."

I finished my blueberry muffin and folded the crumbs into my napkin in a tight, neat square.

"You must have gone there with Luc," she said. "I know how he misses his daughter."

"Thank you for getting him those flowers," I said. "My mother would have loved them."

Thelma touched the back of her lacquered hair with one hand, ever the coquette. "I'd do anything for that man," she said. "Did you know every time he comes into the store he kisses my hand? I just plumb love it when he does that. Hold out your hand to any other man around here and he thinks you want to show him your age spots."

"Really?"

"I only tried it two times, but that was enough."

I laughed.

"Some of those Romeos could take a page from his book, if you ask me. I probably shouldn't tell you this, Lucille, but I've been studying French for a while. Audiotapes. Works real good. How's this sound? *Mon chapeau est sur ma fesse.*"

"You have a good accent," I said. "But you just said something like 'my hat is on my ass.'"

"Lordy." Her color deepened to match her dress. "Maybe I need new headphones." She paused. "I'll miss Luc when he leaves. I'd sure like to visit Paris some day."

She took off her glasses and looked away but not before I saw the longing in her eyes.

"You never know," I said. "And he'll be back to visit."

"Sure he will." She forced a smile. "So he was with you when you found Nicole Martin. What kind of sick person would leave a body out there for all the animals to find?"

"Someone who didn't think she'd be discovered for a while. Did you ever meet her?"

"Why, sure I did. She was in a few days before she ... passed. On the phone the whole time. So annoying. She could have waited two minutes until she was outside before making those meeting plans, couldn't she? Instead she's yakking away right under my nose, just as rude as you please."

"What day was that?"

Thelma had an encyclopedic memory. "Sunday. 'Bout eleven o'clock."

"Any idea who she was meeting or what it was about?"

"I'm pretty sure it was a woman." She tapped her forehead. "Feminine inhibition, you know. At first I thought maybe they were meeting for lunch because she was all dressed up real fancy in a nice-looking suit. Then she said something about 'being over there' as soon as she left the store so I guess she was driving to the other woman's house."

"What color was the suit?" I asked.

"Reddish-brown. Not one of my colors. Makes my skin look sallow. Why?" She turned pale. "Good Lord, Lucille. That's what she had on when you found her, isn't it? That poor woman. Goin' from my store to her death."

"It's also possible she had her meeting and went somewhere else."

Thelma picked up her glasses and polished the lenses on her sleeve without looking at me. "How's Quinn taking this? I heard he wasn't too happy she came to town."

I didn't know whether to answer her directly or indirectly. Quinn didn't kill Nicole and I needed to eliminate that idea from Thelma's repertoire of possibilities before it went any further.

"He once loved her enough to marry her. So he's taking her death like you'd think he would. He's devastated."

Thelma adjusted her glasses and surveyed me through trifocals. "I don't suppose you heard about Hamp Weaver," she said. "He's moving into the postfuneral planning business."

Hampton Weaver was a local carpenter who ran a fireworks company—Boom Town Fireworks—on the side. "Postfuneral?"

"It's kind of a new thing. But I'm sure it'll catch on real big. For those folks who want to give their loved ones an extraterrestrial experience. A wonderful send-off to their next home."

I must have looked startled because she said, "Oh, don't you worry. It's very tasteful. And Hamp knows his fireworks. He sees it as a different kind of way to spread the ashes of your loved one. Everyone's going to want to do it. You can even choose the favorite colors of the deceased. You know, personalize the display for that final send-off. There's lots of possibilities for creativity."

"Fireworks?"

She stood up. "Most everyone has that reaction, Lucille. It surprises the heck out of you but once you think on it, it's pretty clever. Let me get you his new business card. You can slip it to Quinn when you think the time is right."

Which would be never. "I ought to be getting home, Thelma. Thanks for the coffee and I'll pay you for the muffin. I also need some coffee beans and a loaf of that homemade sourdough bread for my grandfather."

She caressed the paper bag that held the bread as she put it in a plastic carrier. "You tell Luc I sent this with my love, you hear me? And tell him don't be a stranger, either. I know he likes red." She smoothed her dress. "I'm wearing this just in case he drops by today."

"He does," I said. "And I'll tell him."

"Au revoir," she said. "And you can also tell him that I've got a nice cross-ant waiting here special for him. *Dans ma poitrine.*"

I knew she meant *vitrine,* which was the large glass case where she kept all the baked goods, including her croissants. No point mentioning she'd told me instead that she was keeping it in her breast.

So Nicole Martin stopped by the General Store on her way to a meeting with a woman. Dressed in the suit she was killed in.

I drove home, making a mental list of possible candidates. It was pretty short.

Chapter 25

I called the winery on my way back to the house. Frankie answered and said a couple of reporters had phoned about Nicole.

"What'd you tell them?" I asked.

"No comment."

"Good for you. I just turned my phone on. Looks like I've got a bunch of messages."

"Listen only if it's someone you know," she said. "I asked Gina to come in today. Hope you don't mind, but I thought the boss could use a day off. We can cover anything that comes up."

I smiled. "The boss wouldn't mind a day off. Have you seen Quinn?"

"Jesus Lord."

"Guess that's 'yes.'"

"He looked like hell."

"He needs some sleep. I hope you told him to take a day off, too."

"I tried. He went to the barrel room to get away from

everything. A reporter showed up on his doorstep and wanted to talk to him," Frankie said.

"What happened?"

"Quinn threw him off the property, then called his hunting buddy to come over and patrol the place. He's supposed to be shooting crows and what have you, but I think he's also supposed to put the fear of God into trespassers."

"The spot near my mother's cross is still a crime scene, Frankie. The sheriff's department is coming by to search the place, too."

"They've been here already," she said. "I think they're out by where you found Nicole now. Look, why don't you let me handle all this? Go home and turn your phone off. Take your grandfather out for a drive or just get lost somewhere. There must be something you'd like to do."

"As a matter of fact," I said, "there is."

When I got home around nine-thirty Pépé was still sleeping. I sat across from the bust of Jefferson in the foyer and listened to the messages on my phone. The only call I returned was Kit's.

She answered on the first ring. "Where the hell have you been? I've been looking for you everywhere. No one answers at your house and your cell goes straight to voice mail."

"My grandfather wouldn't wake up if an army marched through his bedroom. I've been out."

"Are you okay, Luce? I heard you two found Nicole."

"We were visiting my mother's cross. Whoever killed her left her body near there."

"Bobby said she was beaten and strangled."

"I know."

"How's Quinn taking it?"

"Like you'd think. He's in the barrel room trying to work."

"Look, I'm on my way to a briefing at the sheriff's department so I've got to dash. Why don't I call you this afternoon?"

"Sure. You're writing the story?"

"Everybody in the bureau's working on it."

"You make any decision on the Moscow job yet?"

She hesitated and my heart sank. She was going to take it. "Yeah," she said, "as a matter of fact I did. I turned it down."

I smiled into the phone. "I'm really glad. What changed your mind?"

"Maybe it's not so bad writing about school board meetings after all," she said. "And Bobby finally said, 'Baby, don't go.'"

"Really? Things must be getting serious."

"Yeah, sure. Mr. Speedy when it comes to romance. Like watching a glacier melt." She chuckled at her own joke. "What are you doing today?"

"Errands."

"Keep your mind off everything, huh? Take care of yourself. Talk to you later, kiddo."

"Sure."

I hung up and wrote Pépé a note about the coffee, adding a "p.s." about Thelma and the bread—though I left out the red dress. My grandfather was sweet and chivalrous to every woman he met because that was his nature, but my grandmother had been the one and only love of his life. Deep down, I think Thelma knew that.

I put the morning newspaper on the coffee table in the library where he liked to read and emptied his ashtray. He'd left a neat pile of copies of the *Washington Tribune* containing Ryan's columns. I gathered them up to put in the recycling bin on my way to the car.

If Nicole Martin had a meeting with a woman, there was one other woman—besides me—who didn't want her leaving town with the Washington wine. Amanda Heyward. Had she tried to stop Nicole? Our relationship had cooled because of Kyra's vandalism and the fact that I'd made her daughter clean my stone pillars. Quizzing Amanda about Nicole after her body had been found at the vineyard wouldn't be much of a fence-mender.

I opened the side door to the carriage house and stuffed the copies of the *Trib* into the recycling bin. The newspaper on top had been folded open to Ryan's column—the one he wrote about the Washington wine. I picked it up and read it again.

Ryan hadn't only written about the Margaux, though that was the centerpiece of the article. He'd also mentioned the Domaine de Romanée-Conti and the Château Dorgon. Joe Dawson said Valerie had been upset because of something she'd learned in Bordeaux. I'd always assumed it had been the Margaux since both Valerie and Thomas Jefferson had visited that vineyard. The DRC was a Burgundy—but that also left the Dorgon. A vineyard that no longer existed.

The other night I'd finished reading Jefferson's European travel diary. It had been a meticulously kept account of everything he saw, down to such mundane observations as the size and composition of bricks found in buildings along the Garonne River. Unlike me, he missed no details.

I went back inside and knocked on the door to Pépé's bedroom. He answered, sounding sleepy.

"I'm sorry to wake you, but it's important," I said.

"Entrez."

His blue-and-white-striped pajama top had a button undone, revealing a small triangle of pale white skin. His gray hair stuck up in tufts. Seeing him like this instead of dapper in a worn but elegant suit made him seem somehow vulnerable. My throat tightened and I leaned down to hug him, kissing his wrinkled cheek.

"What's wrong? Sit, *ma puce*."

"Do you want to come downstairs for coffee?" I asked. "Thelma sent you some fresh bread, too. In case you change your mind about eating breakfast."

"You woke me at—" He leaned over and picked up his alarm clock, holding it close to his face so he could read it without his glasses. "*Mon Dieu*. Nearly ten A.M., to ask me if I wanted breakfast?"

"No, no. I'm sorry. It wasn't that. I wanted to ask you about the wine Jack Greenfield donated to the auction. Not the Margaux. The other Bordeaux—the Château Dorgon."

"What of it?"

"Do you know why that château went out of business?"

"The family members who survived the war couldn't keep it going so they sold it." He sat back against his crumpled pillow. "Why is this so important?"

"I don't know. Is there any way you could find out more about that family?"

"I can call someone, if you wish. He spent a lot of time in Bordeaux working with the vineyards in that region once we got funds from the Marshall Plan."

"That would be terrific."

He regarded me. "I presume you wish me to make this call now?"

"If you could."

But his friend wasn't home, so he left a message.

"What's going on, Lucie?" he asked.

I told him what Thelma had said about Nicole and the meeting with a woman I guessed was Amanda Heyward.

"What do you plan to do about it?" His eyes were grave. "I hope you're not going to ask Amanda if she met Nicole?"

"I need to talk to her about the auction," I said. "I can find an indirect way to ask her about Nicole."

"Call her."

"I need to do it in person."

"Of course you do." He shook his head. "I don't think that's wise."

I stared at him, arms folded.

"If you insist," he said at last, "then I'm coming with you. But first I need to take a shower and then I must have some coffee."

"Take your shower and I'll make your coffee."

He glared at me. "I do not want dishwater, especially at this ungodly hour. Thank you, but I'll make it myself."

"You sure wake up grumpy," I said.

"At my age, it is a blessing merely to wake up," he said. "And now if you'll excuse me—"

I stood up and grinned. "Of course. I'll see you in the kitchen."

The phone in the foyer rang as I came downstairs. Frankie, calling from the villa. I heard her sigh through the phone.

"What's wrong?" I asked.

"I'm really sorry. I know you don't need this today and it seems kind of trivial." She had lowered her voice so I could scarcely hear her.

"What seems trivial? And why are you whispering?"

"Mac Macdonald came by. He wants to leave a donation

for the auction. Says it's a really good bottle of wine, but he wants to give it to you. In person," she said. "I think he kind of wants to see how you're doing after finding Nicole yesterday. He's worried about you."

Mac owned Macdonald's Fine Antiques in Middleburg and was one of the Romeos. He'd helped my mother acquire many of the American pieces she'd bought for Highland House over the years and he'd been close to both of my parents.

"I'll be right over," I said. Pépé would be a while taking care of his toilette.

"I'm sorry about this," she said again.

"Don't worry about it. Can you give Mac a cup of coffee?"

"He's on his second. I gave him my muffin from Thelma's, too."

"You're a good woman."

I hollered up the stairs to Pépé that I had an errand at the winery and would be back shortly. Then I got my jacket and car keys.

Frankie had put a couple of pumpkins and a pot of bright yellow mums by the steps to the front door of the villa. One of the pumpkins was darker than the others and the color reminded me of Nicole's suit. When I got inside, her two carved jack-o'-lanterns—the witch and the werewolf—sat on either end of the bar. Frankie's smile froze when she saw my face.

"What's wrong?" She turned and stared at the pumpkins. "I saw these in the barrel room and thought they'd look great over here. Someone did a terrific job with them. They are meant for the winery, aren't they?"

"Well, hey there, sugar." Mac Macdonald came out of the kitchen holding a coffee mug. Tall and stooped with a monk's tonsure of white hair, Mac's suits usually hung on his thin, bent frame, reminding me of a well-dressed crane. His eyes traveled from my face to Frankie's. "Something wrong? Am I interrupting—?"

"No, nothing's wrong." I caught Frankie's eye.

Behind Mac's back she pointed to the pumpkins and raised her eyebrows, mouthing, "These?"

I nodded and went over to kiss Mac on the cheek. "Frankie said you brought a donation for the auction. How thoughtful."

Mac and his wallet were close and though he swore every time he sold a piece of furniture or a painting that he was barely making a profit, everyone in town knew better. He and a couple of the Romeos had formed a small investment club that beat the market every year since they'd been in existence, plus Mac had his own portfolio rumored to be in seven figures. It still didn't stop him from peeling uncanceled stamps off envelopes and reading Thelma's copy of the *Trib* each morning when he stopped by for coffee and a doughnut. The donation of a bottle of wine was a surprise.

"I've got it right here." He'd left a cotton tote printed with the logo of Blue Ridge Federal Bank on one of the sofas. "It's supposed to be pretty good."

He pulled out a bottle and handed it to me. A jeroboam of Château Latour à Pomerol.

"It's more than pretty good, Mac. It's fabulous," I said. "A Latour à Pomerol will bring in a lot of money."

"Really?" He seemed surprised and for a moment I wondered if he wasn't going to reconsider. "Well, he said it was worth a lot."

"Who did?"

"Shane Cunningham."

"You bought this at Jeroboam's?"

Mac shook his head. "Shane gave it to me. I just started buying wine futures from him and I purchased a couple of bottles of wine through his Internet auctions. He's advising me since I'm still a novice, but I trust him." He shrugged. "Whatever I buy I usually resell through him and it's made me a tidy little profit. The wine was kind of a thank-you gift after I made a fairly substantial investment."

Some thank-you gift. "You don't ever see the wine you buy through those auctions?"

Mac hoisted his coffee mug. "You know I'm a teetotaler. But I do enjoy investing—and it's fun getting involved in, you know, the world of wine." He smiled like we were co-conspirators.

I looked at the bottle. Jack Greenfield owned a couple of jeroboams of the Latour—I'd just seen them when I walked through his wine cellar on Sunday. And Shane was taking inventory of what Jack owned since Jack seemed to have lost track.

"When did Shane give this to you?" I asked.

"Couple of weeks ago, maybe a month. Why?"

"Just curious. Thanks so much, Mac."

"You all right, sugar? I heard about you finding that young woman yesterday." He put an arm around my shoulder. "What's this world coming to where you kill a person and dump them like a sack of trash? Who would do something like that?"

"I don't know," I said. "But I'm sure the sheriff will find whoever did it."

"Used to be so safe around here," he said. "Now we've got all these people coming in from away. Including *you* bringing 'em in—you're hiring 'em. I say we ought to send those folks back home where they belong. I'll bet you one of them did it."

Fond as I was of Mac, I would never understand his ugly prejudices or his belief that white stood for purity and good. He thought America ought to be populated by Americans, not foreigners, but you could never tell him that the only real Americans had been here for centuries, long before the *Susan Constant,* the *Godspeed,* and the *Discovery* arrived in Jamestown in 1607. When all was said and done, he and all the rest of us were the foreigners.

"If those men didn't pick my grapes," I said, "who would? They work hard, Mac. They send money home so their families can have a better life. A lot of them have more than one job."

"You wait and see," he said. "When it all shakes out one of those people will be responsible for that woman's death."

He said "those people" like he was talking about bird droppings.

"I'm not sure about that," I said.

He bussed me on the cheek and left his empty cup on the bar. The pumpkins, I noticed, were no longer there.

After he left, Frankie came over to me with her hands on her hips. "I moved the pumpkins out to the terrace because I knew they upset you," she said, "but I swear, I was that close to throwing one of them at him." She held up her thumb and forefinger. No daylight between them.

"I wouldn't have stopped you," I said. "He's always been like that. Usually he keeps it to himself."

"I would have called him on it."

I shook my head. "Today I just couldn't."

"I could tell. Especially when I saw the look on your face when he handed you that wine. And what's with the pumpkins?"

"Nicole carved them when she was with Quinn the other night," I said.

Frankie's hand went to her mouth. "I had no idea. I never should have taken them. What do you think I should do now?"

"Put them back in the barrel room and let Quinn decide."

"All right." She eyed the Latour. "Fabulous donation."

"It is, isn't it? I'd better get back to the house. My grandfather's waiting for me."

"You two going to do something nice together?"

"I think I'm going to drive over to Sunny Greenfield's place and drop off the artwork for the cover of the auction catalog."

She looked surprised. "Really? Well, if it will take your mind off everything that's been going on, then good. The auction has kind of fallen by the wayside ever since Jack asked you to return his wine. We still have a lot to do to get ready, you know."

I drove back to the house and wondered about the Washington bottle. Had Nicole gone over to the Greenfields' on Sunday and tried to buy it? Jack would have still been recovering from his concussion the night before. Thelma had heard Nicole on the phone, making plans to see someone she presumed was another woman. Had Nicole met with Sunny and not Amanda as I'd thought?

Then there was Shane, who I now suspected was pilfering wine from his partner's wine cellar. He was also Nicole's ex-boyfriend and nowhere to be found after the burglary the other day. How did he fit into all this?

Pépé had finished his coffee when I got home.

"Change of plans," I said. "We're not going to Amanda's. We're going by Sunny Greenfield's to drop off something for the auction."

"Is she expecting us?" he asked.

"No," I said, "but that's okay. I'll be right back. The papers are upstairs in my study."

He was waiting in the library with his coat on when I returned.

"Everything okay?" I asked.

"Fine. I just wanted my cigarettes." He patted his breast pocket. "The reason we're going to Sunny's is not so you can leave some papers with her, is it?"

"No," I said, "it's not."

"I didn't think so," he said.

Chapter 26

On the way over to the Greenfields, I told Pépé about the bottle of wine Mac had donated for the auction.

"When Eli and Sunny asked me to look around on Sunday to see what had been stolen, I thought it was odd there weren't any bottles pulled partially out of their places," I said. "At the time, I wondered if it might be because the thief or thieves knew Jack's cellar—and I figured Nicole was probably involved."

"Now you believe she was not?" Pépé asked.

"Now I think I understand what happened. Nicole and Shane were partners—he knows that wine cellar inside out. Mac said Shane gave him the bottle of Latour a month or so ago. Maybe Shane was stealing wine from Jack's cellar as he took inventory. Since he's setting up the database, he can make sure it matches what's on hand. Besides, Jack has thirty thousand bottles. That's a lot of wine."

"So why the robbery, if he has been stealing wine quietly and not getting caught? Or at least, until now when you made the connection with the Latour," Pépé said.

"Maybe Nicole pushed Shane to do it," I said. "Though I don't think she was there during the robbery. She had dinner with Mick until nine and afterward went over to Quinn's for the rest of the night. Quinn said she arrived around ten or ten-thirty."

"And between nine and ten?"

"Sunny didn't know what time the break-in occurred. All she knew was that when she went looking for Jack it was after midnight. That's when she found him unconscious in the wine cellar—alone. The earliest he could have gone there was after eleven because she went to bed and left him watching the news."

"Perhaps Nicole showed up just to make sure all was in order," Pépé said. "Then she drove over to be with Quinn."

I frowned. "Could she have done that in an hour? Drive from Mick's to Jack's to Quinn's place?"

"She could have met Shane elsewhere. Or called him."

"You know, their affair was over. I think Nicole's the one who ended it. The timing seems odd."

Pépé smiled. "Perhaps it does to you, but I suspect they did not let their feelings get in the way of committing a crime together."

"Or they did get in the way and after the robbery Shane killed Nicole."

"Lucie," he said, "we really ought to go to the sheriff with all this."

"We will, once I check out whether there's a missing jeroboam of Latour in Jack's cellar."

"How do you plan to do that? I knew you were not planning to drop off any so-called papers with Sunny."

"Of course I am. That's the reason we're going over there. And they're not 'so-called papers,'" I said. "It's the artwork for the cover of the auction catalog. We're using one of Mom's paintings of the vineyard. Sunny's taking care of getting the catalog printed, so she needs this."

Pépé's face grew soft. "May I see which painting you chose?"

I reached into the backseat and got the folder. The photograph of the oil painting, one of my favorites, was of the vineyard in autumn. It was one of her last works during a period when she'd been experimenting with bold, brilliant colors and a more impressionistic style.

He stared at it for a moment and closed the folder. "You haven't answered my question. How do you plan to look around the wine cellar? You can't tell Sunny what you want to do."

"Sure I can. I'm just going to ask her flat out if I can look around again," I said. "Besides, I'm bringing my secret weapon. You. You'll charm the socks off her."

His smile was fleeting. "Even if you are right that doesn't prove Shane stole it. Or that Nicole had anything to do with it."

"A lot of people we know are buying wine from Shane through his auctions and his futures. Mac's never seen a single bottle of wine that he's bought. What if it's all just a sham? A Ponzi scheme?"

"Lucie." Pépé shook his head. "I'm telling you, this is dangerous. Nicole was murdered and that other woman died because someone tampered with her car. Look in the wine cellar if you must, but then we should talk to your friend Bobby. This is no business for us."

I turned into the Greenfields' driveway. The sun had finally come out and the sky was clotted with clouds. I pulled up and parked in front of the house.

"Looks like they're both gone," I said. "No cars."

"Don't forget your folder." Pépé handed it to me as we got out of the car. "If you came to talk about the auction, you should have your papers with you."

"Good point." I rang the doorbell. "I don't think anyone is home. Maybe we should try the wine cellar."

"First, let's check the house more thoroughly. I'll go around back. You wait here in case someone's home after all," Pépé said.

He disappeared and I peered through one of the sidelights. The house was quiet.

"Lucie!" Pépé gestured for me to follow him. "Come take a look."

A split rail fence, with a morning glory twining through it, marked the boundaries of their half-acre backyard. There was a brick patio with the lawn furniture still set out and a small pond with a weeping willow along one side of the property line near the path to the cottage where the wine cellar was located. In the center of the pond, a large white clump of something floated like an ungraceful lily pad.

"What is that?" I asked. "It looks like paper."

"It is paper. Wait a minute." Pépé walked over to the barbecue grill on the patio and unhooked a long meat fork and metal spatula that were hanging on the side.

He handed me the spatula. "Let's see if we can find out what it is."

We splashed the water with our tools like a couple of kids, stirring it up until the mass of paper finally drifted within reach. Pépé speared it with the fork, but by now I could tell it was wine labels. A lot of them.

"All Château Dorgon," I said. "You think the bottles are in the bottom of the pond?"

"It would be logical. Whoever did this did not think

about the glue dissolving and the labels rising to the surface."

"But why put the wine here? Why not drink it or dump it out, if you wanted to get rid of it?" I asked.

"Because someone did not want to get rid of it. They merely wanted to hide it temporarily," he said.

"Sunny told me that Valerie accused Jack's father of stealing wine from the French when he was stationed in Bordeaux during the war," I said. "But Sunny said it was just the opposite and that Jack's father risked his life helping the local vineyard owners. Do you suppose Valerie was right—that this wine really was stolen from Château Dorgon during the war and Jack has been lying for his father all along?"

"Or it's possible Jack told the truth as he knew it," Pépé said. "Maybe he believed that his father really did help the French. Then Valerie showed up and told a different story of a man who was not so noble. You know, some of the vineyard owners were sent to the concentration camps."

"Oh God! What if he did something like that and Valerie found out and threatened to blackmail him?" I said. "So he tampered with her car, or had someone do it for him."

"Possibly."

I gestured to the labels. "But Jack wouldn't hide this wine. He'd want to destroy it once he knew the truth. Someone else did this."

"Shane, perhaps," Pépé said. "Or maybe Sunny?"

"Sunny? Would she?" I stared at him. Maybe that's what Shane and Sunny had been talking about the day I saw them together at the Point-to-Point. "Come on. Let's see if we can get into the wine cellar."

"I guess we could take a look around."

A slate path bordered on either side by azaleas and rhododendron led from the pond to the small building. The door still hadn't been repaired and there was a new-looking padlock through the hasp. I tugged on it. Locked.

"Give me the paper clips from those pages in your folder," Pépé said. "I'll unlock it."

"You're going to pick the lock?"

"Do you have a better idea?"

"Uh, no. It's just that I had no idea you knew how to do that."

"I'll teach you sometime," he said. "It's not so hard."

He opened one of the two paper clips and pulled the wire at a ninety-degree angle.

"Can you hold this, please?" He handed it to me and opened the second paper clip, doubling it back on itself.

I watched as he jammed it in the keyhole, putting his ear next to the lock. As he jiggled the paper clip, he moved his tongue from side to side as though it were following the zigzag trajectory past the lock pins.

After a moment he said, "Please give me the other paper clip."

A few seconds later, he pulled on the lock and it opened.

I rolled my eyes at the satisfied smile on his face. "Ladies first. But let's be quick. This is breaking and entering. Have your look around, then let's get out of here."

I flipped on the lights and Pépé whistled. "Nice, isn't it?" I said.

"Someone spent a lot of money."

"Look. The Washington bottle," I said. It was in a small alcove above the bar on its own, caught in the soft wash of a low-wattage spotlight. "So Nicole didn't get it, after all. I guess Jack or Sunny must have moved it back here after the break-in."

"Let's go see where you found the Latour," Pépé said. "And then I think we should leave."

The tiny twinkling spotlights shining on the dark walls and slate floor made the place seem moodily theatrical. We walked past the stair-stepped freestanding wine racks to the rows of shelves and their floor-to-ceiling racks containing bottles of wine. I led Pépé down what seemed like endless mazelike rows until we came to the Bordeaux. The jeroboams were in a separate location since they didn't fit in the standard racks.

I pointed to an empty space next to a jeroboam of Latour. "I bet Shane took it from here."

"Okay," he said. "Now we go to the sheriff."

The sound of the front door closing—loudly, as though a blast of wind caught it—sent my heart into my throat. Pépé's eyes met mine and he put a finger to his lips.

"Stay here," I whispered. "It's probably Jack or Sunny. I'll say the door was unlocked and tell them about the auction papers."

I walked around the corner and stepped into the light pool of a small spotlight.

"Well, well. What are you doing here, Lucie?"

Shane Cunningham stood in the doorway, dressed as though he'd been out riding. He was holding a hunting rifle and he did not look pleased to see me.

Chapter 27

"I came by to see Sunny," I said. "There was no one at the house so I checked here. It was unlocked so I came in."

"That's odd." He came into the room and closed the door. "I was here earlier working on the inventory and I know I locked up. Sunny's got a meeting in Charlottesville and Jack is at the store. Sorry about the gun, but I thought maybe whoever broke into the place the other night had come back. Didn't mean to scare you."

I laughed, giddily relieved at the reprieve. "Don't apologize. Sorry I scared you, too." I walked over to the marble and redwood bar where I'd left the folder. "I brought this for Sunny—"

"What the hell's going on here?" The door opened once again. Jack Greenfield seemed to block all the available light coming from the outside. He looked from me to Shane and the rifle and his eyebrows knitted together. At that moment I knew he was guilty of something because he looked like the devil himself.

"Good God, Shane. What are you doing with that?"

Jack stared hard at me as though I'd somehow let him down and shook his head. "Why did you come here, Lucie? Why couldn't you have stayed out of it?"

"Shut up!" Shane said. "Shut up, you fool."

For a moment no one spoke. Jack looked at Shane and the light went out of his eyes. "How was I supposed to know? You're standing there with the goddamn rifle."

"And you're supposed to be at the store. She was here when I arrived. I told her I thought whoever broke into the place the other night might have come back." Shane raised his rifle like a club and said to me, "You don't know what you've just done. Jack's right. You should have stayed out of it."

"Stayed out of what?" I said. My hands were slick with sweat and my legs were shaking. I leaned on my cane for support.

"She knows," Shane said to Jack. "Or she wouldn't be here."

"Now what do we do?" Jack asked.

Shane shrugged. "I can make it look like an accident."

"Like Valerie?" I pointed to the Washington wine. "You killed her and Nicole for that bottle of wine? Or was it because of the Dorgon and what your father did during the war?"

At the mention of the Dorgon, Jack came inside the room, slamming the door. "What about the Dorgon?"

"Nothing. I got rid of it." Shane looked Jack in the eye with the smooth assurance of a practiced liar.

"No, he didn't. The bottles are in the pond in your backyard," I said. "The labels floated to the surface."

Shane blinked rapidly and twirled a finger by his temple. "She's crazy. The wine's gone."

"You bastard," Jack said.

"What did Valerie find out about the Dorgon, Jack?" I asked. "That your father was no hero during the war? That he didn't really help the French winemakers protect what was theirs so the Nazis wouldn't confiscate it? He stole and looted just like the others, didn't he? Maybe worse."

Jack picked at something imaginary on the sleeve of his expensive blazer. When he looked up, his face was filled with rage. "You have no right to judge. What choice did my father have? You don't understand . . . none of us do. None of us were there. He did what he had to do."

"Then why did you tell Sunny the wine was a thank-you gift from someone your father helped?" I asked. "Someone grateful for his bravery and courage."

He closed his eyes. When he opened them, they were haunted by betrayal. "Because that is what he told me. Because I believed he was a good man who tried to help others."

Whether Jack's father genuinely believed he was acting as a patriotic soldier for the Fatherland obeying Hitler's orders, or whether he'd been one of the thousands of Nazi soldiers who plundered and destroyed the vineyards of France was something I was sure he'd already answered for when he met his Maker. But he'd heaped even more shame on what he'd done because of the lies and the myth he'd perpetuated so the son believed that his father had courageously risked his life by defying his superiors, that he'd been a man of conscience, and that the bottles of wine he brought home were gifts in tribute to his heroism.

Instead it was the spoils of war. Blood wine.

"What did Valerie tell you?" I asked.

"None of your business."

"Your father did something to the family who owned the vineyard, didn't he?"

Jack shrugged. "He was ordered to confiscate the property. The wine was needed for industrial alcohol. It was near the end of the war. We had nothing. And the château became a hospital for our soldiers."

We. Our. I flinched at his use of pronouns. "What happened to the family who lived there?"

Another shrug. "They were Jewish."

"Your father sent them to the camps?"

"I have answered enough of your questions."

Somewhere behind me, Pépé was listening to the son of a man who had fought against him during the war. I wondered if he was remembering his missions through France, leading those who needed to get to safety while Jack's father condemned a family for the unforgivable sin of their religion.

"Valerie tried to blackmail you. She was broke and she needed money so she came to you and threatened to tell what she knew and humiliate you. You needed to get rid of her and you tampered with her car." I glanced at Shane. "Or someone else did."

"I don't need to listen to this," Jack said. "And you don't know what you're saying."

"You killed Nicole, too. Valerie talked to her before she died, so Nicole knew something was up."

Jack glanced scathingly in Shane's direction. "Nicole was a greedy young woman who stupidly tried to profit off her friend's . . . misfortune."

"Not so stupid she didn't help you set up your phony robbery," I said.

I caught the surprised look that passed between them. "She didn't set up anything," Shane said.

"Then who did?"

They were silent and that's when the pieces fell into place.

Or at least some of them. "*You* did?" I said. "You staged your own robbery? Who knocked you out, Jack? Shane? Sunny? You had to make it look real, didn't you? Then what happened? Maybe after Nicole figured out you killed Valerie, she also learned about the fake robbery from Shane. She didn't have much of a conscience but she did want the Washington wine—and now she had plenty of leverage to make you give it to her, didn't she? So you killed her, too."

"Shut up," Shane said. He looked at Jack. "I'll handle this."

"I'm sorry, Lucie." Jack sounded like he meant the apology. "You understand we have no choice. My hands are tied."

I stared at him with contempt. "I bet that's just what your father said to that family before he sent them to the concentration camps."

He walked over and slapped me hard across the face. "I was wrong. You deserve what you're getting," he said. To Shane he added, "Take her somewhere else. Don't do it here."

"Why do you still trust him? He kept the Dorgon and he's stealing from you," I said. "I'm not just talking about the robbery, either."

"Shut up," Shane said, but I had Jack's attention again.

"Mac Macdonald donated a jeroboam of Château Latour à Pomerol for the auction," I said. "He said it was a thank-you gift from Shane, in return for investing a lot of money in wine futures and the Internet auctions. There's an empty space next to the other Latour jeroboam on your wine rack."

Jack stared at Shane. "One bottle," Shane said. "Big deal. We're making a bundle. Sometimes you need to spend money to make money."

"We'll talk about that later." Jack sounded grim. He gestured to me. "Take care of this. I'll see you at the store when you're done." He left without looking at me and a moment later I heard his engine start.

"Let's go," Shane said. "I haven't got all day."

"Go where?"

"Outside."

The sound of glass on glass like bottles clanking against each other stopped him.

"What was that? Who else is here?" He pointed the gun at me. "Whoever you are back there, you'd better come out. Unless you show yourself she's a dead woman."

"He's got a gun," I said. "Stay where you are, Pépé."

For a moment Shane looked puzzled. Then he burst out laughing and lowered the rifle. "Your grandfather? That old man is here? You think he's going to save you?" He crossed the room and grabbed my arm, twisting it behind my back. "First we're getting rid of that damn cane. I don't trust you with it." He kicked it from my hand and it skidded across the room, disappearing under one of the shelves.

"Okay, Pépé," he said. "Get out here now before I kill your granddaughter. I can even count in French so you understand. *"Dix ... neuf ... huit ... sept ... six ... cinq ..."*

I heard a soft thwack and Shane slumped against me.

"Run, Lucie." Pépé held a wine bottle in his hand. "I don't know how long he'll be out."

"My cane."

"No time." He grabbed my hand and pulled me with him but my leg buckled and I fell.

He helped me up. *"Vite, vite!* Hurry!"

"Don't move. Either of you." Shane's voice was thick behind us.

Pépé hurled the wine bottle across the room like he was

throwing a fastball. Shane turned away as it came toward him, shielding his face.

My grandfather shoved me down one row and dove down another as Shane groaned and I heard the sound of breaking glass. "Go!"

The aisles of Jack's wine cellar were open-ended—we wouldn't be able to hide for long. I saw Pépé's shadow at the end of his aisle. He leaned out and signaled to me. He would draw Shane so I could get to the door. My phone was in the car, but that was a few hundred feet away. I pointed to my leg and shook my head. Then I pointed at him. He could run. I could not.

"I'll kill you both." Shane's voice echoed in the room. "No one's leaving."

Pépé disappeared, silent as a ghost. I heard the sound of more glass on glass and Shane moving toward the noise. Pépé still meant for me to go for help and he was trying to draw Shane away from where I was. But I'd have to go the long way around the perimeter of the wine cellar before I could get back to the tasting area and the door without Shane seeing me. And I didn't have my cane.

"Hey, Lucie," Shane said. "Guess who I've got?"

I heard my grandfather's "ouf" and the sound of something hard connecting with flesh. Then more breaking glass. Pépé must have fallen into one of the wine racks. Had Shane struck him with his rifle butt, or another wine bottle? He could have killed him if it had been a blow to the head.

"What did you do to him?" I shouted. "Leave him alone!"

"Then get over here," he said. "Or I'll really hurt him. You know what damage a broken bottle can do to a soft old skull?"

"Oh my God," I said. "Don't. Please, don't."

I walked around the corner. Pépé lay crumpled on the floor, his silver hair streaked with red. He wasn't moving.

"Let me take care of him," I said. "Please."

"Don't be stupid. Now I've got two of you to deal with. You first. Let's go." Shane jabbed the rifle barrel in the small of my back. "Step around that mess. There's glass everywhere."

He forced me back to the tasting area, his hands and jacket covered with wine and blood from where he'd been cut by broken glass. "Over to the sink," he said. "Grab a towel and get it wet. I've got to clean up."

I reached for the towel and caught a glimpse of my grandfather, bloody and wine-stained, as he peeked around the corner of one of the shelves. Shane, facing the sink, had set down the rifle and was wrapping the towel around his hand. He didn't see Pépé. I looked down so my eyes wouldn't give anything away.

"Don't test my marksmanship." My grandfather's voice was surprisingly strong as he cocked the hammer of Leland's Colt .45 semi-automatic pistol and aimed it at Shane. "Put the rifle down on the floor and move away from it."

"No." Shane reached for his gun as I grabbed the Washington wine.

"Do what he says or I'll drop this," I said.

He swung around. "No! Don't do it!"

I brought the bottle down hard on his arm. He swore and fired the rifle, hitting a bottle of wine, which exploded off the shelf. I hit him again and this time he dropped the rifle. I held the Margaux in my hands, amazed that the bottle had not broken.

Pépé walked over to us, keeping the pistol pointed at Shane. He nudged the rifle out of the way with his foot.

"Put the bottle down and get the rifle, Lucie," he said. "And take it with you when you call the sheriff."

I obeyed and started for the door.

"Oh my God—no! Look what you've done!" Shane was staring at the bottle, now cracked with a spiderweb of tiny fissures. Slowly the wine seeped out like blood from a wound. "We have to save it! My God, do you know what this wine is worth?"

"Two lives too many," I said.

"Let it go," Pépé said. "The man it was destined for never drank it. Go along, Lucie."

"Are you sure you'll be okay?"

"Don't worry about me," he said. "I thought I'd teach our friend to count to ten in French while we're waiting. He forgot six, you know. Besides, I am here with the spirits of two of your most famous presidents. I'll be fine."

Chapter 28

The fresh-faced paramedic who showed up was the one who had treated me the day Valerie died.

"You get around," he said.

"I think my grandfather should go to the hospital," I said.

"Not on your life," Pépé said. "Most of this is wine, not blood. I have a small cut on my head but it will heal. I'm not going to any hospital."

"I see orneriness runs in the family," the paramedic said.

I watched a deputy handcuff Shane and take him over to a cruiser. His eyes met mine as the deputy pushed his head down and he slid into the car.

By the time Bobby Noland showed up, he said a couple of deputies had already picked Jack up at Jeroboam's. Bobby walked into Jack's wine cellar and saw the mess of broken bottles and wine on the floor.

"All this over some old bottles of wine," he said. "Give me a beer any time. If it's old, you know it's bad."

★ ★ ★

Pépé's friend had left a message on the answering machine when we got back to the house. Château Dorgon, he reported, had been taken over by a Nazi officer named Johannes von Gruenfeld. None of the family had survived the camps, but a year or so ago an American woman had shown up, claiming to be a distant relative.

"In English, 'Gruenfeld' translates into 'Greenfield,'" Pépé said.

"A distant relative. *Valerie?* My God, if Valerie was related to the family Jack's father sent to the camps, she must have really wanted revenge," I said. "Why didn't she confront him right away?"

"Maybe she wanted to see the wine first," Pépé said.

"I wonder if Nicole knew Valerie was related to the family who owned Château Dorgon," I said. "Though I think all Nicole cared about was having the leverage to blackmail Jack so he'd sell her the Washington wine—or maybe give it to her outright."

"From what you've told me, I doubt Valerie would have confided something like that in Nicole," my grandfather said.

"So Nicole was telling the truth—she didn't know what Valerie knew. Except I thought it had to do with the Margaux," I said.

"In a way, it did," Pépé said. "Both women wanted it and both of them tried to blackmail Jack and Shane—but for different reasons."

"What do you bet Shane would have resold all the 'stolen' wine through his Internet auctions once they collected the insurance money?" I said. "Though Shane betrayed Jack as well, hanging on to the Dorgon and pilfering from his wine cellar."

My grandfather shook his head. "Such a tragedy. At least now it is finished."

"Maybe you ought to think about postponing your trip home," I said. "You really have quite a nasty cut on your head."

"I'll be fine," he said. "I need to get back to Paris. A few of *les vieux potes* are planning another trip."

The old chums. His buddies. The friends he'd gone to China with. "Another trip? Where are you going this time?"

"Egypt. To see the pyramids." He smiled. "I remember watching when they were built. It would be nice to see what they've done with them since then."

I burst out laughing. "Are you really going to Egypt?"

His smile broadened. "But, of course."

The day before he left for Paris, Pépé planned his own fare-well party, inviting Dominique, Eli, Quinn, Thelma, and me to join him at the villa. He'd brought a bottle of 1945 Château d'Yquem from France, intending to drink it with his colleagues to commemorate the year the war ended in Europe. Instead, he decided to share it with us.

"One last memory bottle," he said. "To lay old ghosts to rest."

We drank it at sunset before going to dinner at the Goose Creek Inn. When Thelma arrived in another flam-ing red dress, Pépé kissed her hand. She blushed and glowed like a young girl. Quinn, to my surprise, showed up in a well-tailored blazer, a pair of wool trousers, and a black crewneck sweater. No jewelry. A first for him.

He caught my stare and held it.

Pépé proposed the first toast, to the future.

"What are you going to do about the auction, after

everything that's happened?" Dominique asked. "I heard Sunny Greenfield left town and she's not coming back. Jeroboam's is locked up with a sign that says CLOSED INDEFI-NITELY."

"We'll still hold it, of course," I said. "I think we'll manage to raise a lot of money—nothing like what we expected—but it will be something."

"I can't get over that Shane," Thelma said. "He was always so nice to me but, you know, there was something kind of fishy about him. Usually I'm pretty good about figurin' folks out, but I guess my extrasensory precipitation wasn't working so hot this time. I just can't believe he killed those poor women." She looked over at my grandfather. "You're a brave man, Luc Delaunay. You and Lucie could have been killed."

Quinn moved so he was standing next to me and laid a hand on my shoulder. He leaned down. "Thelma's got quite a crush on your grandfather."

"Mmm."

Pépé smiled at Thelma and raised his glass to her. "'He did not wear his scarlet coat, for blood and wine are red. And blood and wine were on his hands when they found him with the dead. The poor dead woman whom he loved, and murdered in her bed.'"

"Why, Luc!" Thelma's face turned the color of her dress. "That's real poetry. Aren't you the clever one? Did you make that up?"

"Ah, no." He smiled at her. "I am not so gifted. Oscar Wilde wrote it. 'The Ballad of Reading Gaol.'"

"How funny—it describes Shane perfectly," Dominique said. "The scarlet coat. Killing the woman he loved. Even the blood and wine on his hands."

"Speaking of blood and wine, Ryan Worth is going to

fly to Switzerland to get the Washington wine tested," I said. "He called this afternoon. There was enough left in the bottle."

"I still can't believe you hit Shane with that bottle," Eli said. "Thirty thousand to choose from in that wine cellar and you picked that one?"

"I had to get his attention," I said. "And he was reaching for his gun."

"You know, if Valerie hadn't shown up and scared Jack by threatening to expose his father, Shane would probably still be getting away with that scam," Dominique said.

"I suppose we'll never know," Quinn said. "Or if Nicole hadn't come to town for that Margaux." His hand was still on my shoulder. He said in my ear, "Jaime came to get her yesterday. We went out for a few drinks last night."

"You okay?"

"I think so." He gazed at me and his fingers brushed the back of my neck. "I'm glad nothing happened to you and your grandfather. I'd hate to think about losing you."

My face warmed. "You would?"

"We've got the Cab to blend. I need you for that, don't I?"

"Yes," I said, "I guess you do."

Thomas Jefferson, George Washington, and Wine

"We could, in the United States, make as great a variety of wines as are made in Europe, not exactly of the same kinds, but doubtless as good," Thomas Jefferson wrote in 1808 in a letter to a French acquaintance. Though Jefferson's fondest desire was that his own country would cultivate a wine industry, he developed a strong appreciation for French wines while serving as American ambassador to France from 1784–89 during George Washington's administration. The most knowledgeable oenophile among the Founding Fathers, Jefferson was also the greatest wine expert in Colonial America. Besides acting as an informal wine consultant to many of his famous friends, he advised several presidents on the subject, including Washington and Monroe.

In 1789 when Jefferson returned from France for what he thought was a temporary leave of absence, Washington asked him to remain in America and become secretary of state. Though he'd hoped to return overseas, Jefferson reluctantly accepted the appointment. Once settled at home, he offered to introduce Washington to the world of French wine, helping stock the president's cellar.

It was not the first time the two good friends had

collaborated on the subject of wine. As far back as 1774 when the Continental Congress passed legislation banning imported spirits, Jefferson had enlisted Washington's financial support as a backer of the Virginia Wine Company, which was formed for the purpose of growing grapes and making wine in Virginia.

Though that project failed, Washington gladly took advantage of his good friend's expertise to become acquainted with the best French vintages. According to John Hailman's excellent book *Thomas Jefferson on Wine* (University Press of Mississippi, 2006), in 1790, Jefferson wrote the American consul in Bordeaux requesting thirty dozen bottles of Château d'Yquem for Washington and ten dozen for himself, and twenty dozen Château à Latour for Washington. On another occasion, he ordered forty dozen bottles of champagne for President Washington. Throughout his tenure as secretary of state, Jefferson continued ordering wine for Washington, both for Mount Vernon and during his presidency in the then capital city of Philadelphia.

Like Jefferson, George and Martha Washington entertained most days of the year, opening Mount Vernon to both friends and strangers who passed through the region. Through their letters and diaries, it was evident the Washingtons welcomed hundreds of guests annually, providing food and lodging.

"My manner of living is plain," Washington once said. "A glass of wine and a bit of mutton are always ready."

Plain though he claimed to be, Washington always served wine at his afternoon dinners and evening suppers—both with the meal and afterward. Never a connoisseur like Jefferson, Washington enjoyed a daily glass or two of Madeira, a fortified Portuguese wine, or Claret, the generic term for red wine.

Over the years both men tried and failed to establish vineyards on their properties. Washington ordered vine cuttings from Madeira, which never bore fruit in the soil of Mount Vernon, just as the dozens of species of wine grapevines Jefferson tried to grow at Monticello did not produce a single bottle of wine.

Nevertheless both were successful in other ventures

involving alcohol and spirits. For years Jefferson brewed his own beer at Monticello and Washington enjoyed considerable commercial success as the owner of a whiskey distillery, to such an extent that he may have been the number-one whiskey producer in Colonial America.

Over the years, the two close friends undoubtedly drank many bottles of wine together. However, a few years before Washington's death, Jefferson committed the unpardonable political blunder of writing a private letter to a mutual friend in Italy sharply criticizing Washington. The letter made its way back to America, where it created a firestorm when it was published in a Philadelphia newspaper.

Though he had considered Jefferson one of his most trusted partners since before the American Revolution, Washington was so hurt he refused to write or speak to his old friend ever again. Unlike the prolific Jefferson, Washington left behind no documents mentioning what he thought of all the wines Jefferson had procured for him, or the occasions on which they drank them together. With their decades-long relationship irretrievably severed, the two Founding Fathers never again shared a bottle of wine.

An Introduction to Bordeaux

The region of Bordeaux in southwest France conjures images of imposing chateaux, acres of sun-drenched, vine-covered hillsides, and dimly lit cellars filled with cobwebbed bottles of legendary vintages. The best known and most prestigious wine-growing region in the world, Bordeaux is renowned for wines and vineyards that are the benchmark by which much of the industry sets its standards of quality and winemaking style.

But what *is* a Bordeaux wine? Do we make similar wines in America? In other words, what's in a name? To begin with, it is important to remember that in the traditional wine-growing countries of Europe, many wines are classified by region of origin, whereas New World wines are classified by type of grape. And because Bordeaux is a region, it produces both white and red wines—though it is best known for its reds.

Let's say you want to buy a bottle of wine for dinner and can't decide between a bottle of (red) Bordeaux and a California Cabernet Sauvignon. Are you comparing apples to apples?

Not really.

A Bordeaux red is a blend of grapes that includes Cabernet Sauvignon, Merlot, and Cabernet franc, with maybe a little Petit Verdot and/or Malbec, added in as well. The blend—whether the primary grape is Cab Sauv or Merlot—depends upon where in Bordeaux the grapes were grown. The Gironde River and its tributaries—the Dordogne and Garonne—divide the region into two distinct wine-producing zones. The so-called Left Bank possesses a climate well-suited to growing Cabernet Sauvignon; the Right Bank favors Merlot. So read the label on the bottle to find out whether you're drinking a blend of mostly Cab Sauv or mostly Merlot and remember that anywhere from 15 percent to 50 percent of the wine could be the other grapes mentioned above.

As for Cabernet Sauvignon, it's WYSIWYG on the label. U.S. law stipulates that at least 75 percent of the wine must be Cabernet Sauvignon or else it needs to be called something like "Red Table Wine." The other 25 percent—or less, depending on the winemaker's blend—could be the same varietals found in a Bordeaux, but essentially you're drinking Cabernet Sauvignon.

Back to your dinner wine purchase. You've settled on the Bordeaux so you pull out your wallet and decide money is no object because you want a fabulous bottle of wine. How do you choose? You're in luck, because the French have solved your problem. In 1855, Napoleon III established a five-tier classification system still used today that ranks France's "best" wines. Most of the first tier, or *premier cru*, wines come from several legendary Left Bank chateaux (so they're mostly Cabernet-based) such as Chateaux Latour, Lafite-Rothschild, Mouton-Rothschild, Margaux, and Haut-Brion. If you go for the *premier cru*, your wallet will be considerably lighter.

The primacy of these famed Cabernet-based Bordeaux wines, their excellent ability to age for many years before drinking, and the fact that Cabernet Sauvignon is the world's most widely-planted red grape make Cabernet Sauvignon (and Bordeaux) one of the most popular wines among consumers. With distinct styles that range from fresh and easy-drinking to intense, complex, and full-bodied, there is a wine to please almost every palate.

In Virginia, Cabernet Sauvignon is the third most widely planted red grape after Cabernet franc and Merlot. A late-harvested grape that grows best in warm regions blessed by abundant sunshine, Cab Sauv is more difficult to grow during Virginia's cooler autumns, forcing winemakers to choose between waiting for the grapes to ripen as the weather turns chilly or picking earlier when some of the seeds and stems are still unripe.

Okay, you've brought your bottle of wine home. Now what's for dinner? If you had chosen a lighter, fresh-fruit Cabernet Sauvignon, you should pair it with light cheeses or serve it as an aperitif. But since you splashed out on an intense, full-bodied Bordeaux, serve it with steak, lamb, duck, or game.

Acknowledgments

———— ⌘ ————

I am grateful to many people for the time and assistance they gave me while writing this book, but I'm especially indebted to Juanita Swedenburg of Swedenburg Estate Vineyard in Middleburg, Virginia, who, as always, sat me down and schooled me in the business of making wine. Her death in June 2007 was a loss to her family, her many friends, and to the Virginia wine industry where she was known as the gutsy lady who sued the state of New York for the right to ship her wine across state lines. It took five years, but she finally won her battle before the Supreme Court. All of us miss her.

I would like to thank winemaker Rick Tagg for his assistance in answering my questions with patience and humor, and for reading this book as a manuscript. Mary South Hutchison spent many hours discussing foxhunting and steeplechasing with me, loaning me books from her personal library.

James McGrath Morris granted me permission to use his edited version of *Thomas Jefferson's European Travel Diaries,* which was published by Isadore Stephanus Publishing on the bicentennial anniversary of Jefferson's journey through the wine regions of Europe. At Monticello, Gabriele Rausse, winemaker and Associate Director of Gardens and Grounds, spoke to me in Jefferson's vineyards on a cold March day. Cinder Stanton Shannon, Senior Historian at Monticello, talked to me about Jefferson's wine purchases for George Washington, as did John Hailman, author of *Thomas Jefferson on Wine* (University Press of Mississippi, 2006).

Thanks, also, to the following people for their help and expertise: Elizabeth Arrot, Terry Jones, Cheryl Kosmann, André de Nesnera, Katherine Neville, Martina Norelli, Lois Tuohy, and Mike Willis. Special thanks to MPO J.J. Banachoski of the Fairfax County Police Department's Crash Reconstruction Unit.

As always, I'm grateful to the RLI gang: Donna Andrews, Carla Coupe, Laura Durham, Peggy Hanson, Val Patterson, Noreen Wald Smith, and Sandi Wilson.

At Scribner, my thanks to Anna deVries, Susan Moldow, Whitney Frick, Katie Monaghan, Andrea Bussell, and Heidi Richter. Overdue thanks to Katie Rizzo and Rex Bonomelli. At Pocket I'm indebted to Maggie Crawford and Melissa Gramstad. Finally, I'm grateful for the counsel, wisdom, and friendship of Dominick Abel.

In addition to Jefferson's original diaries and John Hailman's book, several other books were particularly helpful in researching and writing this novel: *Wine & War* by Don and Petie Kladstrup (Broadway Books, 2002), *Passions: The Wines and Travels of Thomas Jefferson* by James M. Gabler (Bacchus Press, 1995), and *Wine: The 8,000-Year-Old Story of the Wine Trade* by Thomas Pellechia (Thunder's Mouth Press, 2006).

For those interested in reading more about the now-famous "Jefferson wines"—bottles of Bordeaux supposedly belonging to Thomas Jefferson discovered behind a bricked-up cellar wall in Paris—I recommend "The Jefferson Bottles" by Patrick Radden Keefe from the September 3 and 10, 2007, issues of *The New Yorker* and *The Billionaire's Vinegar: The Mystery of the World's Most Expensive Bottle of Wine* by Benjamin Wallace (Crown, 2008).

Scribner proudly presents

THE RIESLING RETRIBUTION

Ellen Crosby

Available now in hardcover from Scribner

Turn the page for a preview of
The Riesling Retribution . . .

Chapter 1

We all have a right to our private lives; it's living a secret life that gets us in trouble. At least, that's been my experience. Either the house of cards comes crashing down when the lies and deceit finally catch up with us, or we die with our secrets and someone uncovers them after we're gone. Either way, we break the heart of a loved one, and that's our legacy.

I own a vineyard at the foothills of the Blue Ridge Mountains in Virginia on a five-hundred-acre farm that has been in my family almost as long as this country has existed. Every Montgomery who lived here for the last 250 years is buried in a brick-enclosed cemetery that sits atop a hill near my home and commands a particularly breathtaking view of the mountains. My parents lie in the two newest graves.

Every few weeks I make a point of stopping by the place and always find peace and tranquility there. I spend most of the time at my mother's grave, leaning against her headstone and talking to her as the clouds drift across the Blue Ridge in a pretty tableau of chiaroscuro. I do right by Leland, too—my father preferred his children to call him by his first name—although I don't stay long with him or talk much.

They say God gives us families so we don't have to fight

with strangers. My father somehow managed to be both family and stranger to my brother and sister and me. Each time I stare at his polished granite tombstone with its chiseled epitaph—"The acts of this life are the destiny of the next"—an Eastern proverb that seemed more warning than prophecy in Leland's case, I wonder about the man he was and the layered life he hid from us. Leland had done a good job of keeping secrets about some of the acts of his life, but in the two years since he passed away, so far nothing he had done had altered my destiny, or that of my siblings.

Though that was about to change.

Today's visit to the cemetery on a sultry late July afternoon was brief. I had picked my mother some fragrant pale pink Renaissance roses from her garden. She planted the bush shortly before she died eight years ago, a few months before my twenty-first birthday, and never saw it bloom. If she had, I know it would have been one of her favorites.

When I had finished, I got back in the two-seater Gator and drove to a remote part of the farm where I'd agreed to let a group of men spend a weekend shooting at each other. That probably sounds sinister, but it's not. A person can't tread on a patch of land around here that hasn't somehow been part of the Civil War, a fact that still eats at plenty of folks. Of all the states that fought in the war, none suffered like we did in Virginia. Gettysburg lasted four horrific days. We had four years of misery.

So when B. J. Hunt, who owned B. J. Hunt & Sons Funeral Home, approached me last year and asked if I'd allow Company G of the 8th Virginia, his reenactment unit, to stage the 1861 Battle of Ball's Bluff on my land, how could I say no? Especially when B.J. said the local battle wasn't often reenacted, meaning we'd not only draw spectators and reenactors from all over the country, but the vineyard would also get a healthy shot of national publicity.

I am not martial in my interests, nor do I hunt and shoot, unlike my father who was an expert marksman, but I do honor my forebears and our history. The real Ball's Bluff, now preserved as a national battlefield and a park, is a few miles down the Old Carolina Road at the edge of the Potomac River, and is the site of the third-smallest military cemetery in the United States.

B.J. and his reenactors did not want to fight on hallowed ground, but they did want to stage their event as close to the battlefield as possible, preferably someplace near water. On October 21, 1861, Union soldiers had taken a few small boats across the Potomac from Maryland to Virginia, expecting to find a deserted Confederate camp near the town of Leesburg. What happened instead was a day-long series of skirmishes that ended with the panicked retreat of Federals down the cliffs of Ball's Bluff into the fast-moving Potomac. The sight of dozens of bloated bodies in blue floating downriver to Washington, as far away as Mount Vernon, so horrified President Lincoln and his Congress that a commission was established to oversee the conduct of the war from then on, forcing Union commanders to answer to a bunch of nonmilitary lawmakers.

Goose Creek, one of the Potomac's tributaries, runs through the middle of my farm. Though it meanders mostly through woods, the creek also skirts a large field beyond the vines that B.J. said would an ideal place to hold the reenactment, now scheduled to take place in less than two weeks.

I was a few dozen yards from the field when the Gator, anemic sounding ever since I'd left the cemetery, stalled and died. I turned the key in the ignition and pumped the gas, hearing nothing but dead-sounding clicks. I was about to climb down for a closer look at the engine—though to be honest, I wouldn't know what I was looking for if it hit me in the face—when the ominous sound of wind rushing through the treetops made me look up. The birds suddenly had gone silent. We were in for a storm. A fast-moving one, too.

The weather forecast hadn't said anything about a tornado, but there was no mistaking the ropy-looking gray funnel that had materialized out of nowhere on the horizon, spewing debris like dirty smoke. The dust cloud swelling at its base was shaped like an old-fashioned oil lamp, and the twister, rising in the middle, had the furious torque and spin of an angry genie.

As though its appearance was a cue for what came next, a lead-colored wall of clouds descended from the sky like a curtain slamming down on a stage. The wind picked up, twisting tree branches unnaturally until all I could see were the undersides of leaves flashing like millions of silvered coins.

I fished my cell phone out of my pocket and started to call Quinn Santori, my winemaker, until I remembered that he was twenty miles away at a meeting of the winemakers' roundtable in Delaplane. Instead I hit the number for Chance Miller, our new field manager, and heard him say, "Hello, Lucie," before the display flashed "call lost . . . searching for service" and went blank. The storm must have knocked out reception from the tower.

Across the field lightning arced the sky like God was throwing down pitchforks. I tossed the phone, now a lightning-magnet, in the Gator's open glove compartment and started counting. One-Mississippi. I got only to four when the crack of thunder came, sounding like it had split open the earth.

A hard, slanting rain moved in, slapping my shoulder-length hair in my eyes and tearing at my clothes. In my head I heard the litany of warnings television weather reporters shout as they are lashed by rain and wind in some perilous edge-of-the-world location, moments before they bolt for safety when the camera is turned off. Seek shelter immediately! The safest place is the basement of a house! If you do not have a basement, find an interior room and barricade yourself inside! Cover yourself with a mattress or hide behind a piece of furniture! Abandon all cars and mobile homes! They will not protect you! Seek shelter immediately!

The warnings never provided for the foolhardy soul who wasn't about to be whisked out of the path of destruction by a waiting car. The tornado danced closer, teetering and swaying like a drunkard. If I didn't get out of here soon, I was doomed. I fought against the panic crawling through my mind and tried to focus on my options. How fast did tornados travel? How much time did I have?

The surrounding woods were no safer than the field. The vineyard, where wooden posts could be uprooted and trellis wire become as sharp as a razor, was a worse idea. Get to a low place, that's what they always said.

On my way here I had driven across a stone bridge my great-great-great grandfather built across Goose Creek shortly after the Civil War. Calling it a bridge was a stretch, since it was really more of a culvert. But it was nearer than the winery or my house, both at least two miles away. Another flash of lightning looked like it struck something in the woods. My skin tingled as I heard the crack of timber splitting.

I grabbed my cane from the Gator and began moving toward the bridge. Four years ago an automobile accident left me with a crippled left foot and a devastating pronouncement from my doctor that I would spend the rest of my life in a wheelchair. I changed doctors until I found one who saw things differently. It took surgery and months of therapy and swimming until I finally managed to get around with the help of a walker. Later I graduated to a cane, which I still need for balance and support. But I can no longer run—and I never will—other than managing an awkward lope like I'm half of a shackled team in a three-legged race.

The wind shifted and I glanced over my shoulder. The darkening wall of clouds obliterated the sky and it sounded as though a jet or an out-of-control freight train was bearing down on me. I dragged my bad foot like a reluctant child. The dirt road dissolved into a muddy, rutted stream and my right work boot made a sucking sound with each step.

How much longer until I reached the bridge? What would happen if the tornado overtook me before I got there? Would it pick me up, like Dorothy in *The Wizard of Oz*, and spin me around, depositing me safely somewhere else? At least Dorothy had been inside a house. What really happened to people who got caught in a tornado's vortex? Were they hurled through the air like human javelins? Or was the drop in barometric pressure so intense it literally tore them apart?

The outline of the bridge, blurred and softer looking in the downpour, loomed ahead. I slid down the embankment, grabbing a branch to keep from landing on my rear or tumbling into the creek. Underneath the air smelled of cobwebs and decomposing vegetation. I threw my cane into the darkness, coughing and swallowing what tasted like dirt, as I felt around for a dry spot that wasn't some animal's lair. The rising creek rushed past me in a torrent, but the noise could not drown out the apocalyptic sound of what was happening outside.

The bridge was too low and shallow to stand. Instead I knelt as though I were praying and dug my fingernails into the crumbling mortar between the old stones. The rain changed to hail, dancing like hot grease in a frying pan as it crackled on the ground and hissed on the water. Wind buffeted the bridge, sending debris hurtling at me with such force it seemed to penetrate my skin.

Only one other time in my life did I wonder with the same desperation if these were my last minutes on earth. For months after my crippling accident, I woke from sweat-drenched dreams where I'd relived the slow-motion moment I knew the car driven by a now ex-boyfriend would not make the turn and instead slam with a killing force into the stone wall at the entrance to the vineyard. Now the storm slammed into me with that same violence, inhabiting my body and crowding my mind like a demon that would need exorcising.

The bridge shuddered as the tornado passed by—how close I couldn't tell, but so much debris and dirt rained down that I was sure it would collapse and bury me alive. Gradually the throbbing diminished and the roaring grew dimmer. My arc-shaped view of the world changed from black to gray. Then the rain stopped as suddenly as someone shutting off a faucet.

I found my cane and crawled back outside. My muddy clothes stuck to me like skin and my hair felt like seaweed when I pushed it off my face. To the west the sky was still death-colored, but to the east the tornado seemed to have sucked the storm clouds with it, leaving behind blue skies and improbable sunshine.

The hail had transformed the summer landscape to a winter scene that dazzled and glittered. In the distance, the yellow-and-green Gator—exactly where I'd left it—was a bright blotch of color against a frozen carpet.

The tornado's wide swath stretched from the edge of B.J.'s battlefield through the woods. I squinted at the low-slung Catoctin Mountains to my south, and the Blue Ridge, which filled the skyline to the west, and made some calculations. The twister had traveled from southwest to northeast. On that trajectory it probably sliced right through the vines in the south vineyard, which meant it might have destroyed more than half of our grapes. I closed my eyes and contemplated the loss of a few million dollars' worth of vines and thousands of cases of wine. But my life had been spared, and if the tornado missed my home and the winery—and God was merciful—then everyone who worked here had survived as well.

I retrieved my phone. Still no service. Unless someone came looking for me, I had a two-mile hike back to the vineyard. Before I left, though, I wanted to see up close the gash the tornado had cut through the field.

At the edge of the trench a dome-shaped object gleamed in the late afternoon sunlight. I knelt and brushed away dirt to get a better look at it. The first thing I saw were empty eye sockets staring into space. There was a perfect triangular orifice where the nose had been. The mandible with its lower row of teeth were missing, but the maxilla and top teeth were intact. Distant thunder rumbled like a drumroll near the vineyard.

It was a hell of a way to announce that the tornado had unearthed a human skull.

45713000R00202

Made in the USA
Lexington, KY
06 October 2015